STRIVING
FOR THE
FINISH LINE

A Triathlete's Journey

RUSSELL KOOP

STRIVING FOR THE FINISH LINE
A TRIATHLETE'S JOURNEY

iUniverse books may be ordered through booksellers or by contacting:

iUniverse
1663 Liberty Drive
Bloomington, IN 47403
www.iuniverse.com
844-349-9409

ISBN: 978-1-6632-1086-9 (sc)
ISBN: 978-1-6632-1085-2 (e)

Library of Congress Control Number: 2021902558

Print information available on the last page.

iUniverse rev. date: 02/23/2021

Preface

What on earth would make a supposedly sane person put themself through the arduous task of swimming 2.4 miles, then getting on a bike and cycling 112 miles, and then, as if that weren't enough torture, running a marathon of 26.2 miles? All in the same day? I'm guessing some of you have seen an Ironman-distance race on TV and had the very same question as did I when I witnessed it: "Why would you do that?" Actually, I seem to recall my statement was "What a bunch of idiots!" Oh, by the way, in the interest of full disclosure, as you read the book you should know the character of Curt is mostly me, although I did change a few things (chalk it up to literary license).

I completed my first triathlon in 1999, an Olympic distance, done mostly out of curiosity and as a way of fully recovering from a torn Achilles tendon. I never intended to make it a lifestyle, but isn't that the way life works so very often. Since that time, I've lost count of how many races I've done, from the shorter sprint distance all the way to the Ironman-distance race. Even to this day I don't have a solid answer for why I keep doing it. Just as with the characters in the book, there are often times when I do it simply because it has become part of my life. Or maybe I should be saying the characters are an extension of me and my journey.

There is one thing, though. As I typically do the same races every year, I've discovered each time out is a separate challenge and another opportunity to demonstrate how hard I'm willing to push myself. So maybe that's it for me, for the characters, and, come to think of it, for every athlete—how far are we willing to go? It is my hope that as you read the journeys of our four triathletes, you will be able to get inside their minds, revealing their personal motivations and aspirations for entering and hopefully finishing the most grueling distance in triathlon—the Ironman!

It is also my wish that some, if not many, of you become inspired to participate in a triathlon yourself, though maybe not an Ironman; start small and do a sprint distance. I truly believe that just about everyone could do a triathlon. I'm sure many people would say, "Not me, I could never do that." To which I would say, "You never know unless you tri." (See what I did there?) To those of you who are already seasoned triathletes, keep tri-ing!

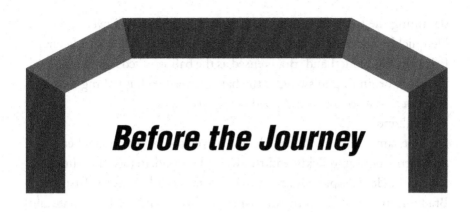

Before the Journey

Curt Emory got up from the bench and picked out his two favorite aluminum bats that were propped against the fence with the others. Stepping out from behind the chain-link fence that served as a dugout, he began swinging them to warm up for his turn at the plate. He could sense the anxiety building up inside. His heart was racing, his breaths coming faster and harder, and he was grinding his teeth despite knowing what he was doing and trying in vain to stop. Surveying the field, he attempted to create a Zen-like approach to the task, which included deep breathing and positive self-talk. On failing, he switched his focus to what was going on around him.

"C'mon, Brad, just a little dinger now!"

The smell of the dust from the infield filled his nostrils; the lingering heat from the early June evening created barely noticeable drops of sweat at his temples and down the middle of his back. The sun was hovering on the horizon, still fully visible as a bright orange ball. The lengthening of the shadows gave notice to anyone who might be paying attention that it would soon be lost behind the mature trees—an end to another day. A smattering of comments from the sparse crowd of mostly family intruded upon his focus, and he returned to providing verbal encouragement to his teammate.

"Let's do it, Brad. Just a single scores the runner!"

Brad Jenkins stood next to home plate, swinging his bat in wide arcs over his head. Stepping into the batter's box, he took a few last practice swings. The pitcher bent at the waist and peered at the catcher, first slamming the ball into his mitt and then turning the ball over and over. He quickly stood up, leaned back, and brought his arm in a wide circle, firing the ball underhand. Brad tensed as the ball streaked in a blur toward the plate, beginning to swing as the ball approached but jerking to a stop at the very last second as it dipped below his knees.

Ball one.

The same scenario on the field was played out, as the pitcher bent over and then stood up quickly and threw the ball underhand, this time in a slow arcing lob, despite his arm moving as fast as it had on the first pitch. Brad was unable to correctly time when the ball would reach the plate and swung too soon, missing the ball completely.

Strike one.

There's one out, Curt thought to himself. *If Brad gets a hit, it scores a run and we're behind by only two runs, making me the potential tying run. And if Brad gets out, that's two, and I'll be the potential third out.* He began to mentally play through all the possible outcomes of his teammate's at-bat, continuing to take practice swings, all the while aware the tension was not only there but was also continuing to build. The pitcher reared back and let the next pitch go—another fast one this time. Brad correctly guessed the pitcher would go back to "the heat," and he was able to make contact, sending a low bouncer down the third base line, just barely into foul territory.

Strike two.

Not that he felt himself to be a "sure out," but Curt was not exactly the kind of athlete that wanted that last shot. He had always liked to play it safe most of the time, going all the way back to Little League in elementary school and other sports throughout junior and high schools. He never wanted to have the game resting on his shoulders. If pressed for details, he would be able to relate times of purposely allowing others that opportunity, even with the possibility of ending up the hero. The prospect of being the goat most often outweighed his chance of being celebrated at game's end. He flashed back on the city basketball championship during high school. He had a completely open shot in the last few seconds that would have won the game, one that he had hit several times in that very game, but he chose to pass the ball when his anxiety about "less than" got the better of him. All these years later, not much had changed; he still didn't relish the

2

idea of being in that position now—especially not in this game, with the Fairview Municipal Class A Softball Championship on the line, and with Maxey's Mad Minutemen leading his team, the Fairview Flying Fajitas, with a score of 6–4.

The pitcher threw the next pitch high and hard so that the catcher had to leap up to prevent the ball from sailing over his head to the backstop.

Ball two.

"Please God, let Brad get a hit." Curt increased the fervency of his encouragement, as if by force of will he could somehow bend the cosmos to achieve the desired outcome. "Let's go, Brad! You can do it, buddy! No problem-o! You da man!" He wasn't sure if his efforts made any difference, but it didn't matter once he saw the ball streak off Brad's bat about head high, right in between the shortstop and third baseman. The runner on third base loped to home plate as Brad did the same toward first base. He was really feeling the pressure now, although it was tempered with the knowledge that if he did get out, at least it wouldn't be the final out. High-fiving the teammate that had just scored, he made his way to the batter's box, digging his feet in and taking a few practice swings. The pitcher slammed the ball into his mitt with a rather menacing look on his face, which Curt took to be a result of his being quite displeased with having given up the hit and run. He crouched again and peered at the catcher to get the sign. Curt locked his gaze at where the pitcher was holding the ball in his mitt, and he crouched slightly himself, in anticipation of the pitch. The pitcher stood up quickly and flung the ball underhand toward the plate—just low and outside.

Ball one.

Curt stepped back out of the batter's box, adjusted the Velcro on his batting gloves, and then stepped back in. He took a deep breath and another practice swing. The pitcher heaved his next pitch with a loud grunt, again low and outside, but this time Curt swung. The ball jumped off the bat at an angle and crashed into the chain-link fence in front of his team's bench.

Strike one.

Once more the scenario was repeated by both batter and pitcher. This time the pitch was waist high, and Curt hit a ground ball that took a very high bounce to the shortstop's right. He began racing toward first, knowing there was only a slight chance of beating the throw if he could just get a good enough jump out of the batter's box and run as fast as he ever had in his adult life. Halfway to first he caught sight of the shortstop out of the corner of his eye just starting to jump up to get to the ball sooner. Evidently the shortstop knew it was going to be a close play too. He increased his effort, but in his anxiousness to reach first, he felt as if he were running through water. He spied the shortstop, who by this time had the ball in his hand and behind his head, ready to release the throw. That was the last thing he remembered about his run to first base.

Once the fog lifted, he became aware of lying in the dirt on his butt, and he looked around, wondering how he had ended up in that position without knowing how. He saw his teammates anxiously looking at him, not knowing if he had been hurt or just tripped. Once he realized where he was and what had happened, he continued to just sit in the dirt to make sure there hadn't been any injuries. After several seconds with no sensation of pain anywhere, he began laughing, somewhat in embarrassment and somewhat in relief that nothing serious had happened. The first baseman sauntered over to tag him out with the comment "So, been runnin' long?" His teammates started laughing with him and two of them walked over to him to give him a hand up. Curt grasped each of their hands as they pulled him up off the dirt, and that's when the wave of excruciating pain shot up from his left ankle. He bit off a scream of agony and dropped to the ground. His teammates dropped to one knee as several others sprang off the bench and rushed over to where he was sitting hunched over in the dirt.

"Keep your weight off it!"

"Somebody go get some ice!"

"Just relax and stay on the ground for a while!"

He was vaguely aware of myriad voices calling out, but he couldn't connect any statements with the people making them, as his eyes were shut tight in reaction to the sudden pain, which now felt like fire from his foot to his hip. He clenched his teeth in anguish, his breathing now becoming labored. His teammates gently eased him down so that he was lying on his back. After a minute or two, he opened his eyes to view a hazy kaleidoscope of concerned faces. Gradually his vision returned to normal, and he was able to unclench his teeth and begin breathing slower, with deeper breaths.

After several minutes of lying on the ground, his breathing returned to somewhat normal, and he braced himself as the two teammates put their shoulders under his arms and lifted him up, supporting his weight as they did so. The three hobbled off the field, and they eased him onto the dugout bench with his leg propped up. He very slowly and carefully untied the shoelaces on his cleats and sat back against the fence. Another teammate had gotten a bag of ice, which was gently placed on his ankle. He tried to keep his breathing steady and relaxed, which proved to be increasingly difficult, as waves of nausea began to wash over him. To take his mind off the pain, he focused on the game, and with time the nausea gradually subsided.

He sat there for the remainder of the game, which the Mad Minutemen ended up winning, although he was quite fuzzy on the details. When it was over, he gingerly sat on the edge of the bench, stood up, and tested putting his weight on the leg. Upon discovering he was able to do that without much pain, he picked up his glove, shoe, and bat, and he began ever so slowly walking to his car. Several teammates walked with him, and many others called out their ideas on various methods of handling the injury. As he slid into his car and drove home, Curt was thankful it had been his left ankle and not his right, and that his car had an automatic transmission.

Sarah trudged wearily down the hallway of the dorm, having to make a concerted effort to keep her backpack from slipping off her shoulder while focusing on putting one foot in front of the other. She had never known walking could take such effort. Almost all of the other students on her floor took notice of the state she was in and sidestepped out of her way to creep along the wall until they were past her. That is, all except Heather. She seemed to be in constant obliviousness to her surroundings, even when her nose wasn't in a book, as it was now. Heather didn't see Sarah approaching down the hallway and very nearly knocked her over in her hurry to make it to her next final on time while she did some last-minute cramming. Fortunately for Sarah, Heather somehow looked up at the last second and pulled up short with a loud "Oh!" and then "Sarah, I'm sorry. I ... um ... didn't see you there. I ... uh ... that is ... well ...

omygosh! ... I'm gonna be late! And everybody says Professor Franks locks the door during finals. *Bye!*" Heather scurried off in a near panic, causing the remaining students in the hallway to flatten themselves against the wall as she flew past. Sarah softly groaned as she continued the march to her dorm room. Once there, it took her several attempts to get the key into the door lock and heave the door open just enough to squeeze through. She let her backpack slide off her shoulder and drop to the floor, not caring where it fell; shuffled to her bed; and flopped down on her back with a long sigh.

A few minutes later, just as she was dropping off into the sweet bliss of unconsciousness, her roommate came into their room and unceremoniously set her books down on the desk with a loud thud. When she saw Sarah lying down, she scrunched her shoulders to her neck, whispered, "Oops!" and began to step softly, attempting to make as little noise as possible. Without giving any other indication she was now awake and knew her roommate was in the room, Sarah asked, "Hey, Brittany. How did the bio exam go?"

Brittany noticeably relaxed and turned to face Sarah. "Not bad. I'm just glad it's over. Only one more to go, and then I'm outta here! Good-bye State U. for three months." She paused and then added, "You look like death warmed over. Please tell me you were able to stay awake for your final in chem."

Sarah chuckled. "Barely. It's a good thing for me it was mostly multiple choice and all I had to do was memorize stuff and then spit it back out. I don't think I could have passed it otherwise. So what are you up to now?" She sat up, leaning on one elbow.

Brittany grabbed her purse off her bed. "I'm going to head over to the Rusty Bucket and cut loose for a while! I need to clear my head of all this junk that's in it before I can start stuffing it full of other mindless drivel that we'll just forget in a few years anyway. Wanna come?"

Sarah paused a moment, her face suggesting she was deep in thought and torn between two conflicting desires. "Maybe a little later. I'm gonna try and get in a short nap first, but if you're not back by the time I get up, I'll see you over there."

Brittany headed for the door. "OK, but don't stay in this prison cell for too long." She was almost out of the room when she called out over her shoulder, "Oh, I almost forgot. Your mom called and said I was to be sure and tell you to call back this time. Later!"

Sarah fell back onto her bed with a loud groan and put a forearm across her face. She felt trapped, knowing she had to call but desperately wishing there were a handy solution to the inevitable. She fought an urge to jump off her bed and run to catch up with Brittany. *At least that would buy me some time*, she thought to herself. She lay in bed for a few minutes, not being able to doze off as planned owing to her rumination about the phone call. Finally she hoisted herself out of bed with a loud sigh and picked up the phone, murmuring to herself while dialing the number, in an obvious mimic of her mother's voice, continuing right up to the moment she heard her mother's voice.

"Hello." She steeled herself for the conflict that was sure to ensue.

"Hi, Mom. It's Sarah."

There was a short pause. "Sarah? Let me see. Sarah … Do I know a Sarah? I have a daughter named Sarah, but she so very rarely calls me. Might you be the Sarah that's my daughter? Or are you a different Sarah?"

She bit off a quick, rude reply—one that was sure to get a rude reply in return. "Sarcasm does not become you, Mother. You know it's me, and I called a couple weeks ago."

"Time must be passing slower where you are, sweetheart, because it was a month ago at least since your last call," her mother replied in a voice that was quite intentionally overly sweet.

"OK, maybe three weeks," Sarah conceded, "but it couldn't have been any longer than that."

Her mother sighed. "Well, I guess we'll just have to agree to disagree. How are your finals going?"

Sarah began pacing around the tiny dorm room. "Fine. I have two more, and I already know most of the material for both" she replied, slapping her head at the implication she was sure her mother would identify.

"Oh, good. So when will you be coming home?" her mother asked in a suddenly excited and inquisitive tone of voice.

Sarah thought for a moment. "The dorm is still open a week after the last day of finals, and I'd like to get in a few more workouts with the team."

Her mother tsk-tsked and said in an exasperated manner, "I don't see why you need to. You've been swimming all year long, and a few less workouts couldn't possibly make any difference. Besides, it's not like you're training for the Olympics, and one more season and you won't be swimming competitively anymore. Couldn't you cut your training short just this once? Dad and I want to spend some time at the lake house this summer."

Sarah consciously and with great effort controlled her anger as she replied, "Mother, I may not be training for the Olympics, but the swim team has a chance to do really well this coming year—maybe even win our conference. Every little thing we can do together to make that happen is worth it!" She noticed her voice becoming louder and more emphatic with each word. She stopped, took a long, deep breath, and continued. "I know you want me home as soon as possible, but I'll be home the entire summer. We'll have lots of time together."

Apparently her mother picked up on her emotional state, as she said, "I'm sorry, dear. I didn't mean to imply that swimming isn't important to you. But you're almost done with school now, and it's time to start thinking about what you're going to do after college. You know Dad can arrange an internship for this summer. It would be good experience. And who knows, you might like it."

Sarah bit her tongue. *Well, there it is.* She had known it was sure to come but didn't think her mother would bring it up so soon in the conversation. She tried to mentally calculate how many times her mother had tried to push—or, rather, guide—her into the appropriate career. Of course, it was always what her mother thought was the most appropriate career. She purposely forced herself to talk in a pleasant voice. "Thank you, Mother; that won't be necessary. Rob said last year I could have my job back at Peabody's for the summer. I'll let you know what day I'll be leaving. I'm pretty sure Brittany and I are going to drive together. She only lives an hour away, and I thought Geoff could come pick me up when I get to her house. I'll call you when we've worked out the details. I need to go now. I'm meeting some people in the library for a study group."

Her mother hesitantly said, "Oh, all right, dear. Study hard, and—"

Sarah interrupted quickly with "I will, Mom, thanks. Talk to ya later. Bye." She leaned against her dresser and exhaled noisily while stomping a foot on the floor. "When is she going to stop trying to run my life?" she asked the empty room. Closing her eyes, she stood propped against the dresser for a while, then put the phone back on its base. "I'll never be able to rest now. Might as well go over to the Rusty Bucket." She sighed as she picked up her purse and left the dorm room. She was only partially aware of other students' greetings as she headed over, returning their calls of "Hey!" and "What up!" though her mind was still rehashing not only the conversation she had just had with her mother but also all the conversations in which her mother tried to subtly (and sometimes not so subtly) manipulate Sarah into doing what she thought was "an appropriate course for a young lady in these days and times."

She suddenly found herself standing in front of the Rusty Bucket without being aware of how she had gotten across campus. She pushed through the glass doors and was immediately engulfed in an avalanche of sound: music blaring from four large speakers in the corners of the large pub, people talking loudly to be heard over the music, glasses tinkling, and pool balls smacking into each other. She stood in the doorway for a moment, acclimating herself to the noisy environment after the relative quiet and calm of the university campus. When her senses were finally adjusted to the extreme sights and sounds, she began searching for Brittany, who was at a table against one wall with several other girls. As she navigated her way through the tables and chairs, Brittany saw her coming and pulled a chair around to face the table they were sitting at. "I'm going to guess that call didn't go so well," she said as Sarah plopped down into the chair.

"And your guess would be correct" came the response as she nodded to the other girls. "It took her all of about thirty seconds to hit me up again about my major and choice of career. She's just not going to get it. I'm a big girl now, and I can decide for myself what type of life I want, where I want to live, and … and … *everything!*" All the other girls quickly murmured their assent, commiserating with Sarah.

"I feel your pain," added Brittany with a sympathetic look, "but you don't have to go home for another two weeks, and right now we are going to forget about that and *paarrrttaayyy!*" She grabbed a pitcher of beer that was on their table, filled an empty glass, and handed it to Sarah as she raised her own. "A toast to the best days of our lives!" The girls laughed as they clinked their glasses together.

As Patty swallowed and put her glass on the table, she looked around at the other girls and asked, "So what's everybody doing this summer?"

Brittany was the first to answer. "My plan is to do as little as possible. Lie out, catch some rays … and maybe some Jordans and Brandons," she said with a mischievous grin. The other girls began giggling, immediately comprehending her implicit message.

Lisa, who was on the swim team with Sarah, said, "My boyfriend wants me to train with him to do a triathlon in September, but I don't know. He says I'll be a natural because of all the swimming I do. He ignores me when I remind him I haven't even been on a bike since I was a kid. And who wants to do all that running? But I probably will, just to get him off my back … and because he's my boyfriend, yadda, yadda, yadda." Lisa paused for a moment and then looked pointedly at Sarah. "Ya know, Sarah, you're on the swim team too. If I can do this triathlon thing, so can you. Besides, it would be sooo nice to have a training partner. Whadda ya say?"

Sarah looked back at Lisa with one raised eyebrow. "A triathlon, huh? Swimming, biking, *and* running?" Lisa nodded. "All in the same day?" Sarah clarified. Lisa nodded again. "Without stopping in between?" Sarah asked, again emphatically, shaking her head.

Lisa nodded once more and then added, with a pleading tone, "But we're already in good shape, and all we have to do is finish. It's not like we have to work hard enough to win anything. Come on, Sarah, please, please, please?"

Sarah was still shaking her head in doubt. "I don't know. I'll think about it. Maybe." Lisa leaned back in her chair, content with that minor victory, but a seed had already been planted. Sarah couldn't help but begin to scheme how training with Lisa might be a way to avoid her mother this summer as much as possible.

"Good, Mr. Wilson, good," Michelle said encouragingly. "You're making good progress. Not much longer and you won't need me anymore."

The middle-aged man looked at her skeptically, responding in a playfully sarcastic manner, "Then I'll have to hurt something else so we can keep spending our 'quality time' together." They both laughed and walked to the next machine Michelle was using in his physical therapy.

Just as she was assisting him in setting the machine and getting started, they heard a loud voice from the other side of the workroom. They looked at each other knowingly, and Michelle remarked, "Looks like Matt is on duty."

Mr. Wilson nodded. "Ya think?"

They burst out laughing, and as they were still laughing, Matt strutted over with a quizzical facial expression. "So what am I missing? Must have been pretty good!"

Michelle suppressed an urge to put her hands over her ears. Staff and patients alike had learned that when Matt became excited, particularly as it related to a patient making progress, his volume tended to increase. Michelle suppressed an urge to tell him the truth, opting instead for a simple "inside joke" explanation. When it became obvious he would receive no further explanation, Matt headed off to assist another patient. He quickly became immersed in the daily routine of working with patients who were rehabbing from injuries. It didn't take long for the time to pass, and he ended the final workout with his last patient of the day. He was standing at the counter, completing his charting, when Peter came over to work on his own charting. "Done so soon? Seems like you just got here."

Matt hesitated while finishing a notation on a rough diagram of a human body. "Yep. Got to get going so I can make it to meet the cycling group."

Peter shook his head. "Ya know, you could make a heck of a lot more dinero if you put in more hours. There's certainly enough business to go around."

Matt hesitated again while making another note. "I know, but it would cut into my training schedule."

Peter hesitated, as it took a moment for his memory to connect the dots. "Oh yeah, working out with those professional cyclists, right?," Peter asked.

"Affirmative," Matt responded. "And I want to start increasing my distances so I can keep up with them over the long haul and eventually start doing longer races."

Peter raised both eyebrows. "Longer races? What are you doing now?" he asked.

Matt placed a chart back in a cubby and said, "Right now I'm doing basic criterium-type stuff."

Peter waited for an explanation that never came and asked, "So what distances are those?" Matt grabbed another chart and explained, "The ones I've been doing are short or relatively short races, usually about thirty-five to forty miles or so. They're not very long, but it's mainly about speed."

Peter shook his head again in disbelief. "Not that long? And you want to go farther than that? So what would those distances be?"

Matt put the chart back in the cubby and the pen in his pocket. "That would be about one hundred twenty to one hundred sixty miles."

Peter couldn't help but look at Matt skeptically. "You actually want to go that far? In one day? Without stopping?"

"Uh-huh," Matt replied, nodding his head.

Peter began chuckling. "Which begs the question: even if you could, *wwhhhyyy?*" Suddenly a lightbulb came on in Peter's mind. "Oh, I get it. You want to eventually compete in something like the Tour de France. Don't take this wrong, but isn't something like that for the younger guys?"

Matt paused and pondered the question for a moment. "No, I'm not planning on competing in the Tour de France, although that would be the dream of a lifetime. It's because I want to push myself as far and as hard as I can—you know, 'be all I can be' and all that."

Peter patted him on the shoulder as he turned to meet his next patient. "I think you're insane, but whatever floats your boat."

An hour later, Matt was gearing up for one of several weekly rides to which he had become accustomed. The group engaged in cycling chit-chat and good-natured banter as they got their bikes down off their cars and put on their cycling shoes and helmets. As they were preparing for the ride, Matt noticed someone he hadn't seen before, and as they began mounting their bikes, Richard came over and made introductions. "Hey, Matt, this is Kyle. He's gonna start riding with us." The two men exchanged pleasantries and shook hands, and the group took off.

Matt ended up riding close to Kyle, and as they were riding, they began engaging in small talk. "So, Kyle, how long have you been biking?" he asked.

"About three and a half to four years," responded Kyle. "I've been doing shorter distances up till now, but I wanted to increase my mileage, and Richard told me about the group. It fit into my schedule, so here I am."

Matt nodded as he took a long swig out of his water bottle. "If you're looking to increase your mileage, then I'm guessing you must have some kind of goal in mind?"

Kyle nodded in return. "Yeah, I've been doing triathlons for a few years—sprint and Olympic distances—and now I want to try doing an Ironman."

"Oh, yeah, I've heard of triathlons, but what are the different distances you're talking about?"

Kyle hesitated as a large truck drove by. "A sprint-distance race is usually about a 400-yard swim, 8- to 12-mile bike ride, and a 2- to 3-mile run. An Olympic distance race is about a 1-mile swim, 25-mile bike ride, and a 6-mile run. And an Ironman race is a 2.4-mile swim, 112-mile bike ride, and a 26.2-mile run."

Matt whistled. "That's a lot to do in one day. That's got to be every bit as hard as one of the longer legs of the Tour de France."

Kyle nodded in agreement. "That it is. I don't know if I'll get there, but I'm going to give it one hell of a try. Speaking of which, since you already have the biking background, you ought to give it a try yourself."

Matt shook his head. "No possible way. I've never been a very good swimmer, and running is just not my thing."

Kyle nodded in an understanding manner. "I hear what you're saying, but you could always start with the shorter distances, and I do swim workouts at the high school. There's a guy in the group that I know could give you a few lessons. Swimming isn't that hard; it just requires proper technique. And I don't necessarily enjoy running all that much, but by the time I'm on the run, I know I'm on the downhill side of the race and I'm almost home. And that finish line looks so good at the end."

Matt was listening while Kyle talked, but he still shook his head slightly. "I don't know. It might be something to try. Cross-training is the big thing these days, so maybe doing a few triathlons now and then would help my biking." Just as he finished talking, the group of riders began trading places, as the front riders switched with some from the middle and back, with Matt and Kyle being separated by several other riders. But the seed had been planted yet again.

Angie slowly eased the car into the garage, careful not to knock over Michael's golf clubs that were propped up along the wall of the garage. She tsk-tsked as she stopped and turned the car off. *"When is he going to clean this place out so we can have more room … like he promised?"* she thought to herself as she got out of the car, struggled to get the three bags of groceries out of the backseat, and then awkwardly arranged them in her arms in an attempt at not having to make a second trip. Tottering to the door, she clumsily fumbled at getting the key into the lock and opening the door, managing to heave the bags onto the kitchen counter just as they were about to slip out of her hands. She plopped onto one of the stools next to the counter, taking several deep breaths.

After a few moments, she began going through her normal postwork preparing-for-meeting-the-needs-of-the-family routine. This included putting the groceries away, making sure the cat had food and water, checking the mail to see if there might be anything of interest (which there almost never was—only bills), deciding what to make for dinner that night, retrieving her selection from the freezer, defrosting it in the microwave. Once the routine was finished, she changed her clothes and sat down on the computer to play a couple games of backgammon before starting to cook dinner. After playing more games than intended, she jumped up and scurried into the kitchen, chastising herself for spending too much time on stupid computer games. Just as she had begun cooking, the phone rang.

"Hey, Mom! MelissawantstoknowifitsOKformetoeatdinneratherhouse tonightandthengotothebasketballgameatschoolafterthatsocanIhuh?"

Angie couldn't help but chuckle. "Sandra, I could not understand a single word you just said. Try again, and this time remember to put some space in between each word."

She heard Sandra take a deep breath and begin talking in a deliberately labored manner, overenunciating each word: "Melissa … wants … to … know … if … its … OK … for … me … to … eat … dinner … at …

her ... house ... tonight ... and ... then ... go ... to ... the ... basketball ... game ... at ... school ... after ... that."

Angie shook her head, censoring herself before she said what had popped into her mind. There was no use in becoming upset, and besides, she had to choose her battles. Teenagers can be so trying. "First, did Melissa's parents invite you? Second, when does the game start and finish? And third, how are you going to get there and get home afterward?"

Sandra went back to her usual conversational pace, which was to talking what an Indy 500 race is to driving. "Yes, they invited me. I'm not so rude as to invite myself. It starts at seven o'clock and ends at about nine o'clock, and her parents are taking us and picking us up. OK?"

Angie couldn't help but wonder, for the gazillionth time, whether she had talked like this to her parents and, if she had, how she had made it out of adolescence without serious injury. "All right, I guess that will be OK. And you two *will* have *all* your homework done before going to the game, correct?"

Sandra sighed heavily and in an exasperated tone of voice replied, "Yes, Mother. *All* our homework will be done before going to the game. Thanks. Bye."

Angie hung up the phone with an exasperated sigh herself and went back to cooking. A few minutes later, the phone rang again.

"Hey, Mom, what up? I'm not gonna have time to make it home for dinner before the game, so don't make anything for me. Thanks! Later."

She had just enough time to stammer, "Jonathan, what ... where ... when ...?" before realizing she was talking to herself. Issuing another exasperated sigh, she jammed the phone back on the base. "Somebody please tell me again *why* we have children?" she yelled. Gazing around the kitchen at all the food in midpreparation, she began pulling plastic containers out of the cupboard for the leftovers that were sure to be there once she and Michael had finished eating.

Angie had just finished with the final touches on the meal when she heard Michael's car pull into the garage. She began putting dishes on the small table in the breakfast nook when he walked into the kitchen. "You're right on time," she greeted him as he put his lunch container on the counter near the sink. "Dinner will be hot off the stove and ready to go as soon as you wash up." Michael glanced at her with a somewhat puzzled expression,

"Huh? Oh, right. OK. I'll be right there." He began plodding back toward the bedrooms like a zombie. Angie started to ask him whether everything was all right, but he was around the corner and out of sight before she could get the words out. She continued setting the table, dishing out portions on each of their plates, and sat down at the table. After waiting for several minutes, she began picking at her food. It usually didn't take this long for Michael to get ready for dinner, and she was debating whether to go see what was taking him so long when he rounded the corner and sat down. She could tell by his facial expression and body posture that there was something bothering him. He had a pained look on his face, as if someone had just died or he had been fired, and the way he sat made him seem all tense, as if he was under a great deal of stress and about to either explode or break down in tears.

Michael turned, searching the breakfast nook, kitchen, and dining room. "Why are we eating in here and not the dining room? Where are the kids?" he mumbled in an absentminded manner, as if he were saying one thing but thinking of something else entirely different.

Angie stifled her own questions while answering his. "Sandra is eating dinner at Melissa's and then going to the basketball game, and Jonathan didn't have enough time to come home before the game. Looks like it's just you and me," she responded in an upbeat and perky manner. She was hoping her mood would rub off on him, but when he continued to appear morose, she couldn't help but blurt out, "Michael, what is it? What's wrong? You look like something terrible has just happened."

He turned to face her, but for the first few moments he seemed to be looking right through her, at something behind her. Finally he blinked slightly and shook his head, as if waking up out of a stupor. "Oh, the kids are gone. OK. What's that? What's wrong?" He just sat there staring at Angie, and she could tell by past experience and the look on his face that he was deliberating about whether or not to say anything and how much to say.

After what seemed like hours, he took a deep breath and said, "I'm not sure how to say this. There probably isn't a simple way or an easy way. But with the kids gone, perhaps now is the best time, although I don't know if there is a 'best time.' I knew I would eventually have to tell you, but I kept putting it off, hoping to find the right words that would make it easier."

As Michael spoke, Angie slowly became aware of a feeling that she couldn't quite put into words—fear, maybe, or dread, although she didn't remember ever having felt dread in her life. Would that be the correct word for it? Michael continued to make the same statements using different words. Finally he realized he was rambling and quit talking, almost biting off the last words. "What I'm trying to say is, I'm seeing someone else. And she wants to get married."

Angie just sat in her chair, trying to get control of her emotions, which made her feel as if the room were spinning. She also had a vague sensation she had been physically slapped in the face. Hard. All she could do was stammer incomplete and incoherent sentences. "You're seeing …? You don't …? Best time …?" She had a sudden urge to laugh hysterically and tell Michael that he was not funny, it was not a good joke, and he shouldn't kid around about something like that. No sooner did that urge come upon her than a competing urge hit her—one of wanting to cry hysterically. It took her several minutes to fight alternately first one urge and then the other, all while Michael sat in his chair looking like a little boy who had stolen a piece of the apple pie on the window ledge and now had to face the consequences. With much effort, Angie managed to regain some semblance of composure.

"Let me make sure I'm understanding you correctly," she began, with her lower lip quivering. "You are 'seeing' someone else?" Michael nodded silently as he hung his head. "And by 'seeing' someone, I take it you mean having sex with her? It is a her, isn't it?" Michael raised his head and began to give Angie a look of incredulity at the idea, but he then thought better of it, given the circumstances. He simply nodded silently and reverted to gazing at his plate on the table. "And how long has this 'seeing' been taking place?" Angie became aware that as she was talking, she was twisting her linen napkin tighter and tighter.

Michael looked up and just barely managed to make eye contact. "About nine months. And I know what you're going to ask next. We work together and for the past couple of years just seemed to really hit it off. We starting enjoying one another's company and went to lunch a few times, and … well … it just happened. It's not like we were planning it or anything."

Angie suddenly reached a breaking point and could no longer control what was welling up inside her. The volume and emotion in her voice skyrocketed as she shot to her feet and towered over him. "Just happened? *Just happened?* Oh no! Oh no! Oh no, no, no, no, no! 'Just happened' is when your car goes out of control on an icy road, or when you cut the grass too low, or when you burn the meatloaf because your son skinned his knee while riding his bike and you have to take care of it. That's 'just happened.' What you did didn't just *happen*. You could have seen it coming. If you had any brains or any morals, you would have seen it coming. And you kept on doing it for nine months? That is not 'just happened'!"

As she ranted, Angie started waving her arms around, becoming louder and louder. Michael stood up, making shushing sounds and unsuccessfully attempting to grab her arms. "Angie, please calm down. You're getting overemotional." He winced as soon as the words were out of his mouth, as he realized that probably wasn't the best comment to make at this moment. And he was right, as it just made Angie yell louder and begin hitting at his hands and arms to keep from being restrained.

"Overemotional? *Overemotional?* You go around screwing some bimbo behind my back, betraying our vows, ignoring how I would feel when I found out, throwing all the years we've had together in the toilet, and then *accuse me of being overemotional?* I'll *show* you overemotional!" And with that Angie picked up her dinner plate, which was still full of food, and threw it at Michael. Fortunately for him, in her agitated state, Angie fumbled with the plate long enough for him to see what was coming, move out of the way, and run out of the room so that the plate broke against the wall behind him, splattering the food in a pattern reminiscent of a piece of modern art.

Angie stood transfixed, staring at the food-splattered wall before giving in to the drive to stomp her foot on the floor while screaming as loudly as she could. That act served to drain away the adrenaline and emotional energy that had built up during the brief exchange with Michael, and she crumpled to her chair and then slumped over on the table, letting her head bang heavily on her forearms. Sobbing uncontrollably, she heard Michael walk down the hallway from the bedroom, turn at the entryway, and go out of the house through the front door. A minute later, she heard his car start up, back out of the driveway, and drive off.

Angie lost all sense of time while ruminating over myriad thoughts: what Michael had just told her, all the enjoyable times they had shared, recurrent self-recriminations about things she could have or should have done differently so that he would not have done what he did, and what would happen to their marriage now. After what seemed like weeks, Angie lifted herself out of the chair and began picking up the pieces of the broken plate, which she found reminiscent of the pieces of her broken marriage. She moved like an automaton, going through the motions, but the part that was Angie was a million light years away. She cleaned the wall and floor of the breakfast nook and put the remaining food into plastic containers and then into the refrigerator. Walking down the hallway in a stupor, she turned into her bedroom and flopped facedown on the bed. The last thing she was aware of before drifting off into unconsciousness was Sandra opening the front door, yelling good-bye to Melissa, walking to her room, and closing the door.

Exposure

Curt grimaced as he awkwardly attempted to climb out of the car's passenger seat, swinging his right leg out first, placing both hands under his left thigh, and then gently and cautiously lifting his left leg to rest beside his right. Given his injury and the heat of the June sun, his forehead began quickly beading with sweat. The fact that his foot had started swelling again and he was very nervous about walking on it, even the short distance to his doctor's office, didn't help matters. He barely put any weight on the foot at first, but with each step his confidence grew, and soon he was limping rather than hobbling, all the while waving off Katie's attempts at assistance.

She eventually gave up and just walked beside him, remarking, mostly to herself, "Fine, you want to fall flat on your face, go right ahead. Then the doctor can put some stitches into that big head of yours."

Curt grimaced again, not from pain or anxiety about his walking but rather from Katie's statement. "I'm wonderful; thank you for your concern. And as you can see, I'm walking just fine. I don't need any help."

Katie mumbled "Whatever" under her breath while striding ahead of him to open the door.

He shuffled into the doctor's office, thankful for air-conditioning as a wave of cool air blew into his face, then located the nearest seat that had an opening next to it and plopped down with a sigh of relief. He didn't want to admit it to Katie, but perhaps her idea of dropping him off right outside the door instead of walking to the office had probably been a good one. But he suffered in silence, not wanting to give her the satisfaction, knowing what her response would be. She would get that amused look on her face and sarcastically say something like "Oh, really? You mean I'm capable of having good ideas once in a while? Well, thank you for noticing." Women could be so difficult.

Katie sitting down next to him with a copy of *Good Housekeeping* broke his musing. They both sat quietly for several minutes until Katie, without looking up from her magazine, interrupted the silence by whispering, "So how's the foot?"

Curt sensed the irritation building; he knew what she was trying to do, and he was not about to let her get the best of the situation. "Great," he murmured. "Peachy. Never better. In fact, I could run a marathon right now." She showed no overt signs of response, but he saw a sly smile briefly cross her face as she peered intently at the magazine. He decided to let it drop and instead passed the time observing the other patients currently sitting in the waiting room.

After what seemed to be several hours but which in actuality had been only twenty-five minutes, a nurse came out from the examining rooms and said, "Mr. Emory?" Curt gripped the armrests of the chair firmly and grunted as he pushed himself to a standing position, pausing for a moment before limping across the waiting room and through the door the nurse held open. He hobbled to the scale, knowing what was going to come next. Planting his good foot on the ground, he pushed off and quickly hopped onto the scale, grabbing the top as he began to lose his balance. "Two nineteen," she stated in a matter-of-fact voice, and she wrote the number on his medical chart. *There's no way I weigh two nineteen*, he thought to himself. *It has to be because I have clothes on.* The nurse handed him an electronic thermometer and in the same unemotional, professional tone of voice, said, "Hold this under your tongue." In just a few seconds, a barely audible beep emitted from the part of the device the nurse was holding. She removed the thermometer from his mouth and, while writing the number on his chart said, "Second door on your left." He limped down the hallway into the exam room with Katie close behind. This time he let her help him up on the examining table, since there was no way he was going to hop onto the table as he had the scale.

After what seemed like another several hours, which this time was only twelve minutes, Dr. Jeffries opened the door with Curt's chart in his hand. "Morning, Curt." Nodding to Katie, he gave a brief "Katie." Dr. Jeffries scanned the chart once again and then asked, "Curt, what on earth did you do to yourself?" He listened with a smirk on his face while Curt described how he had been injured, and he then responded, "I guess we're not getting any younger, are we?" He received a rueful chuckle in return. Dr. Jeffries put the chart on a counter, pulled a stool from a corner of the small examining room, and sat down in front of Curt. He gently lifted his foot, pushed down on the top of it, pushed on the arch, and then began pushing and pulling on his ankle. He noticed Curt wince and said, "OK, lie down on the table on your stomach."

Curt leaned back and, with considerable difficulty, first rolled onto his side and then flopped on his stomach, breathing heavily with the exertion. Dr. Jeffries began pushing on various spots on Curt's ankle again, gradually moving up to push on his calf. That's when the pain hit like a searing-hot branding iron being thrust into his leg. Curt, unable to control his reaction, arched his back so high that his shoulders and stomach were lifted off the exam table. The only thing that kept him from screaming at the top of his lungs was that his teeth were clenched tight, but even that didn't keep him from giving a long, loud groan. Dr. Jeffries released Curt's leg as soon as he saw his reaction, and he quickly stepped around to the side of the exam table to make sure Curt didn't roll off. Although the initial pain, the most extreme, lasted only about fifteen to twenty seconds, to Curt it felt like half an eternity.

He continued to lie on his stomach on the exam table for several minutes, unable to do anything except try to catch his breath and relax all the muscles in his body. He slowly propped his body on one elbow and then rolled around to a sitting position, wiping his forehead with his arm. Dr. Jeffries didn't attempt to use any humor after that and said, "Well, Curt, it looks like you tore your Achilles tendon, and it appears its severed completely in half. That's why you feel that little bump on your calf; that's the end of the tendon. And the only way to fix it is surgery. If it were only a slight tear, maybe we could keep you off it for a couple of months, let it heal, and then do some physical therapy to strengthen it up again. But now ..." He let his comment trail off and shrugged his shoulders.

Curt sighed and looked up. "So when does this surgery happen, and how long am I gonna be off my feet?"

Dr. Jeffries reached for his medical chart and a paper tablet. "It's best to get it done right away. I'm giving you a referral to Dr. Harold Davidson. He's done a lot of these, so you'll be in the right hands. I'll call his office today and they should be calling you either later this afternoon or tomorrow. He'll look at it and schedule the surgery after that. The surgery shouldn't last longer than about an hour or two. After that, you'll have a cast and then a special orthopedic boot for about three months. And after that you'll have to go through physical therapy for about two to three months, depending on how fast you heal and how often you do the exercises the physical therapists tell you to do. Gradually you'll be able to walk, and after about six to eight months, maybe nine months, you can start running." He finished writing on the tablet, tore off the sheet, handed it to Katie, and exited the exam room.

No sooner was the door closed than Katie commented, "Boy, when you do something, you sure do it right." Curt could only look at her, as he couldn't think of anything witty to say. She quickly added, "And if you think I'm going to wait on you hand and foot, you've got another think coming. I'll give you a pillow for your foot, a soda, and the remote. After that, you're on your own." She harrumphed and folded her arms across her chest for emphasis, but Curt detected a very slight grin on her face, so he just smiled at her without saying anything. Fortunately they didn't have to wait long for a nurse to come in with a pair of crutches. As this was the very first time in his life he had ever needed to use crutches, he awkwardly walked out of the exam room and down the hallway, bending his knee and lifting his left foot slightly so it wouldn't drag on the ground.

The next day, Katie pulled up in front of the Pacific View Orthopedic Center, as close to the entry doors as she could get. This time she wasn't going to put up with any of Curt's machismo. Once checked in at the front desk of Dr. Davidson's office, he plopped down on a chair with as quiet of a grunt as he could manage. They didn't have to wait long for Dr. Davidson, who entered with his head down, reading Curt's medical report from Dr. Jeffries. Dr. Davidson eventually looked up and exchanged pleasantries; he then had Curt lie down on his back and lifted his leg up, prodding and poking from his foot to his calf. Curt was extremely relieved and grateful Dr. Davidson didn't push on his calf as hard as had Dr. Jeffries. Finally Dr. Davidson sat back and confirmed Dr. Jeffries's assessment of the injury.

"Yep. You've torn your Achilles tendon, all right. And Dr. Jeffries was correct when he told you it would require surgery. I've already checked my surgery schedule, and we'll do it this Tuesday morning."

Curt gulped. "That soon?!"

Dr. Davidson noted the obvious panic in his voice. "I know you may not be looking forward to it, but it's best to get it done ASAP. No sense in putting it off. That way you can begin the healing process and rehab that much sooner. I'll have someone come in and give you all the details about the procedure. As surgeries go, this isn't all that involved, so you should be up and around in no time." The last comment was given in a rather upbeat manner as Dr. Davidson attempted to ease Curt's anxiety. He shook hands with them both and left the room.

Curt sighed loudly as the door swung shut. This time Katie looked at him sympathetically. "Sorry, love, but I'll be waiting for you when you wake up. Plus the kids and I will do everything we can while you're recovering." This was said in a somewhat questioning tone to see what kind of reaction he would have.

He silently laughed while sighing again. "Thanks; I'll need all the help I can get."

For the remainder of the time, both were silent, as Curt went into an introspective mode and Katie just wasn't sure what to say and didn't want to say the wrong thing. The silence was broken by a nurse entering the room with several pieces of paper, which she handed to Katie after a quick look at Curt. Katie reviewed the information that was provided on the handouts, and after answering a few brief questions, she smiled as she exited the exam room, opening the door for Curt as he lumbered out of the doctor's office and toward the elevators.

By the time Tuesday morning rolled around, Curt had had an entire weekend to become quite adept at getting from place to place on his crutches. In fact, once he acknowledged the necessity of being on crutches for a couple of months, he insisted that Katie and the kids do as little for him as possible. This meant he was able to get out of the car, walk into the outpatient surgery center, check in at the front counter, and sit down with a minimum of effort. He vacillated between wanting to wait a long time to be called into his presurgery room and focusing on his newfound desire to get it over with as soon as possible. He was still experiencing those conflicting thoughts and emotions as Katie came to sit by him, as the nurse came to escort them into the pre-op room, and as she instructed him in what he had to do to prepare for the procedure.

Once Curt was in the hospital gown, Katie helped him climb onto the bed and arranged the sheets around him. Several minutes later, the anesthesiologist came in to describe what he would be doing and what the likely effects might be. Curt's wide-eyed, anxious demeanor remained consistent throughout the entire time the nurse was inserting the IV needle into the back of his hand and as he waited for the anesthesiologist to give him a pre-anesthesia "cocktail." As soon as he had removed the needle from the IV tube, Curt asked the doctor, "Hey doc, how long does it take for this stuff to wor …?" He was unable to finish the last word, as he was overcome by a wave of euphoria. From that point until they wheeled him into the operating room, Curt couldn't help but giggle at just about everything Katie said. They both knew he couldn't control it, which made him giggle even more. As the nursing team rolled his bed into the OR, he began singing "Sweet Caroline" at the top of his voice, despite Katie's repeated attempts at quieting him, and he was still singing as the doors to the OR swung shut. When the anesthesiologist came to give him the shot that would knock him out, Curt exclaimed "Hey, doc! What's in this stuff? This is great! Can you give me some more?" The doctor smiled as he held up a syringe. "Why, yes, I can." Curt rested his head on the pillow as the anesthesiologist inserted the needle into the IV tube and pushed the plunger all the way down. "Suhweeet! Happy juice!" he declared. Within a few seconds, he quickly dropped off, the last word he was capable of uttering being "Hey."

Regaining partial consciousness occurred quickly at first but proceeded slowly after that. Upon opening his eyes, Curt had to blink several times and make a conscious effort at focusing, and even then there was a general haziness to his vision. Gradually he saw that he was in an area surrounded by a curtain, and there was just enough of a gap to see other patients in beds surrounded by curtains as well. Katie was sitting near the head of the bed, reading a magazine, when she saw that he was awake. "Well hello, sleepyhead. How is our happy boy?" she said with a smirk and a tone of voice similar to that which mommies use with infants. All he could do was groan and close his eyes. He was in no condition to get into a battle of wits, especially since he was still groggy from the anesthesia.

He tried to focus on the hustle and bustle of the post-op area. Katie, guessing about his condition from his facial expression, asked, "How's the foot?"

It took him a few seconds to formulate a response. "Not too bad now. But I can tell it's going to hurt like hell later." She put her magazine down and said, "Well, let's make sure we get a prescription for painkillers before we leave, and I'll stop by the pharmacy on the way home." They talked about how living conditions would be for the next few months. While they were discussing logistics, a nurse came in every fifteen minutes or so to check on his progress. Finally, after about an hour and a half, the nurse who came in went through the process of taking out the IV and helping him prepare to leave, and another nurse came in with a wheelchair and handed her a piece of paper. "The doctor has already written a prescription for a painkiller, and we're going to give him a lift out to your car just to make sure he doesn't fall from any lasting effects of the anesthesia." Katie nodded and went to get their car so it would be by the door when he got there, while the nurse assisted him with getting into the wheelchair.

"Whoa! Good thing I've got this thing," he murmured to himself as the nurse pushed him out of the post-op area. After the exertion of getting dressed, and still with some remaining anesthetic in his system, he felt certain he would not have made it far without falling. In fact, he felt quite woozy simply rolling down the hallway to the pickup area, where he could see, through the double glass doors, Katie pull up and open the front passenger door. With what felt like his last remaining strength, he pulled his legs into the car and straightened out into a sitting position. Closing his eyes, he let out a long, deep sigh while sinking into the padded car seat. He hadn't intended on sleeping, but upon opening his eyes again, he observed Katie slowly guiding the car into the garage.

"*Hey!* Can a guy get a little help here?" Curt bit off a sudden impulse to use a few choice words, knowing it wouldn't achieve his desired goal of getting any family member to bring him something to drink and would more likely result in all of them staying away on purpose just to spite him. He had discovered that his initial mental images of him sitting around with his family at his beck and call were quite far from the reality of having to lie around and wait for someone to come to his aid. After a few days of Katie and the kids making sure he was comfortable and had everything he needed, life returned to disgustingly normal. Katie had to return to work after a few days off, Justin was probably off to soccer practice or baseball practice or who knew what other kind of practice. And Ashley—dear, sweet Ashley, the apple of Daddy's eye. OK, so she was only eight years old, but when did Barbie become more important than Daddy? And when did she learn how to roll her eyes like that?

To reduce excess movement, he resorted to watching TV, bemoaning the lack of "guy" programming, but at least today was Saturday and there were plenty of sports to watch. Like a typical American male, he channel surfed for several minutes until finally settling on a baseball game. Neither team playing was a favorite of his, but it would have to do. When that station went on a commercial break, he resumed channel surfing. At most stations, he would pause for several seconds to see whether anything caught his interest. If not, he would press the up or down channel arrows to move to the next station. If the channel were on a commercial, he would press the button immediately.

That pattern continued when he came to a station that showed some guys riding bikes across the countryside. He noticed some numbers on the bikes and concluded they must be in some type of race. Something the race narrator said aroused his attention, and he turned the volume up, as it had been down all morning so he could catnap. He caught the last few comments as the narrator was explaining that the riders were currently biking through lava fields and that the temperature and humidity made it like riding inside an oven. A type of morbid curiosity took hold, and he continued to watch incredulously, dumbfounded that any person in their right mind would choose to ride a bike under those conditions. After about twenty minutes of the coverage switching between riders at various stages of the race, he changed channels while muttering under his breath, "What a bunch of idiots!"

He returned to channel surfing, but after about twenty minutes something inexplicable kept drawing him back to the station showing the bike race, and each time he returned to that channel, he stayed there a little longer. Not only that, but he gradually began sitting straighter and straighter on the couch until, returning to the channel for the final time and staying there, he was sitting on the edge of the couch, leaning slightly forward, with his elbows resting on his knees. By the time his full attention was devoted to watching the race, most of the riders had gotten off the bikes, slipped on running shoes, and were running along residential streets. He listened with amazement as the narrator explained the racers were running a marathon of 26.2 miles. He didn't think he could run at the speeds they were for even one mile. His disbelief heightened as the narrator, with the race leaders about three quarters of the way through the run, summarized the accomplishment as swimming 2.4 miles, biking 112 miles, and running 26.2 miles, all of which was done in one day *and* in the extreme heat and humidity of the big island of Hawaii.

Being so focused on the TV, he wasn't aware of Katie coming in through the door from the garage with two bags of groceries in her arms and with Ashley in tow, who was combing the hair of one of her Barbie dolls. Katie tried to get his attention but quickly noticed it was going to be a lost battle and walked past the couch and into the kitchen. Ashley followed, giving Curt one of her by-now patented eye rolls. This, of course, didn't register into his awareness, because he was so completely enthralled while watching the finish of the race that some country could have dropped a bomb, and if it didn't interfere with the broadcast, he wasn't about to notice. The lead runner had now reached a narrow lane created by long, continuous banners on either side with various product logos on them. Thousands of people were standing behind the banners, screaming, shouting encouragement, and waving small flags and pennants.

Curt continued to watch with rapt attention as several minutes later another runner crossed the finish line. Then, about two minutes after that, another runner came in, and then the racers began finishing in small packs, each runner being separated by only a few seconds. Once the top ten to twelve finishers had completed the race, a sportscaster began interviewing the winner, who was draped in the flag of his country of origin and drinking out of a sports water bottle. He listened as first the winner and then the second- and third-place finishers were each interviewed, talking about how they approached each stage of the race. By that time, several female racers were only a couple of miles from the finish line, and coverage focused on the battle that was being waged between the leader and the runner then in second place, who was a few minutes behind.

The remaining women finished in a pattern similar to that of the men, and after several more interviews and race summaries, Curt turned off the TV and sank back into the couch, his thoughts about what he had witnessed racing through his mind. He lounged for a while in a semiconscious state until a barely audible noise tugged at his awareness. He listened closer and noticed it was coming from the bedroom. "Katie?" he called. He heard more noises from the bedroom, and shortly Katie appeared from the hallway. Before she could say anything, he jumped in and excitedly recounted all the information he had heard from the race narrators about the conditions of the race, the distances, and what the racers had to go through to compete in the race. Katie simply smiled and listened patiently. "I wonder if there are races like that but shorter distances?" he mused aloud. "I think it would really help my rehab if I had a goal that I was trying to reach—something to keep me motivated until I was back at 100 percent."

"I don't know," she responded with an amused smile, "You could always get on the internet and do a search for triathlons and see what comes up."

Even though he still couldn't walk, the idea of competing in a triathlon consumed him. He began to spend hours on the internet, searching for local races first, and then for races that were within two to three hours' driving time. There weren't any problems finding an abundance of races and bookmarking them on his computer for future reference, knowing that even with starting rehab next week, it would be quite a number of months before he could begin thinking about doing much of anything, much less biking and running in a race. For the next few days, he was antsy around the house, not only from the boredom of not being able to do anything except watching TV, reading, or playing video games on the computer, but now also because he couldn't wait to get started on rehab. He'd checked the name and address of the rehab clinic so often he had them memorized. Because of his increasing restlessness, his sense of time changed; minutes seemed like hours, and hours seemed like days. Finally the day arrived for his first therapy session.

He found the clinic, Fairview Physical Therapy Center, easily and walked in about ten minutes before his scheduled appointment. After checking in, he was shown to the locker room. He changed his clothes and still had time to spare before his physical therapist came out to take him to the therapy room. The therapist gave him a towel folded lengthwise, instructed him in how he wanted him to stretch out his calf, and left to check in on other patients. As he stretched, Curt surveyed the room. There were many machines in the room, some of which he recognized as being similar to those in a typical gym, such as a stationary bike and weight machines. He had no clue as to the functions of some of the others. In a few minutes, the therapist returned to show him how to perform several exercises with the towel, all of which were designed to further stretch out the tendon and his calf muscles.

Once Curt had done the stretches to his satisfaction, the therapist brought out a bag of marbles and had him pick up the marbles with his toes. The last exercise of the session involved one of the machines he couldn't figure out. The therapist had him sit in a padded seat, strapped his ankle into a brace below the seat, and had Curt flex his ankle back and forth, stretching out the tendon. He explained as Curt flexed that they would gradually add weight in order to strengthen the tendon. The session ended with a specially designed cold pack wrapped around his ankle. Although the few exercises he had done today had gone well, it demonstrated to him just how far he had to go. Still, he couldn't help but feel invigorated with having taken this first step toward his goals.

His life settled into a pattern that became somewhat monotonous in its regularity and predictability: work every day, helping Katie make dinner and then helping out around the house, some gardening on the weekends, and therapy twice a week, always on the same day and at the same time, with the same therapist and the same people in the workout room. The only thing that broke up the routine was that after four weeks of therapy, he had begun taking walks every day—sometimes in the morning before work, and sometimes after dinner with Katie. After another six to eight weeks of therapy, he began jogging—very slowly at first while his legs became accustomed to the new level of use, and then slightly increasing his speed every few weeks. Once he had completed twelve weeks of therapy, the therapist had him go through all the exercises and all the machines he had used as somewhat of a final exam before releasing him as having met the goals of physical therapy. *Finally I can start preparing for a race,* he thought with a wide grin.

— — — — — — — — — — — — — — — — —

The hum of the air conditioner was muffled by the whirring of the exercise machines, which were lined up in neat rows and arranged according to type of machine. Angie was thankful for the gym membership during this time of year, when she could work out in a cooled facility rather than having to exercise outside in the heat. She tilted her head back and closed her eyes, letting the breeze from the air conditioner wash over her sweating face. She had hoped, however small that hope might have been, that by closing her eyes and focusing on the flow of air on her face she could drown out Sylvia's incessant chatter. Having failed at that, she glanced down wistfully at the magazine she had wanted to read before giving in to the inevitable, noting that Sylvia was yet again giving her opinion on what she thought Angie should do about Michael and getting on with her life.

"I'm telling you, Angie, you need to put that part of your life behind you and write a new chapter of The Book of Angie," Sylvia stated emphatically. Trying to hide the big smile she wore by wiping her face on her sleeve, Angie observed that Sylvia was talking a *lot* faster than she was pedaling. "This is the new millennium, after all, and women these days have *all* kinds of opportunities to live life the way *we* want to, not the way our mothers did. And that life doesn't always have to include a man—especially a man that cheats on you." Angie winced as Sylvia made that last comment but said nothing, as she knew it wouldn't do any good. Sylvia had her opinion on everything, and once she had her mind made up, she was not going to change it for anything or anybody.

In response to the emotions that Sylvia's remarks were dredging up, Angie increased the difficulty of pedaling the bike, which required her to use more energy just to keep the pedals going at their current speed. She had discovered that exercising was a good way to cope with the emotional impact of the separation, and since Sylvia had talked her into going to the gym five months ago, she had gradually increased the number of days she went from two to three and then to four or five. In addition to the frequency, she had also increased the intensity of her workouts, as the stress of acting as a single parent had begun to take its toll. She was thankful the kids were as old as they were; being in high school, they were mostly self-sufficient. It was difficult to imagine what she would have done if they had been toddlers or even small children. Because of the changes in her lifestyle, both negative and positive, she was slowly but steadily losing weight and becoming more and more physically fit.

Even with focusing on the increased effort, Sylvia's constant prattle was beginning to take a toll on Angie's nerves. When was she going to get off her soapbox about "starting a new chapter"? Angie searched the mirror in front of them until she located the reflection of the clock on the wall behind them, and it took several seconds to calculate the time, since it was backward. It was worth the effort, as she noticed they only had about five more minutes until their agreed-upon end time. She calculated that she would be able to hold on for that short amount of time but picked up on a statement just on the edge of her consciousness.

"Look at me. You don't see me sitting around feeling sorry for myself. Oh, no. I got up, brushed myself off, and began creating the new me! Yes, ma'am! I'll say it again—that's what you need to do Angie ..."

"All right! I get it!" Angie burst in, a little more emphatically and emotionally than she had intended, immediately wishing she could take it back, not only because of Sylvia's reaction of stunned silence but also from other people in the area stopping what they were doing and looking over at them. She hung her head and quietly murmured, "Sorry, Sylvia. I just get tired sometimes of people telling me what I should do. But I know you're right. I do need to make the best of this, because I still have a lot of life left, and I don't want to spend it being miserable."

Sylvia smiled, "That's OK, Angie. I know I tend to go on and on. I'm just trying to encourage you, and sometimes I don't know when to stop. Now that you've decided to do something, what's your first move?"

Angie gazed off into the mirror. "Oh, I've got a few ideas."

About a half hour later, after they had showered and changes clothes, Angie strolled out of the gym with Sylvia toward their cars. When they got to their cars, Angie waved good-bye to Sylvia and tossed her gym bag into the backseat. Flopping down into the driver's seat, she adjusted her sitting position, buckled the seat belt across her shoulder, put the key into the ignition, and … froze. She suddenly became aware of a thought flittering through her mind. This was one of those proverbial forks in the road. She could decide to keep her life as it was now—safe, comfortable, doing what she had always done. Or she could take a risk and radically transform herself into an entirely different creature. Taking a deep breath, she removed the key from the ignition and hurriedly, before changing her mind, strode back into the gym.

She stopped abruptly just inside the double glass doors, as there were people around the front desk. *This is silly*, she thought to herself. *First of all, they don't even know me, so who cares if they see me taking some flyers. And second, I have just as much right to enter a race as anyone else …* There were a number from which to choose, ranging in distances from 5K all the way to a marathon. She took two flyers that were for 5Ks and two for 10Ks. As quickly and unobtrusively as possible, she slid past the small crowd and raced back to her car. Once back in the driver's seat, she leaned her head back against the headrest and breathed a loud sigh of relief. "I did it!"

Her pulse quickened again with the realization that she had chosen to embark on a new journey and was so caught up in the thrill of what she was planning that, pulling into the driveway, she couldn't remember a single thing about the drive home.

"You what!" was Sylvia's reaction when Angie told her about taking some of the flyers at the gym and sending in the registration form for one of the upcoming 5Ks. Actually, that was only Sylvia's first reaction. Her second reaction, closely following the first, was "You?" For a few seconds she thought Sylvia was being demeaning, as there was a pause while she processed the information Angie had just shared with her. But it didn't take long for Sylvia to exclaim, "You go, girl! I'm so proud of you. I can't believe you would do something like that. That is soooooo not like you. Oh, Angie, that is so awesome. I want to help! How can I help? What can I do? I know! We'll start running more. And strength training. We'll start strength training!" Angie bit her lip to keep from laughing out loud into the phone. Sylvia was getting more excited about the race than she was. "Ooh! We'll have to go shopping. You can't race in those beat-up gym clothes; you just have to have a genuine race outfit. You know what they say; if you look fast and feel fast, you'll be fast."

Angie had to break in and stop Sylvia before she gave herself a mild heart attack. "Sylvia, thank you so much for the support, but get a grip. It's only one race, and I don't even know if I can finish it. Well, I'm pretty sure I can even if I have to walk part of the way. And shopping for a race outfit? Oh, please."

Angie heard Sylvia's tone and volume lessen slightly as she conceded, "OK, maybe the race outfit is a little premature, but I still think we need to increase our training. Tell you what, the gym has a personal trainer. How about we sign up for a consultation and let an expert guide us in what level of workouts we need to be doing to finish the race."

Angie caught on to the word "we" in Sylvia's assertion. "We? *We?* What do you mean, we?"

She could almost see Sylvia puff herself up. "Well, you don't think I'm going to let you do this all alone, do you?" All she could do was sigh and chuckle. When Sylvia took that tone of voice, she knew she might as well give up, because she wasn't going to win.

As with so many things in life, race day came far too quickly, and the night before the race Angie was back to her old self—dreading the decision, feeling greatly unprepared, and coming close to simply not going the next morning. A fitful night's sleep didn't help her mood any upon waking, especially when the doorbell rang unexpectedly. She shuffled to the door, dreading what was going to be on the other side—Sylvia and her bubbly, enthusiastic, hyperactive self. She barely had time to get the door all the way open before Sylvia bounded in, grabbing her by the upper arms, and jumping up and down in her best Tigger imitation. "Ooooh, Angie, isn't this so exciting? This is going to be so awesome! I can hardly wait!" Sylvia appeared as if she was going to say more, but she abruptly stopped. "Boy, you look like death warmed over." She gazed at Angie while gradually awareness seeped in. "Oh … must have been a bad night, uh? Couldn't sleep?"

Angie nodded. "I know its irrational, but I couldn't stop worrying about the race. I keep feeling that I haven't done enough to prepare—that I'm going to embarrass myself. You name it, and if it's a negative thought, I've had it."

Sylvia guided Angie to one of the stools by the kitchen island and made her sit down. In a deliberately calm and emphatic voice, she said, "Angie, you have to trust me on this. You are ready, and you will do well. Right?" When there was no answer forthcoming from Angie, Sylvia sighed and positioned herself squarely in Angie's line of sight. "OK, repeat after me: I will do well." She paused expectantly, making it obvious that she wasn't going to stop until Angie said it as well.

Angie sighed herself, shrugged, and said, very unconvincingly, "I will do well," her tone of voice sounding remarkably like Eeyore's.

Sylvia give Angie a look that showed she meant business. "Now say it like you mean it."

Angie smiled ruefully and, in as cheery a manner as she could, responded, "I will do well."

Sylvia gave a firm nod. "That's more like it. Now get your stuff, and let's go show 'em what we've got!"

Despite Sylvia's encouragement, Angie felt the anxiousness building within her with each mile closer to the race site. She was silently thankful Sylvia was driving, knowing that if she were driving by herself, she would turn around and go home. She knew intellectually this was what she needed to do, but emotionally it was happening too fast. She found herself wishing yet again that there had been more time to prepare or that she had chosen a race that was still several more months away. She made a conscious effort to ask Sylvia questions about her job, children, and family—anything to change the topic of conversation away from the race. While this provided momentary relief, all too soon they were at the park that served as the starting and finishing lines for the race.

As they were finding a parking space, they could see multicolored balloons in the middle of the park arranged in a semicircle over a table. The process of checking in, getting their race numbers, pinning them to their shirts, and stretching and warming up seemed very similar to her experience of the last few days in general, and of this morning in particular. It was all happening too fast. Even though they had gotten to the park an hour before race time, Angie felt as if it were mere minutes before the race director yelled, "Five minutes to race time!" into a bullhorn. Angie looked around at the other participants as they all headed over to the starting line. She was keenly aware of feeling out of place, and she even thought to herself, *What am I doing here?* Suddenly feeling an arm around her shoulders, squeezing tightly, she realized Sylvia was giving her some last-minute encouragement. Sylvia smiled from ear to ear and whispered, "Here we go! We're gonna be just fine!"

They gravitated toward the back of the group of runners as the race director went over the course and other last-second details. Then, before she could mentally psych herself up, an airhorn blew and everyone began running, slowly at first until the pack separated itself into small groups and individuals, and then gradually picking up speed. Angie, her anxiety and inexperience getting the better of her, began running at a pace that was almost sprinting. It wasn't until the huffing and puffing began that she realized she had started out too fast and slowed down until she reached a more manageable pace. The rhythm of her feet pounding on the asphalt trail that circled the park and listening to conversations helped take her mind off the physical exertion.

In fact, she was so caught up in the atmosphere that her arrival at the one-mile marker was a most welcome surprise. She checked her watch to see how long it had taken to reach that first milestone and was gratified to see it was only about ten seconds behind the goal she had set for herself. This resulted in a quickened pace for a few strides to make up the time before she had the presence of mind to slow back down somewhat, reminding herself there were still two miles to go. Reaching the two-mile marker, she looked at her watch again and calculated being another ten seconds off her goal pace. But before becoming too negative about it, she realized the race was two thirds over and knew she had the stamina to finish the race at her current pace. A sense of excitement began building within her—small at first but increasing with each minute.

Eventually she rounded another gradual turn and saw the balloons of the finish line. Her heart started beating faster than her running could account for, and she knew it was from the excitement of knowing she was about to finish her first race. About a hundred yards from the finish line, she could no longer hold in her enthusiasm and sprinted the rest of the way, throwing her arms up while crossing the finish line, to the cheers of those who had already finished the race and those who had come to watch. She had a slightly difficult time controlling her breathing—not so much from the exertion of running as from the elation of the accomplishment. Within a minute, Sylvia came trotting in, whooping and cheering in Sylvia-like fashion, which became even louder, as if that were possible, when she spied

Angie already across the finish line. Sylvia's demeanor was infectious, and the two friends hugged and screamed as only women can. Angie found herself almost in tears, relieved and excited and happy and feeling so many other emotions she couldn't quite name them all. In time, the adrenaline wore off and both ladies were ready to head home. Angie didn't remember much about the drive or getting into the house. All she knew was that she was both excited and sore—and that she had finished her first race. The first chapter of her new life had been written.

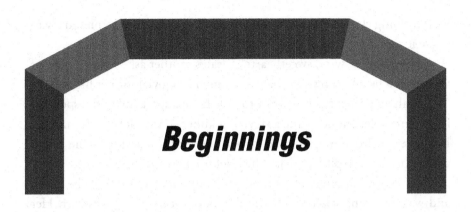

Beginnings

Sarah languorously stroked through the cool lake water as she crossed from one side of the small cove to the other. She relished the effects of the water temperature on her skin; goose bumps popped up all over her arms and legs. It was a nice reprieve to the hot afternoon sun. As she reached the other side of the cove opposite their lake house and turned around, she was just able to make out her mother and another woman walking the short distance from the house to a deck near the water's edge. She managed a cringe despite her swim stroke. Although from this distance she couldn't quite make out exact facial features, she didn't need many guesses to figure out the woman was the wife of the man who owned the company with which her mother was trying to arrange the internship.

She deliberately slowed down her pace, delaying the inevitable. If she had been far enough away for her mother to either not see her or not recognize her, she would have swum around the entire lake, such was her feeling of dread at having to be introduced to the woman, putting on the fake smile and pleasant demeanor, and pretending to be interested in the position. She further slowed her stroke until she was swimming just fast enough to stay afloat in the water and make some progress, knowing her mother was sure to say something about it later if it became obvious she was treading water and purposely staying away. Unfortunately, even with the reduced speed, her perception was that she reached the shore way too quickly. Sighing deeply, she trod out of the water and removed her goggles, catching herself at the end of the sigh, but too late to stop it from sounding like anything else, so she inhaled and loudly exhaled several times to try to make it sound as if she were winded from the physical exertion.

"Have a nice swim, sweetheart?" Sarah's mother asked with a tone of voice and a facial expression that were much too jovial for her liking.

Sarah made a conscious effort to hide her exasperation and responded in an agreeable, but not quite as jovial, manner: "Yes, Mother, thank you. It was very exhilarating." Grabbing her towel off the deck rail, she began drying her hair, hoping to delay the grief for a few more seconds.

Her mother jumped in as soon as Sarah had the towel off her head and was wrapping it around her body. "Sarah, this is Liz Westcott. Her husband is the CEO of Westcott Industries. You know, the company I told you about?" Sarah's mother didn't even wait for an acknowledgment. "Anyway, your father and Mr. Westcott have been talking this past year, and we all thought that since you were majoring in business anyway, and there is a branch of the company close to where you're attending college, *and* you must complete an internship somewhere, why not do it with Westcott Industries? So, whadda ya think?"

Sarah knew her mother would get around to the subject eventually but was totally unprepared for the abruptness of the question. All she could do was stammer a few incomplete phrases. "Well … Um … I dunno … Er … I guess I could … I mean … Uh … I hadn't thought that far ahead yet."

Her mother didn't wait for a denial. "We all think it would be an excellent opportunity. I'll have your father make the arrangements for an interview. Liz, would you like something to drink?" The two women turned and walked up to the house, leaving Sarah feeling as if she had just been slammed into by a semi. She stomped a foot on the deck and made a sound that was part growl and part groan, but as she walked up to the house, she reminded herself about having all summer to come up with a plan to get out of the situation. But for now, she was going to have to put up with her mother for who knew how long.

Sarah's mother and Liz were engrossed in talking about their various clubs and the women in them as she walked through the sunroom and into the kitchen. She had to admit, though, that their gossip meant her mother wasn't focusing on her. As she was getting a snack of peanut butter and apples, the phone rang. "Sarah, honey, could you get that please?" her mother called out.

She grabbed the cordless phone and returned to the sunroom. "Hey, Sarah, it's Lisa. What's up?"

"Oh, nothing much. Just hangin' out at the lake house ..." Sarah responded. Then, deliberately lowering her voice, she added, "... and trying to avoid my mom. I should have stayed at the college this summer instead of coming home." She felt her level of anger beginning to rise.

"Why?" Lisa asked with genuine concern.

Sarah had to grit her teeth and work hard to keep from screeching. "Because my wonderful mother," she began, with sarcasm dripping heavily from "wonderful mother," "took it upon herself to contact the wife of a guy my dad does business with to line up an internship for this coming year." After finishing the statement, she became aware she was digging her fingers into the arm of the chair. She loosened her grip and flexed her fingers.

"Oh, snap!" Lisa exclaimed. "I feel your pain." She hesitated a moment and then added, "You know, Sarah, I may have a solution to your dilemma."

"What sort of solution?" Sarah asked cautiously.

"You know that triathlon my boyfriend is doing, and wanted me to do with him?" Lisa continued quickly. "I told you about it the last week of school, while we were in the Rusty Bucket."

Sarah thought for a few moments, putting the query into the context of "Rusty Bucket conversations" until she finally dredged up the question from among all the other information that was packed into her brain from that last week of school. "Oh, yeah, a triathlon. To be honest with you, I haven't even thought about it since you asked."

Lisa threw out her sales pitch. "You may have some objections, like almost never biking or running, but we're both in good shape from swimming, and we've got another three months to train for the other two parts. Plus ..."—Lisa paused for effect—"it would get you out and away from your mother for extended periods of time this summer. So wadda ya think?"

Sarah had to ponder the issue for only a brief second once Lisa put it to her that way. "All right, I'm in." She could almost hear Lisa jumping up and down and clapping her hands.

"Sweet!" Lisa exclaimed, "I'll call my boyfriend right now to arrange our first training session and call you back with the time and location. Thanks so much Sarah! Bye."

She began reading a magazine, although in truth she wasn't really reading so much as simply looking at the pictures and letting her mind wander over school, the impending internship, training for the triathlon, and a variety of other subjects. Before she knew it, her mother was escorting Liz Westcott out the front door and waving as she drove off down the gravel road. She came into the room where Sarah was half reading and half zoning out, and she sat down in one of the other recliners. "So what did Lisa want, dear?" she asked, trying to strike up a conversation.

"Oh, nothing much. She just wanted to ask me to enter a triathlon she's going to do in a few months with her boyfriend," Sarah replied nonchalantly.

Her mother raised one eyebrow. "A triathlon? What's a triathlon?"

Sarah lowered the magazine to her lap. "It's a race that includes swimming, biking, and running. Her boyfriend has been doing them and wants her to do one with him, but she doesn't want to do it by herself. I think she wants me along for moral support."

True to her nature, it didn't take Sarah's mother long to figure out the implications of Sarah's spending time with Lisa. "But I thought you would be spending most of your time here or at home this summer. How much time is all this training going to take?"

Sarah didn't dare say what was on her mind, which was "As much as possible," so being conscious of starting a potential argument, she responded with, "I really don't know, Mom. I've never done this before, but I don't think it should take too long. We've got the entire summer, so we can space out the training. It shouldn't take too long." Sarah hoped that last statement would appease her mother, and it seemed as if it worked. From the look on her mother's face, it appeared that she was trying to formulate an objection but was having difficulty finding anything specific to object about—that is, without admitting the truth, which was that *she* wanted Sarah to spend all, or at least most, of her time at home with her.

Matt strolled along the chain-link fence that enclosed the pool at one of the local high schools. As he walked through the gate, he noticed a group of adults sitting in the bleachers, and he recognized them as the group he had joined a few months ago for swim training. They all made the rounds of hellos as he sat down, and they then went back to their conversations. Shortly thereafter, the swim instructor arrived and barked out orders for warm-up drills, and soon after the real workout was underway. True to past patterns, Matt lagged behind most of the others in speed and tried to make up for it in effort. Thankfully, the hour didn't last long when he simply focused on improving his technique.

The next morning, he got up at 5:00 a.m. and drove to a local shopping center that was across the street from a large city park. There was a store that specialized in running shoes and other running apparel in the shopping center, and while buying a pair of shoes there, Matt had learned there was a running club that did regular early-morning runs in the park. As he got out of his car, he noticed a group of people congregating in front of the running store and performing various prerun stretches. A few minutes later, one of them remarked that it was slightly past the time the group was supposed to meet and asked whether everyone was ready to get started. With murmured assents, the runners shook their legs a few more times and began heading toward the park. Once in the park, Matt fell in with two men and two women that seemed to be moving at a pace he felt he should be able to maintain over the length of the run.

About midway through the run, he suddenly became conscious of their pace and was surprised at how seemingly effortless it was. "Maybe there is something to running with others," he mused to himself. Sooner than he would have anticipated, one of the men remarked that it was time to start heading back to the running store. If anyone had asked him, Matt would have had to agree that one of the benefits of doing something as a group is how it affects perception of time. Checking his watch, he was astonished at how far they had run in what had seemed like a short amount of time. He silently made a commitment to make running with a group part of his regular training routine, even though it was so early in the morning!

Over the next several months, Matt stayed true to his commitment. In fact, not only did he continue with the early-morning run; he also began running with a group that met on a weekday evening, as well as adding in a longer run on the weekend. Since he had kept up with his cycling and had added swimming three days a week, most of his free time was taken up with training. Within about six months from the time he had heard about, and planned on competing in, a triathlon, his life became little more than working and training. And if he could have paid the bills without working, he probably would have given up his job.

A quick walk-through of his apartment would have also been a tip-off to his lifestyle. Although no one would've accused him of being an outright slob, there was always a general clutter about the small living room, bathroom, and two bedrooms. The second bedroom, which had been a home office, now had the computer desk and bookshelf pushed into one corner to make way for a treadmill and stationary bike trainer. The sliding door on the shower almost always had assorted types of workout clothes hanging off it in varying stages of drying. And if someone were to open the kitchen cabinets, they would find them stocked full of energy bars, gels, electrolyte replacement drinks, and many other nutritional supplements, but not much of what most people would call "real food."

A similar pattern emerged at work. The physical therapy facility had begun to increase its client and referral base, which resulted in an increased need for therapist services. Rather than hiring more physical therapists, the owner of the company opted to offer more clients to the therapists that had started with the company when the facility opened. All of them had jumped at the chance to earn more money, even though it meant working longer hours—all of them, that is, except Matt. In the beginning, he did accept a few more clients each week just to get the supervisor off his back. But a month after that, he would thank him for the opportunity and politely refuse the extra work. Finally the supervisor stopped offering him additional clients because he knew Matt would always refuse them with the excuse of it cutting into his training time, responding with what had now become a pseudomantra: "Sometimes there are more important things in life than money."

Beep! Beep! Beep! Beep! Beep! Sarah groaned as she rolled over and fumbled with the small alarm clock. Her fingers located the minuscule off button, which got pushed with exaggerated emphasis. She threw it against the wall of the tent in a last act of groggy defiance at being awoken so brusquely. After dressing within the confines of the bag, a wave of cold air hit as she unzipped the bag and stood up to put her shoes on. She immediately began hopping up and down, rubbing her hands on her arms to try to warm up a little. Unzipping the tent door, she stepped out awkwardly, deeply breathing in the cold, crisp air.

Lisa and Connor were already up, warming their hands over a camping stove. "Good morning, sleepyhead!" Lisa called out as Sarah stiffly ambled over to the picnic table. "I thought about waking you up, but we're all going to need as much rest as possible today."

Sarah nodded in acknowledgment through a jaw-creaking yawn. "That's OK. I had to get up sooner or later anyway. Oooohh! Is that coffee I smell?" Lisa poured her a mug full and they began talking about the race. Connor had done this race before, so he explained what they could expect from each event—particularly what the cycling and running courses were like. Once they had finished their coffee, the trio packed up their gear and headed down to the transition area.

As the trio organized their transition stations and warmed up, there was a constant stream of commentary from one of the race directors, who was making announcements and giving course and safety instructions to the pack of participants over a loudspeaker system. Sooner than they expected, he completed his instructions by announcing, "All right, fifteen minutes to the start of the long swim! Fifteen minutes!" The group of participants, about 360 in all, milled around the boat ramp as the long-course racers hustled to the edge of the water and the short-course racers slid back up the ramp to get out of their way. They had barely accomplished separating themselves when the race director's voice came over the bullhorn: "Five minutes! Five minutes!"

Although Sarah wasn't sure where to stand in the pack, Connor had assured her and Lisa that, given their swim training, they would be among the fastest swimmers of the day. Trusting Connor's word, she went to the front of the group that was forming. "One minute! One minute!" the race director cried, giving them one last warning. Sarah and Lisa glanced at each other, shrugged, and edged into the water themselves. Once more the race director yelled into a bullhorn: "Here we *gooo!* Ten … nine …

eight …!" The crowd picked up the count and then screamed while the swimmers ran into the water.

Since Sarah had been in the water for warm-ups and knew how cold it was, she braced herself for the initial shock as she jumped in. Even so, it took her breath away a little, but then her swimming instincts kicked in, and she began a freestyle stroke, putting her brain on cruise control and letting the body memory that had developed after so many years of swimming take control. Once she had reached the first buoy, Sarah reminded herself this was her strongest part of the race and she had to make as much time as possible on the other athletes because many of them were sure to catch up and pass her on the bike ride or the run. Increasing the intensity of her stroke, within a minute or two she had passed the person just in front of her; and a few minutes after that, she passed the next person. After rounding the last buoy, she put on a final burst of speed and cruised into the boat ramp, observing only one person in front of her who was just reaching the top of the boat ramp, which gave her renewed energy as her competitive juices revved up.

Once in her riding gear, there was no need for her to worry about which way to leave the transition area, as a couple of volunteers saw her running with her bike and began shouting, "This way! This way!" and wildly waving their arms. Approaching where they were standing, Sarah could see a straight chalk line across the exit of the transition area. "On your bike at the line! On your bike at the line!" they barked out. Once one of her feet was in a pedal, she pushed off and headed in the direction they were pointing. There were a few turns inside the small park, and at each one there were chalk arrows to point the way.

In a little less than two minutes, she had exited the park and was cruising along the boulevard, on which the riders would stay for most of the bike course. The race organizers had chosen a street that had intersections every one-half mile, and there were police officers at every intersection, stopping the few cars that were out this early in the morning so the racers could ride through the intersections without stopping. She chuckled to herself at the somewhat childlike feeling that it was rather exhilarating being able to ride through a red light and having cars being inconvenienced by bikes for a change, instead of the other way around.

Sarah soaked in the experience of the race, taking great pleasure in the wind as it washed over her body. She occasionally lifted her head up to feel the wind on her face. A deep breath of the moist, cool morning air was accentuated with smells from nearby fields of vegetables. She could hear other racers yelling, "Left!" to notify the cyclist in front of them that they were being passed and should stay as far right as possible on the road. Although she was passed every so often by other racers and heard "Left!" directed her way several times, she felt comfortable with her pace and made no attempt to reel them in. Soon the turnaround point popped up in the distance, marked with cones and a wooden easel-type sign.

Once past the cones on the other side of the turn, she stood up from the saddle, used her weight to help crank the pedals at maximum effort, and, about fifty yards past the turnaround point, got back up to race speed. About two miles from the turnaround, the course made a left turn and headed toward some small foothills. Soon she had shifted all the way down to the lowest gear and was still having to huff and puff her way up the hill. Within several minutes, she came to a bend in the road that curved around to the right and appeared to be the top of the grade, only to find that it merely turned to follow the hill and kept heading up and to the left. "Jeez Louise! How much more of this is there!" she exclaimed. Three more times she thought she saw the top of the road, just to make it around the next turn and see that it kept going up. Eventually she quit expecting to see the top and focused on grinding it out, which by now felt like a snail's pace.

She began wondering whether it would be faster to get off her bike like a few of the others and walk however much farther uphill there was to go before rounding the final bend and seeing that this time the road was truly beginning to head downhill. It didn't take her long to build momentum and coast down the hill, letting gravity do its thing so she didn't have to expend energy for a few seconds. The last eight to nine miles stayed level, which allowed her to maintain a consistent effort. Before she knew it, they were turning onto a major street. Glancing up at the street sign on the corner, she realized it was one of the two streets that bordered the park. Feeling revitalized, she increased her pace during the last mile.

As she was approaching the race site and reentering the park, there was a volunteer on each side of the chute that led to the transition area, and they both yelled "Dismount here! Dismount here!" as she coasted to a stop just in front of a chalk line on the ground and jogged alongside the bike until coming to her own transition area. Taking off her helmet and pulling on a visor, she began searching for the sign that read "RUN EXIT." It took her a few seconds to get her bearings, but after locating the sign, she headed for it at a slow jog. There was yet another volunteer stationed underneath the sign, and he waved her through while shouting out, "Two thirds done! You're almost there! Go! Go! Go!"

Sarah began running as she rounded the waist-high tape barrier. The excitement from finishing the cycling leg, and all the shouting and encouragement resulted in her adrenaline kicking into overdrive. She ran away from the transition area and out onto the running leg at a pace she could not have possibly maintained for the entire 6.2 miles. As on the bike, she flashed back to conversations she and Lisa had had with Connor. "When you get off the bike, you're going to want to run at a sprint. Don't! Start out at a pace that you feel is slower than what you think you can run. That will be the right pace, even though you may be frustrated with how slow you think you're going. Remember: you can always increase your speed later, but if you start out too fast and bonk early, three or four miles is a long way to walk when you're dead tired." Coming back to the present and taking Connor's advice, she slowed her pace, putting her stride on autopilot.

A short distance from the race site, the trail left the park and veered onto an asphalt multi-use path that paralleled a stream. She was thankful to find that the path was lined with mature trees, as the sun was now almost directly overhead and it was starting to heat up. She ran on the packed dirt on the side of the asphalt path to stay in the shade as much as possible and tried to distract herself from the heat by watching the other runners. Her little mental game did just the trick; in a very short time she reached the turnaround point on the run course, which was marked with a semicircle of chalk on the ground and another easel that read "MILE 3" propped up in the middle of the half circle.

Before long she completed the second half and reentered the park, feeling like shouting upon scanning the horizon and locating the inflatable arch that was placed at the finish line. Her excitement supplied her with a burst of adrenaline, and she couldn't keep herself from increasing her speed. As her competitor's instincts took over, she sprinted the remaining distance, bursting past the finish line under the arch. Being so winded from that final push, all she could do was coast a couple of yards and bend over with her hands on her knees, gulping air fast and hard. As she stood there focusing on regaining her breath, a volunteer bent down to one knee and removed her timing chip from around her ankle. Another volunteer handed her a bottle of water, and all Sarah could do was smile and nod at him. He nodded at her in return, seeming to read her facial expression that she wanted to say something but was unable to at that point. "It's OK," he remarked with an encouraging smile. "I've been there myself a few times."

Surveying the area while sipping her water, she scanned the crowd to see whether Connor or Lisa had finished yet. After a minute or two and no sight of them, her gaze drifted across the tableau to various tents filled with samples of products, and groups of finishers standing around the award stage, talking excitedly about the race. Eventually the area around the finish line grabbed her attention. Every time someone crossed the finish line, there was still a crowd of people there to applaud their efforts, regardless of when or how the person finished. One would have thought each person was winning the race from the way the spectators reacted.

Her line of vision led her to notice Connor walking over from the award stage area. "Hey, Sarah!" he said enthusiastically. "How long have you been done?"

She couldn't help but smile broadly at his demeanor. Connor was usually quiet and tended toward shy, not to mention even reticent at times. "About five to ten minutes ago," she estimated.

"That's great! You must have made really good time. I'll bet you and Lisa beat me on the swim, since you two are experienced swimmers." His comment led to them engaging in their own discussion of the race, which was brief, as Connor spotted Lisa nearing the finish line. "Go, Lisa! Go! Go! Go!" he chanted as he rushed over to the finish line. By the time Sarah was able to get over to Lisa, her timing chip was already off, she had a bottle of water, and Connor was administering a bear hug. "You did it!" he yelled.

"Ow!" Lisa responded. "You big moose! My ear is only a few inches from your mouth. Keep it down … and let go. You're gonna break a rib or something." The look she gave Sarah strongly suggested her reaction was only for show, and that she was actually very pleased at being fawned over.

Connor only partially tempered his actions, continuing to hug her, swing her around, and talk about how proud he was of her.

The three of them ambled toward the food tent, their path zigzagging as they walked around groups of racers and well-wishers. After about fifteen to twenty minutes, Connor pointedly asked Sarah and Lisa, "So what do you think about triathlons? Fun, huh? Challenging? Exciting?"

Sarah made eye contact with Lisa and waited a moment. "Yeah, it wasn't too bad. Fun? Maybe if I was more used to biking and running it might be fun. Whadda ya think, Lees?"

Lisa paused for a few seconds and then added her own affirmations. "Yeah, I'm with you. If we trained for the other parts, I might be willing to do this again. *Might!*" She stated this with a hard look at Connor.

He threw up his hands and leaned back. "OK! OK! I get the message. I won't push. Whatever you want to do is fine with me. It's just nice to have someone to do these things with." Sarah and Lisa nodded to each other as they stood up to start making the trip home. Sarah couldn't help but let out a satisfied sigh of accomplishment.

Matt was awake before the alarm clock went off. Once the grogginess wore off, he lay in bed mentally rehearsing the race, going over the details again and again, taking special note of the equipment he would need for each stage, and comparing it to what he could remember packing in his small duffel bag back home. Upon visually completing the race from start to finish for the umpteenth time, he made plans to visit several booths that held items of interest, having developed the athlete's philosophy of "If some is good, more is better." The alarm clock's sudden beeping interrupted his ruminations. He took his time about getting up, walking over to the other side of the bed, and turning it off, standing between the bed and window for a while and watching the headlights of what few cars there were at that time of the early morning on the freeway.

He dressed in layers, having checked the weather the day before. It would be a little chilly while setting up and warming up for the race, necessitating a warm-up suit over his race clothes. Sure enough, the air was cool and crisp on the walk out to the car. He tilted his head back slightly, taking deep breaths and relishing the fresh air after the stuffiness of the small hotel room. Arriving at the race site, he located the "Pre-Registered" sign on the tent and got in line behind four other racers. After receiving a bag with his race numbers and brief instructions on where to put each one, he made his way to the transition area. Once his station seemed to be properly organized, he made his way to some volunteers who were using large markers to write each person's race number on their body.

While he was engaged in that task, someone with a microphone and sound system began talking to the racers—giving race instructions, mentioning all the various products available at the expo, and interviewing racers that happened to be walking by. Matt completed various warm-up exercises, paying vague attention to the guy with the mic, and when he heard "Thirty minutes until the first wave ... age groups fifteen to nineteen! Age group twenty to twenty-four, you're on deck! Thirty minutes to the start of the fifteenth annual North Bay Triathlon!" Matt ambled back to his station, knowing there were two waves before his but wanting to watch them go off to see what it would be like when it was his turn.

When he got down to the lake, it looked as if most of the first wave had already formed a group at water's edge. A short time later, the announcer yelled, "Five minutes to race time!" He then called for anybody still in the water to exit. He alerted them when there were three minutes to go, then two minutes, and then one minute, and finally he yelled, "All right now! Let's hear it! Ten ... nine ... eight ... seven ..." He stopped at seven and let the throng take the countdown the rest of the way until they reached one and then in unison yelled, "Go!" As one, the racers splashed into the water, lifting their legs high for several strides before diving in. The crowd kept cheering until the last of the first wave was well away from the starting line.

No sooner had the roar die down than the announcer bellowed into the mic, "Three minutes! Three minutes to the start of the next wave! Twenty to twenty-four age groupers!" A large group of racers in green caps began entering the water for a final warm-up. "Two minutes to the start of the twenty to twenty-four wave! Anybody still in the water, time to get out! Two minutes!" The countdown was repeated as with the first wave, and the next group splashed into the water.

Matt followed several yellow caps into the water for a few last strokes before his own start. It wasn't long before the announcer began the now familiar process of counting down the minutes, then seconds; and before he could really get himself set, the countdown reached one, the racers were entering the water, and the race was on! After the first couple hundred yards, Matt began reciting a mantra to help keep his stroke smooth. "Reach ... pull ... lift ... reach ... pull ... lift ..." he said to himself, striving to maintain his rhythm. It wasn't long before the monotony of continually repeating swim strokes began to wear on him and his sense of time and distance became skewed. *Man*, he thought, *Why is this taking so long? I should be farther along than this. I feel like I'm stuck in molasses.*

After what seemed like forever, he finally caught a glimpse of the inflatable arch that was over the swim finish line. Despite what it might do to his efficiency, he was so eager to get out of the water that he put all his effort into going as fast as he could. Upon reaching the ramp, he lurched up the embankment, pulling off his goggles and swim cap, managing an unsteady jog past the cheering multitude, following his fellow competitors toward, and into, the transition area. After donning shoes and helmet, he forcefully jerked his bike off the rack and followed the flow of racers through the transition area until they came to a chalk line on the edge of the racks. Volunteers were continually calling out instructions and pointing to the line as each athlete approached. "Mount here! Mount here! Past the line, then mount! Mount here!" The bike course began on the paved road inside the park, which meandered past groves of trees and picnic areas before exiting the park onto the street. There were several volunteers to direct the athletes through a right turn, and there was a police officer to hold up traffic to avoid accidents.

Within several miles, the course came to a section of the road that consisted of curves and rolling hills. As the course entered the hills, houses became fewer and farther between. Instead of wooden and brick fences, the properties were now separated by multiple strands of barbed wire. Most of the driveways were dirt or gravel, and single mailboxes usually stood near the road-and-driveway intersections. The road continued to snake through the foothills, gradually rising and falling. Glancing down at his bike computer, he noted the halfway point should be in about one to two miles. He checked his speed and began revising his estimated finishing time for the cycling leg, and glancing up again, he noticed for the first time that the road didn't seem to curve up and down anymore. It just seemed to curve up, and up ... and up.

Taking a few deep, energizing breaths, he continued to maintain an even pace, preparing himself for a different type of pedaling—what is often referred to as "grinding it out." As he began the climb, Matt had to suppress a slight feeling of annoyance and frustration, feeling as though he had just hit his stride on the flatter sections and now here was some hill-climbing. He resigned himself to maintain as fast a pace as possible given the gradient. Then, to his surprise, before having done much climbing at all, he came around a corner and saw the valley floor, with a large group of trees in the distance. The relative evenness of the terrain suggested the trees had to be the park that served as the race site.

A rush of adrenaline hit his muscles as he sped down the rest of the way out of the hills and into the valley proper. He kept up his pace until he was forced to slow down at the corners of the last couple of streets that eventually led to the park. As there had been at every major turn on the bike course, there were several volunteers to guide the riders as they turned into the park. "Almost there! Almost there!" they yelled encouragingly. Matt noticed there was quite a bit of chalk on the road and saw that in addition to the line curving around into the park, there were numerous signs on the road for individual riders: "Go Stacy!" read one. "Go Team Trigeeks!" read another.

After spotting the finish line, he put on a final burst of speed. About fifty yards away from the chalk line with the "BIKE IN" sign overhead, he heard the volunteers yelling, "Stop here on the line! Dismount here!" Entering the transition area itself, he cruised past row upon row of racks. Then, after sprinting the last few yards, he heaved his bike up on the rack and clunked it down. After taking several deep breaths, in one fluid motion he bent down, slipped on his running shoes, unsnapped his helmet, tossed it on his duffel bag, and snatched up his running cap. He stumbled away from his transition area, not exactly sure where he was going, but just remembering the beginning of the run exited the transition area somewhere to his left.

The beginning of the run followed an asphalt path paralleling the road that circled the perimeter of the park. After about half a mile, the path veered off to the right, leaving the park and entering an area that looked as if it might be a protected habitat. There were trees and bushes along the path, but on both sides for several square miles were various types of reeds and rushes, with small pools of stagnant water dotting the landscape, giving the locale a marshy feel. Even though it was somewhat hot, the runners benefitted from being in the middle of vegetation and receiving shade periodically while running underneath trees; a slight breeze now and then also provided some relief.

Matt began recalling all the tips and advice from the running group he had joined several months earlier. He had just enough running experience to judge the pace he could sustain for this distance, but he kept his speed a little slower, since he had no experience running after swimming and biking. The focus centered on establishing steady breathing and an efficient stride technique, which was not as easy as it might have seemed. Several times his labored breathing provided the feedback that he had inadvertently sped up, necessitating a refocus on his mechanics.

He was so caught up in his form that arriving at the outskirts of the park caught him totally unaware, and shocked, that he had run as far as he had, which from what he could remember of the map, was about two thirds of the run distance. Now all he had to do was run one lap around the park itself and he would have successfully completed his first triathlon. The excitement of being so close made him increase his speed even without knowing what he was doing. Roughly twenty-five minutes later, he spotted the large "FINISH" banner in the distance, about 250 to 300 yards away. Being suddenly overwhelmed with the zeal that comes from finishing a race, adrenaline flooded into his muscles and he began running faster and faster until he was almost sprinting during the last fifty yards, flashing underneath the inflatable arch. Matt couldn't help but beam in satisfaction at his accomplishment.

He meandered around the finish line area for a while, the adrenaline still coursing through his veins, giving him a runner's high now that he was no longer using all that energy. Gradually he made his way toward the race expo, continuing to enthusiastically congratulate the other participants, at times even initiating high fives with several racers who looked as excited as he was. Little by little, the euphoria from finishing the race subsided while he was strolling through the race site. Eventually his rumbling stomach served notice that, except for energy gels, he had not had anything to eat since before the race, and even that had been minimal. He made his way toward the food tent.

Matt took his time eating, and a few minutes after he finished, the race organizers made a final preawards announcement that the race results were all in and were being checked one last time before the ceremony could begin. Once it started, he perked up when the age group of males ages twenty-five to twenty-nine was called out. Although he did not expect to win anything, he nevertheless felt a small letdown when the time of the third-place finisher was reported and, looking at his watch, he knew he would not be heading up to the stage. The final remaining question was where in his age group he had finished. After pausing for a few moments while debating whether to stay for the entire ceremony, he finally opted to check the times for his age group and begin the three-hour drive home.

Locating the page in the middle of a large board with "AGE GROUP 25–29" printed on it in bold, a quick inspection of the entire list showed him there were 118 competitors in his age group. Beginning at the top of the list and working down, saw his name at number sixty-three. He gazed at the number with mixed emotions. This was his first race, and he had finished near the top half of his age group, but he still felt a disappointment in not having finished higher. He chose to focus mainly on the accomplishment and let any unrest serve as a motivator for future races. He completed packing up and driving home mechanically, his mind totally taken up with plans of how he could amp up his workouts to increase his performance enough for a podium finish at his next race.

"Katie!"

Silence.

"*Kaatttiiieee!*"

"*What!*" came the response, in an annoyed tone of voice.

"I'm almost ready to go. How are you comin'?" Not waiting for a reply, he bent down, opened a cabinet door, and loaded his arms with sports bottles. Putting them on the counter, he bent down again and pulled out a large canister of a sports drink. Using the scoop inside the canister, he began pouring one scoop into each bottle. "Katie," he called out again. "You ready to go?" This time he stopped what he was doing and strained to hear her reply.

Silence.

"What is she doing?" Curt mumbled to himself, leaning around the wall that separated the kitchen from the living room. Not seeing her in the living room or hearing any noises in the house, he walked to the family room, thinking that would be the most likely place she would be. Sure enough, there she was, sitting in the big stuffed chair while peering at her laptop. "Katie," he said emphatically, and he then repeated her name when there was no response.

"Yes" came her one-word reply.

Taking a deep breath to keep from sounding too annoyed, Curt asked his question a third time. "Are you ready to go?"

Katie stared at him with a confused facial expression. "Go where?" she eventually asked. Then, just as he inhaled to say something that was sure to be delivered with an irritated or even angry tone of voice, she smiled and ever so sweetly said, "Yes, I've been ready for some time now. Are you ready to go?" She hadn't been able to resist needling him a little for all the gruff responses she had received in the past two weeks as his anxiety about the approaching race began to escalate.

He exhaled his deep breath and swallowed what he was about to say. In as calm a voice as he could muster, he replied, "I will be in a couple of minutes. I just need to fill my bottles and throw them into the ice chest with a few other things and I'll be ready." He finished gathering his race drinks and food, stuffed them into the collapsible ice chest, grabbed the strap, and hefted the full chest onto his shoulder, once more mentally running through all the things needed for the race. "Pphhh, I'm sure I can get something there if I've forgotten anything." He retrieved Katie's bag from the bedroom on the way to the garage, wondering how on earth it could be heavier than his, given they were going to be gone only overnight. An inner voice told him it might be prudent not to mention it at the moment. This time he listened to the voice and simply lugged it out to the car.

Katie was asleep when they arrived at the city that was hosting the race. Curt glanced over at her and considered dropping her off at the hotel first, before making an "executive decision" and taking the exit that led to the race site instead of the one that would have taken them to the hotel. In no time at all, they were pulling into the parking lot that, come tomorrow, would serve as the transition area for the race. Walking toward the general direction of the race area, he surveyed the many tentlike coverings containing the registration table, race sponsor tables, and vendors. There were only a few people milling around the vendor tents, and the largest grouping of people by far was a line snaking away from the registration tent. When it was finally his turn, Curt stepped forward and gave a woman working there his name. They exchanged pleasantries while she checked his driver's license and marked his name off on a list with a yellow highlighter. She then called out his race number to another person behind the table, who scanned a row of plastic bags, found his number, and handed it to him across the table while wishing him luck.

Curt was lying in bed the next morning when he was awoken by what sounded like mariachi music. "What the hell …?" he pondered, rolling over on his back, being unable to do anything but stare at the ceiling. Gradually becoming oriented to his surroundings, he listened more closely and looked around to discover the music was coming from the clock radio.

Katie stirred next to him and groggily mumbled, "Who's playing Spanish music at this time of the morning?"

Curt hastily reached over and pressed several buttons on the clock radio until it went silent. "Sorry," he whispered, turning over to kiss her on the cheek. "Go back to sleep." He tiptoed into the bathroom, got dressed in his race clothes, and then got their bags ready to go. The drapes were partially open, revealing that it was still pitch-black outside. "Who gets up this early?" he mumbled. "Why am I getting up this early? Why did I think this was a good idea?"

Arriving at the race site, he followed the cars in front of him, pulling into the parking lot of large industrial-looking buildings. On the walk to the transition area, he picked up on the hum of hundreds of people talking and laughing. He continued to follow those walking their bikes through an intersection and then through the gates and into the parking lot that, as with many races, now served as a transition area for the racers.

As he passed rack after rack, Curt noticed several balloons and flags sticking up where people had marked their areas so they could find them easily as they ran in from the swim. He made a mental note to do the same if he ever did another one of these things. Copying numerous racers around him, he laid his towel out first and placed the remaining items on the towel in the order in which he would need them. He wasn't sure whether it was all exactly right, but that was another thing to adjust in future races. He struck up a conversation with several men who were setting up their stations near his. When they learned this was his first race, they offered several tips for first-timers.

Curt was surprised to hear the race organizer announce that the first wave would be going off in fifteen minutes, not thinking they had been talking that long. His wave was the sixth, and given that the waves left at five-minute intervals, he knew it wouldn't be necessary to line up just yet. But he grabbed his wetsuit off the rack anyway and tagged along behind those who were rushing to get in some warm-ups before the starts of their waves. His sense of time became skewed while watching the other racers. He thought he had plenty of time before his wave but was completely taken off guard when the announcer called out the two-minute warning for his group. And he hadn't even put on his wetsuit yet!

He had just gotten it zipped up and was in the process of fitting the goggles to his eyes when the horn went off for his wave. He shoved down a quick spike of frustration, trying not to let that deter him from focusing on completing the race, and began stroking as evenly and smoothly as possible. He worked on getting his breathing and stroke synchronized, finally managing to develop some semblance of rhythm. Even with the increased efficiency, it still felt as if it were taking forever. It also didn't help when he was passed by many who had started after he had. At long last, he reached the edge of the river in front of the finish line, standing up as soon as the water was shallow enough and sloshing his way up the bank.

Fortunately for his sagging spirits, he was able to remind himself the swim was over and he didn't have to do it again.

Knowing his swim time was slow not just within his own age group but also among all competitors, Curt consciously opted to sit for a few moments and catch his breath before putting on his bike gear. Once he wasn't hyperventilating anymore, he stood up, slapped his helmet on his head, jammed his feet into his shoes, yanked his bike off the rack, and began trotting toward the "BIKE OUT" sign posted at one end of the transition area. Close to the sign, he could see a double chalk line on the pavement, and two people on either side of the makeshift gate were calling out to the racers, "Pass the line! Mount here! Pass the line! Mount here!" Once past the line, he paused for a few seconds to take another several deep breaths before swinging his leg over the bike and pushing off to coast while working his feet into the pedals.

The first few miles of the course took the riders through a mostly suburban area, with street after street of houses that were very similar in appearance packed close to each other. Taking in the scenery, he noticed the suburban streets were slowly but steadily beginning to be mixed with areas in which the houses didn't have that cookie-cutter look about them and were not as close to each other. Their facades gave the general impression of houses that had been built decades earlier. A rider from behind calling out "*Left!*" brought him out of his survey of the countryside.

As she sailed past, he once again realized he had been paying more attention to the surroundings than to the race. He was eventually able to ignore what was on either side of him, focusing on the road itself by purposely choosing a spot about ten yards in front of his bike and keeping his gaze fixed on that spot. Before long he was passing others, and soon he was the one calling out "Left!" or "On your left!" while overtaking first one rider, then another, and then another. For the first time, Curt began enjoying the race.

That enjoyment was short-lived, as a few miles later the course began to go up and it became necessary to put maximum effort into each turn of the pedals. The same frustration from earlier set in, but he stoically pushed on, now competing more against his emotions than against the course, and he began muttering to himself to work up some type of emotional momentum. "Come on! Let's go! You can do this!" The trick worked somewhat, as he was able to increase his speed slightly until he reached a plateau where the road leveled off. A mile or two farther and he was sailing downhill, resisting the urge to put out 100 percent effort, keeping in mind there was still a six-mile run after finishing the cycling portion.

Soon he was back in the suburbs, with all the houses differing only by color. While he did not recognize the streets, given that everything looked the same, sensing he was now within a mile or two of the park where the race had started gave him an unexpected psychological boost. Suddenly he had a newfound well of energy, and he used it for a burst of speed, sprinting the rest of the way. Shortly after beginning his final push, he saw a volunteer pointing and yelling something, which he guessed was a directive to turn the corner she was pointing toward. Rounding the corner, he could see the park up ahead—the promised land! Putting everything into it, he gave one last surge of effort before slowing down while turning into the parking lot and reaching the chalk line just inside the park entrance.

Arriving at his area and lifting his bike onto the rack, he unclipped his helmet and hooked it on one of the handlebars. Rather than taking off for the run right away, he took a few moments and stretched out his legs. Satisfied with at least being able to jog, he began walking toward the opening in the transition area with the sign that read "RUN OUT." Closer to the gate, he began a very slow jog perhaps best described as a shuffle. His feet were barely off the ground, and it was very disappointing to him not to be running as fast as he desired, but for now he had to be content with knowing at least there was forward movement.

Trying a mental trick from a magazine article, he adjusted his thinking from focusing on how far he had to go to how far he had already come. "OK," he said, talking out loud to himself, "I've got almost one mile down, only five more to go." Even knowing he was among the last group of racers still on the course, Curt felt better about his performance, as there were still dozens of people running on the trail. True, most were running in the opposite direction, meaning they had already completed the part he was just starting, but there were plenty of runners up ahead. Just as he was starting to feel good about his performance again, the first of what would be many bouts of cramps hit.

It started in his thighs. After about a minute or two, he started getting cramps in his calves, and soon after that the cramps radiated into his hamstrings. Each step was so painful. Even as gingerly as he was walking, each time his feet met the ground, pain radiated throughout his legs. The only positive to take from the situation was that at least he was still moving, and as much as he wanted to stop moving, he kept on. Just when it seemed he would have to finish the race under the present circumstances, the cramps gradually began to diminish.

After about a hundred yards and no cramps, he increased his pace from a slow jog to alternating between a fast jog and slow run. Despite his pain, Curt had to laugh at the thought that anyone watching him now would have to guess he was about ninety years old, given the way he was rocking back and forth. It seemed he was moving from side to side just as much as he was going forward. After jogging for the next several minutes, a sense of optimism that the worst had passed began to sprout. Continuing to run past one self-chosen marker after another—a sign here, a type of tree there—the optimism grew. He couldn't stop himself from yelling "Hallelujah!" when arriving at the mile-three marker.

"You're halfway there! All downhill from here!" called out one volunteer as the other one reached out to give Curt a high five.

That was all he needed to boost his flagging spirits. After pivoting around the marker, he took off at a pace he hadn't been capable of since starting the run. He kept plugging away, and after what seemed like a "mini forever," he eventually arrived at the mile-four marker. After another short eternity, he reached the mile-five banner, and shortly after that he heard some sounds coming from a loudspeaker, although he couldn't tell exactly what they were. Soon enough he came to a clearing in the path, which opened onto the park. Once out into the open and on the outskirts of the park, he could hear music playing over the speaker system, and he occasionally heard a voice, although at this distance he couldn't quite make out what it was saying.

He looked in the direction from which the sound was coming and saw the entire triathlon area: the vendor tents, the transition area with all the bikes racked, and, best of all, the inflatable arch that was over the finish line! The excitement of being so near the finish caused him to completely forget about all the negative emotions and his fatigued physical state. He started running at the fastest pace manageable, until, estimating he had about one hundred yards to go, he put on a final sprint—well, maybe not a real sprint. In truth, it wasn't much of a sprint at all. But at that moment in time, with his body feeling the way it was, it was the only sprint he could manage, and after having walked and run so slowly, it certainly felt like a sprint to him.

About twenty yards from the inflatable arch, the announcer saw Curt and yelled into the mic, "And we have number 659! Curt Emory! Give it up!" Even though he was one of the last few racers, there were still several dozen people along each side of the chute, cheering those remaining stragglers. He practically jumped over the finish line, ran a few more steps, and came to an abrupt stop in front of a volunteer, who stooped over the tear off the lower part of his race bib. "Good job!" he said enthusiastically. "You did it!" Another volunteer came over to hand Curt a bottle of water and offer her congratulations. He was breathing so heavily from sprinting that all he could do in response to both was smile and nod. Walking and gulping as much air as he could get with each breath, he scanned the crowd on this side of the finish area to locate Katie.

He finally spied her hurrying toward him, dodging around various small groups of racers and what had to be friends and family congratulating them. When she reached Curt, she stood up and lightly kissed him on the lips, barely making contact. "Ugh!" she said with a purposely contorted face. "You're sweaty!"

The remark caught him off guard. He tried to think of a snappy comeback, but all he could think of was "I'm sweaty? Do you have any idea what I've been doing for the last four hours!" He attempted to give her a stern look of reproach, but he couldn't quite pull it off, owing to her goofy ear-to-ear grin.

He chuckled as she took both his hands in hers and practically hopped up and down. "I'm so proud of you!" she exclaimed.

Curt, continuing to smile in return, managed a sincere "Thank you" despite his feelings.

Katie, sensing that his response was less than heartfelt, asked, "What's wrong? You certainly don't look as happy as I am that you did it." He hesitated and then recounted how the race had gone, focusing on all those things he had not done well. Katie patiently listened, and when she was sure he was done, she quickly and firmly stated, "You are an idiot!"

It was obvious from the look on Curt's face he was completely flabbergasted. His lips made the beginnings of "What ... how ... I ..." but he was unable to finish any thought or question. At long last he finally managed to blurt out, "What do you mean I'm an idiot?!"

She leaned forward on her tiptoes and stabbed a finger in his chest to emphasize her comments. "You, sir, are an idiot because you just did something that very few people *ever* do in their entire lives! You're an idiot because you can't see what you have accomplished and all you can do is whine about what you didn't do!" Curt kept trying to interject comments here and there, but Katie steamrolled right over him. "You're an idiot because when other people were in bed or in front of the TV, you were out training and working hard. You're an idiot because you kept going when you wanted to quit—and when many other people probably would have quit. But you kept going and finished the race, making you a winner, and all you can think of is that you're a loser, when you're not; you're a winner. That's why you're an idiot!" She punctuated the last three words with a particularly emphatic finger-push that made him stumble backward.

Following her remarks, she stood back down on her heels, glaring at Curt for several moments, silently daring him to disagree with her. After a while, the look on his face softened, and he smiled and warmly said, "Thank you." After rubbing his mouth off on the back of his arm, he kissed her on the lips, ignoring her protests.

"So what now?" she asked after wiping her own mouth off with her arm.

"Now I go get something to eat, and then I believe I saw some outdoor showers by the bathrooms near the transition area. And then ... it's time to head for home."

Katie grasped Curt's hand as they strolled to the food tent. "Sounds like a plan" she responded enthusiastically.

───────────────────

Angie counted and recounted in her mind how many bottles she was taking versus how many she thought might be needed. She then made the decision that one more couldn't possibly hurt, so she got down one more water bottle and added it to the others in the ice chest. She got out a box of energy gels and energy bars and, grabbing a handful of each without even bothering to count, tossed those into the ice chest as well. She then retrieved her checklist and scanned it one last time, at last feeling finally ready to hit the road and, to quote Sylvia, "take the next step in her journey toward establishing a new life for herself."

On the way to pick up Sylvia, Angie tried hard not to think about Michael and what had transpired in the last two years. For quite some time, she fought to stop the obsessions, eventually becoming aware of her hands gripping the steering wheel until her knuckles were white. Through that awareness she was able to finally break the cycle. "Take a deep breath and start thinking about the weekend," she said to herself audibly. Although it was a relief to finally focus on something else, it concerned her that, when she found herself turning onto the street on which Sylvia lived, she was hit with the realization she had been thinking about Michael for the entire drive, having no recollection of how she had gotten to Sylvia's.

Pulling into the driveway and turning off the car, she looked at herself in the rearview mirror. There was an intention of trying to say something to build up some morale, to buoy her flagging spirits; but after several moments passed by with her drawing a complete blank, she gave up. It was surprising how much effort it took to push open the car door and trudge instead of walk to Sylvia's front door and timidly knock three times. She could hear music playing inside, which didn't exactly help her mood. In keeping with Sylvia's usual upbeat style, the music had a driving beat and was something one might hear in a dance club, which was almost the exact opposite of how she was feeling.

She had raised her fist to knock on the door again when she made out the faint sound of footsteps approaching the door. Sylvia flung the door open with an excited look on her face and started to launch into what Angie knew was going to be another litany about starting a new life. But before Sylvia could get half a sentence out, she saw the look on Angie's face and, once she noticed that, took a more careful look at her body posture. After a brief pause, during which she sized up Angie even more closely, Sylvia asked pointedly, "OK, what's up? Even I can tell that something is seriously wrong this morning!" This time it was Angie's turn to pause as she contemplated whether to lie outright or just make up something so Sylvia would not press the issue. She began to stammer out some halfhearted excuse for her demeanor but quickly realized she was dealing with Sylvia, who knew her far too well to accept anything less than the truth. Against her desires, she was forced to describe her obsession about Michael during the entire drive over.

Sylvia led Angie over to the couch, turned off the stereo, and, surprisingly enough, was true to her word. She listened to Angie talk about how she felt about Michael, the kids, and her feeling frustrated that she was still adjusting when she had thought that by this time she would have gotten over it—whatever "it" was. Finally, after forty-five minutes, Angie felt as though she had released what had been building up for the past few months. Sylvia's only comment was to ask her if she needed anything else. After much contemplation, Angie said, "… No … no, I think I've talked enough for now. Besides, I know you said we had plenty of time, but we were going to get a look at the course, right? So we'd better get going. Got your stuff ready?"

Angie's pulling it together served to prod Sylvia into her normally bouncy self. "Am I ready? I've been waiting for this for months!" With that she sprang up off the couch and practically hopped into the kitchen to sling her own gear bag over her shoulder. "Lead on!"

The talk with Sylvia served to finally take Angie's mind off what had transpired so far that morning. She genuinely felt at ease as they entered the freeway and headed out of town to the triathlon and found herself able to focus on planning for the race without mental distractions. When they finally arrived and pulled into the parking lot that would later serve as the transition area, she felt an excitement that she had never felt before and was practically bouncing around as much as Sylvia. As they walked to the registration table, she couldn't help but feel as though they were giggling and carrying on like a couple of young teenage girls.

After they finished the check-in process, they jabbered all the way back to the car, the only break in their dialogue coming when Sylvia got out the small race program that was in her goody bag, and they began to study the course map. The two budding triathletes resumed talking excitedly and emotionally as they got out of the car and bounced into the hotel lobby. After checking in and finding their room, Angie suggested as they deposited their bags on their beds, "Whaddya say we get freshened up and find a good restaurant. Oh, and no more talking about the race for a while?"

"Sounds good to me," Sylvia responded as she flopped on her own bed. Angie decided to mimic her friend, and soon the room was silent as each woman was lost in her thoughts.

Just before nodding off, Sylvia shook herself and then murmured "You awake?"

Angie kept her eyes closed but responded, "Yeah."

With big yawns, they sat up, giggling at the unexpected siesta. After changing clothes, they obtained the names of a few restaurants nearby, choosing an Italian one with the rationale that they needed to carbo-load.

Dinner was one of the most pleasant activities Angie had had in the previous two years; she and Sylvia talked about everything except the race and relationships. Of course, it didn't hurt that the conversation was fueled by copious amounts of wine. When they staggered into their room that night, they both agreed that if they ever did another race, they should leave the drinking until after it was over.

By the time they reached the race site the next morning, the sun had peeked over the foothills, providing just enough light for them to assemble their bikes after pulling them from the trunk. "Does it matter if the chain is on the exact gear it was on when we took it off the bike?" asked Angie, having never taken a wheel off prior to the race.

Sylvia paused in the act of putting on her own rear wheel. "I have no idea. I guess we're going to find out." After getting their wheels mounted, they looked around and noticed some other racers lifting first one wheel and then the other off the ground and spinning them quickly by hand. Neither of them was exactly sure why that was being done, but in their desire to give the appearance they knew what they were doing, they followed suit.

"Oh!" exclaimed Angie. Then she quietly said to Sylvia, "If you spin it, you get to see if the wheel is rubbing on the brake pads, and make sure it's in the right gear." Sylvia didn't say anything verbally but nodded in understanding.

Upon arriving at the transition area, the two rookies stopped to scan the signs that were at the entrance to the bike racks, as well as the signs that were mounted on the top of each individual bike rack. Zeroing in on the number signs, it didn't take long for them to figure out they should rack their bikes on the rack that contained their personal race numbers. Once they put that together, it was simply a matter of walking through the transition area until they came to the correct rack. Given this was their first time putting their bikes on a rack, they experimented with a couple of different ways, all the while watching how those around them were racking their own bikes.

As they proceeded to set up their stations, they continued watching those around them to get some tips on how to make their transitions as efficient as possible. Since this was their first race, they didn't have any preset routines to go through, so it didn't matter to them how they set up this time. Once satisfied with how all their gear was arranged, they walked through the transition area back to where they had entered. As they were walking, a race organizer began talking through a loudspeaker system. "All right! All right, race fans! Approximately forty-five minutes to race start! Forty-five minutes to race start! Get your stuff together, get wired, get ready to go, 'cause we are going off in forty-five! Spectators, you have thirty minutes more in the transition area; then you gotta be out! Racers, you gotta be out by ten minutes before the race start. I repeat, the transition area needs to be empty by ten minutes before race start!"

They divided their attention between keeping limber and listening to the countdown to race time. When the announcer called out there were only fifteen minutes to the start of the first wave, they slipped out of their warm-up suits, shoes, and socks and, in imitation of others around them, pulled their wetsuits on up to their waists. Grabbing their goggles and swim caps, they shadowed a group of women out of the transition area and over to the edge of the small lake, gravitating toward a large group of women that had on swim caps of the same color. "Ten minutes to race start! Ten minutes to race start! Those of you in the water, if you can hear my voice, you need to start making your way back in! We are goin' off in ten!"

There was a palpable increase in the buzz coming from the shoreline. The first group of racers stepped into the water as far out as they were allowed by one of the race directors, which was about neck deep for most of them. A few in the group hung back and were only waist deep but still not too far behind those that were treading water in the front. The pack in the front formed such a straight line that, even though there was no physical barrier, an imaginary rope could have been stretched across the water and they would have been perfectly aligned with it. The race announcer began a steady stream of commentary, at first primarily directed at the racers and then gradually mixing in statements designed to get the crowd of spectators excited. Soon the announcer was calling out, "Three minutes to the start of the first wave! Three minutes to race start!"

The throng on the shore, both spectators and racers alike, began yelling louder, building to a crescendo as the announcer called out, "Thirty seconds! Thirty seconds!" Angie and Sylvia caught the enthusiasm of those around them and commenced bellowing their own support to those who were preceding them in what they were about to undertake that day. It didn't matter to either of them that they didn't know anyone else racing; they just knew what it took to get there and, even with not having officially finished a race yet, knew something of what it was going to take to accomplish the feat. The announcer screamed, "Let's send 'em off! Ten … nine … eight … seven!" and the two soon-to-be-legitimate triathletes raised their voices in unison with the crowd in giving the first wave of racers as much verbal support as possible.

Somewhere off to their left, a horn sounded, and the racers on the front line began churning the water. As space was slowly created, cluster after cluster of swimmers entered the water to commence the first leg of the race. As if it were an unspoken rule, the second wave of swimmers hung back for a few seconds after the last few stragglers were well away from the shoreline before entering the water themselves. "Three minutes to the start of the next wave! Three minutes! Blue caps only should be in the water!" As the next wave went off, the ladies commented on how there seemed to be a certain rhythm or flow to this first leg of the race. There was a wave start, a three-minute notice, a countdown, another wave start, and so on.

Whereas earlier the cacophony of sound was restricted to fleeting intervals whenever a wave went off, now it was continuous as the lead swimmers of the first wave arrived on the heels of the fourth wave beginning their race. "Oh my gosh!" exclaimed Sylvia. "Ang, do you realize these guys just swam almost a mile in a little over twenty minutes?"

Angie thought back to their swim practices and what their expected finishing times were. She could only shake her head and murmur "Wow" in disbelief. She had heard and read about how fast some of the top triathletes were in the water, but hearing about it and seeing it in real life were two different things. The first three or four swimmers finished relatively close to each other, and there was a space between them and the next several racers to slosh out of the water. After that there was pretty much a continuous stream of people running from the lake to the transition area.

As each wave left the shore, the next wave occupied the space at the starting point. Then, unexpectedly, Angie had an unobstructed view of the entire lake, and it took several seconds, and Sylvia grabbing her arm and shaking it in anticipation, for her to grasp the fact their wave was the next to go off. Sylvia said something to her that she didn't really hear as they hiked into the water. Out of the blue, she began having a minor panic attack, reminiscent of what a bride experiences as she is walking down the aisle.

"Wait ... wait ... wait!" her own voice screamed inside her head. "No! No! No! Stop! I change my mind! I'm not ready for this! I can't do this! What was I thinking!"

She looked around for a way to get out but was completely hemmed in by similarly colored swim caps. Her perceived lack of preparedness had no effect on the race, as the announcer once again shouted, "Three minutes! Three minutes to the next wave!" It didn't help her anxiety that she felt as if he were looking straight at her. The group was so tightly packed at that point that she had little choice but to follow the others into the water and was waist deep upon hearing the announcer call out, "One minute to the next wave! Those of you in the water, one minute to your start! Get back to the starting line!"

The announcer suddenly gave them their own countdown, yelling, "Ten ... nine ... eight ... seven ...!" That panicky urge hit again—the one that caused her to want to turn around and run back to her car until the whole thing was over. Even that feeling didn't have time to linger, as she heard "One ... *Go!*" Abruptly, the water around her was a maelstrom of choppy water and body parts. Being the novice, she talked herself through each length, focusing on creating as efficient a stroke as she could manage. One benefit from focusing on her form and making it a goal to simply get from one buoy to the next was that in her perception of time, the swim didn't take all that long. In what seemed to be only a few minutes, she rounded the last buoy and the far shore entered her peripheral vision.

Growing ever closer to shore, she saw various numbers of women climbing up out of the water—a small clump of three here, one there, two more right after her. As fast as Angie felt she had been able to swim up until that point was how slow she felt for the final several hundred yards. It seemed that every time she looked up, the shore was farther, not closer, even though she knew intellectually that couldn't be right. After what seemed like an eternity, she could discern the arch drawing closer and was able to hear the cheering again—faintly at first but quickly increasing with each few strokes. By the time she was stumbling up the bank, it was all she could hear.

Her efforts at getting out of her wetsuit and into the cycling shoes and helmet reminded her of videos of newborn colts. None of her limbs felt coordinated, the helmet fell off before she could buckle it on, and it seemed to be quite difficult to get the bike off the rack. When she had struggled through those tasks, she headed toward the line that had the "BIKE OUT" sign over it. A volunteer was stationed on each side of the opening, and they were shouting to the racers, "Over the line! Mount just over the line!" Angie followed the example of the few people ahead of her and pushed her bike to get a rolling start so she could get her feet into the stirrups without falling over.

Remembering the bike course was basically laid out in the overall shape of a square, she arrived at the first "corner" of the square after about twenty to twenty-five minutes but wasn't exactly sure, since she hadn't specifically checked her watch when leaving the transition area. Once around the corner, she glanced ahead to spot the next set of landmarks and had to do a double take. If her eyes were functioning properly, the road inclined slightly until reaching what might be considered small foothills. *Where did those come from?* She didn't remember seeing any foothills mentioned on the course map. Continuing to inch upward, she discovered that suddenly it wasn't all fun and games anymore. Now it was starting to require some work, and when cresting the top of the first hill, she observed that even though the road declined a short way, it went back up again, and when it did, it was an even steeper climb than what she had just finished.

Although it took her longer than calculated, eventually she struggled through the hills to reach the city limits and relatively level ground once again. The hills had taken more out of her than she cared to admit, and she pedaled at a moderate pace, not even trying to push herself. After turning around a few more corners and weaving throughout the residential area, she almost jumped out of her seat when she spotted the sign for one of the streets that went by the park. She wasn't sure how much farther there was to go and didn't really care at that moment. All she knew was that the cycling leg was almost over, and that knowledge fueled a final push that lasted for the two-plus miles it took for her to arrive at the park.

The encouragement of the volunteers served to awaken her flagging spirits, as she knew that in a short time, she would be crossing that finish line and people would be cheering for her. She ripped off her helmet, grabbed her visor, and started jogging toward the part of the transition area where the "RUN OUT" sign would be. The run course curved around the finish area, giving her a wide view of racers and spectators alike sitting around laughing and eating, the first finishers continuing to cross under the arch to the praise of the crowd. The course meandered through the park, eventually leading the runners out into the residential area. She used the scenery to distract herself from how tired she was and from the letdown of not running as fast as planned. It also helped that the aid stations were at every mile marker, which gave her the opportunity to interact with more volunteers and further take her mind off how she felt.

Even with the physical pain, Angie began enjoying the experience. She resumed observing the neighborhood, noting that there were now people out and about walking, washing cars, gardening, and watching the participants run by. One person sitting in a lawn chair rang a cowbell every time someone came past his house. Angie waved and held up her thumb as he rang the bell when she passed. A few minutes later, she really started feeling the effects from all the physical activity she had done that morning. Besides the muscle soreness in her legs, she now had the sharp pain in her side runners get so often. Grunting in frustration, she put her hands on her hips while continuing to walk at the best manageable speed.

The only consolation to her came after what seemed like hours, when she looked up and spotted the next banner, which turned out to be the mile-three marker, and, in the near distance, a sandwich board for the turnaround. She dragged into the aid station, changing her hands from her hips to her knees and staying like that for a while until one of the volunteers asked her if she was all right. She nodded her assent while straightening up, taking a deep breath, and blowing it out forcefully, and she then remained at the station as several runners went by.

As Angie was heading back in, it took a while before she felt comfortable enough to start walking a little faster. A few minutes later, a familiar figure approached. *Sylvia!* It didn't take long for Angie to discern her friend was in as bad of shape as she was—maybe even worse. As the two got closer to each other, Angie slowed down until she finally stopped and waited for Sylvia to reach her. Sylvia had her head down and didn't see she was drawing near to where Angie was standing. Not being confident Sylvia would notice her as she ran by, Angie yelled, "Sylvia!"

Sylvia jerked her head up, and it was as Angie suspected. Even though Sylvia was still jogging, whereas Angie was walking, she didn't look like she was doing well at all. But seeing her seemed to revive her energy. "Angie!" she hollered in return.

The two briefly hugged each other once Sylvia reached her. "Whose idea was this anyway?" Sylvia exclaimed while laughing heartily.

Angie laughed along with her before agreeing, "I know, right!" Angie filled her in on where the mile-three turnaround marker was, and after talking about their options, they decided Angie would keep walking toward the finish line rather than go back with Sylvia and cover the same route over again, while Sylvia would make her best effort to catch up. Once they were together, they would pick a pace both could maintain for the last couple of miles and finish the race together.

Once Sylvia caught up, Angie gave her a couple minutes to catch her breath, and then the pair started off again. This time Angie tried to match Sylvia's speed and was pleasantly surprised to discover she no longer had any pain in her side and was able to sustain that pace, such as it was. The two expended just as much effort talking as they did running. Angie shared with Sylvia her method of taking her mind off the race, pointing out a few houses she had redone. Sylvia expressed her own style of coping with the exhaustion, which was to talk as much as possible with the other racers, which didn't surprise Angie in the least.

Whatever tricks the two hit upon, talking certainly helped, as it seemed that no sooner had Angie and Sylvia started running together, they were at the mile-five marker. Angie saw the marker first and pointed it out to Sylvia, who shrieked when she saw it. Since they were so distracted from the actual race by their conversation, they didn't notice the path reentering the park until they were already in the park itself. They spied the arch and heard the race announcer and crowd simultaneously, which led to yet another shriek. Sylvia grabbed Angie's hand, and they covered the last hundred yards together, raising their hands in the air as they crossed the finish line and passed underneath the arch.

It was all Angie could do to remain upright, but she wasn't able to stop herself from bending over and putting her hands on her knees while trying to regain a stable breathing pattern. She did manage to look up at Sylvia and was treated with the sight of Sylvia doing the same thing.

While recuperating from their exertions, Angie and Sylvia discussed the race, what they had done right, and what they might need to improve for next time. As they were conferring about that aspect of the race, Sylvia gazed pointedly at Angie with a sly grin on her face and asked, "So ... does that mean you're going to do another one of these things?"

Angie's facial expression suggested she was deep in thought. "I don't know," she replied. "Give me about a month to recover from this race. But who knows, ya never can tell," she added with her own sly grin.

The Next Level

Matt coasted in to work on his bike, gently applying the brakes to stop just after rolling up the wheelchair access in front of the physical therapy center. He then walked around to the side of the building and through the door that led directly into the room, lifting his bike onto his shoulder until he got into the staff locker and break room. After a quick rinse-off in the staff shower area, he got dressed in comfortable clothes, putting on the company smock over that. Acknowledging waves and nods from the three other physical therapists in the large exercise room, he pulled the client files from the file cabinet. Sitting down at the counter that faced the room, he began poring through the information to make sure he recalled what kind of progress his clients had made. Once satisfied that he was up to speed, he arranged the files in order of his first client's file on top, and he then slid the thick stack to a corner of the counter.

Still a few minutes early for the first client of the day, he casually strolled around the exercise room, making idle conversation with the other therapists. When the first client rushed through the door and they began their work together, he soon lost himself to the rhythm of the workday, greeting each client, inquiring as to how the client had felt since their last session, picking up where they had left off, and so forth. It was somewhat surprising when, during a lull in activity, a glance at one of the clocks showed his workday was half gone. During the brief respite, he struck up a conversation with another therapist, Stephan. After a few minutes of the usual inquiries about how the week was going, Stephan asked Matt about his plans for the evening.

"Let's see, this is Thursday, so that means it's a running night," he responded.

Stephan paused before asking, "Don't you ever do anything besides training anymore?"

This time it was Matt's turn to hesitate before admitting, "Well, sometimes I do other things. But yeah, I guess I do spend a lot of time training."

Stephan chuckled, "Other things? Oh, really? OK, tell me something you've done besides work and training in the last three to four months." Matt didn't have to verbally respond to let Stephan know he had him in a corner. They both already knew what the answer was.

"Mmm ... let's see ... I ate and slept?" he threw out weakly, which earned him an incredulous gaze while Stephan waited to see whether Matt would dig himself a deeper hole. Sure enough, that's exactly what he did. "Hey, maybe I have spent most of my time training, but in my defense, I've got a really big race coming up, and I think I may have a legitimate chance of a podium finish."

Stephan pondered his next angle for a few moments before asking, "Yeah, I get the part about having this as an interest, and wanting to be competitive and all, but ... is it all worth it? Eating, sleeping, working, and training—and that's it? I mean, that can't be good for you, can it? Don't you miss going out with people, going to the movies, or maybe a barbecue? Not to mention, when's the last time you actually had a vacation? And don't count going out of town to a race as a vacation. C'mon ... admit it; you haven't had a vacation since you started doing triathlons, have you?" He tried to put on his most engaging smile as he finished the confrontation.

Thankfully, Matt took the needling as playfully as Stephan had hoped he would. He smiled weakly, knowing he'd been had. "OK, I guess I've had my nose to the grindstone," he admitted.

Stephan didn't respond right away. Much as he might not think it was a healthy lifestyle, at least for most people, he had to acknowledge it did seem to fit Matt's personality, and there didn't seem to be any signs he was suffering from some type of undue effects of social isolation. "Yeah ... yeah, I can see where you're coming from. I mean, it's not the type of lifestyle that would fit me, but I can see it might be right for you. It's just that we've worked together a long time, and I was beginning to get a little worried."

Matt turned back to face Stephan. "Well, I want you to know I do appreciate your asking. I know sometimes the easiest thing to do is not say something because you don't want to say the wrong thing, or something like that. Just to show I'm listening, I'll make more of an effort to get out and be more social. It can't hurt, right?"

Over the next several months, he did make more of a conscious effort to get out more and do something besides training. This only meant he was on the go more and more, as he wasn't about to give up training. As the days turned into weeks and weeks turned into months, he continued and, as race day approached, intensified his training regimen. He had truly meant what he had said about believing he had a shot at the podium, which implied no less than a third-place finish. But after looking up the race organization's website, specifically the results from the previous two years, his jaw almost hit his chest.

Mentally comparing the times of the top ten finishers to what his own times had been in the handful of races he had under his belt led him to the conclusion that he was either going to have to make some big-time improvements in his performance or was going to have to completely shred himself during the swim and bike ride to have a decent shot at taking it on the run. He let out a very long, deep sigh and kept staring at the screen for quite a while without really seeing it as his mind calculated how to improve his times, knowing it was going to be an uphill battle. As he was engaged in this process, he began dreading how much work and dedication it was going to take. Finally, just before scrapping the whole plan he'd developed by that point, he audibly reaffirmed his commitment to that all-important podium finish. "Well, there's no way of getting around it. If I really want that medal, I have to be willing to put in the work."

"Well, what are you all doing standing around yakking for? The pool's sittin' right there!" bellowed the swim coach. The group got a good laugh out of the comment, but they did collectively jump into the pool in ones and twos. The coach allowed them time to do some brief warm-up laps before organizing them into lanes based on previous finishing times. This was the first step in Matt's plan for improvement—being able to keep up with at least the top ten swimmers. Given that he had spent so many years cycling, he wasn't too concerned with that part of the race. Consequently, he began spending more time and effort in first swimming and later running. Gradually his efforts began to pay dividends. The week before the race, he was finally able to finish in the top third of the swimmers throughout most of the routines, and he almost kept up with the fastest runners on the final prerace run around the park.

As he stuffed his race gear in the small duffel bag, Matt experienced a certain sense of undefinable, nebulous foreboding about the race, which he couldn't figure out. Logically, he reminded himself how much progress he had made in the past couple of years and how well he had done in his first few triathlons even before that. Shaking his head, he zipped up the bag and tossed it by the front door. He had never been very adept in the emotion and intuition departments and decided to put such things out of his mind while finishing with the remaining preparations. He made an attempt to tell himself his anxiety had to do with worrying about forgetting something, but that thought lasted only a few seconds before even he knew there was something else responsible for his unease.

After his third time of checking his equipment, he finally conceded that everything was indeed packed and it was time to load it in his car and head for the race. The rest of the day was a blur as he went through the usual routine of heading to the race site first, getting his race numbers, driving to the hotel, eating an early dinner, and watching some TV before going to bed early. The next morning, he went through the same routine as always on race morning, but this time he was anticipating a podium finish and was hyper-focused on every minute detail to ensure he was as prepared as possible right up until the horn went off. While putting on his race jersey, and his warm-up suit over that, he was amused at wishing he could be this attentive every morning without having coffee.

The heightened alertness to every sight and sound lasted from the drive to the race site and throughout setting up his transition station and warming up. He had just bent over to retrieve a prerace drink from his bag when he heard what sounded like someone tapping a finger on a microphone coming through the PA system, followed shortly by the race announcer's voice. "Good morning, good morning, racers and race fans! It's an absolutely gorgeous day for racing. According to the weatherman, it shouldn't be too hot out there today, so we're looking for record times from some of you. At this time, we want to ask anybody who is a spectator to please leave the transition area. Again, all spectators need to leave the transition area now. Athletes, you have about fifteen to twenty minutes until you are going to have to leave the transition area too. Get your stuff together. Official race time is 6:30 a.m.; we go off in exactly thirty minutes!"

Matt stood around his station, shaking out his arms and legs and watching the other racers. A few were already taking off their warm-up suits and pulling on their wetsuits. Wasting no time, he quickly pulled off his warm-up suit, jamming his legs into his wetsuit and pulling it up to his waist. He then made his way to the water. There was an excited buzz that he noticed when he drew close. Some of the participants began psyching themselves up by talking about the race course and expected finishing times, and spectators were searching for and calling out the names of racers they had come to support. As with previous races, the race announcer, who by now was standing on a short, small dock, made a few last-minute reminders to the competitors and then gave a five-minute notice.

Shortly the announcer called back the first wave, which had entered the water and begun warming up. "Two minutes! Two minutes to race start! All of you in the water, you need to be behind where I'm standing!" Once he had finished his instructions, the multitude of spectators began yelling in earnest, becoming so loud it was very difficult to hear the "One minute to go" and "Thirty seconds" cues from the announcer. Matt figured the announcer must have noticed he was being drowned out as well, because even with the bullhorn, he yelled, "OK, time to count 'em down! Ten ... nine ... eight!" He stopped after that and let the throng carry the countdown the rest of the way. Then the horn sounded and the first wave scampered into the water.

Once they were well underway, the announcer called out the color of the next age group's swim cap, continuing the pattern until it came time for Matt's age group. Matt followed the other athletes into the water, not getting in much of a warm-up, since there were so many guys in his wave that the area became a churning mass of arms and legs. He had just taken his position when the announcer gave the one-minute cue, and as before, the noise from athletes and bystanders alike began climbing toward a crescendo. He managed to catch the announcer yelling, "Three … two … one …!" Rushing into the water until chest deep, and then bending his legs to submerge himself the rest of the way, he pushed off and began stroking. It was difficult to judge exactly how many were in front of him, but he felt good about passing roughly a dozen guys from the starting line to the first buoy. He passed about that same number throughout the rest of the swim; soon after passing that one last swimmer, he spied the inflatable arch signifying the finish to the swimming leg of the race.

The beginning of the bike course included several turns through city streets; at about the two-mile mark, the course reached the first straightaway, and Matt took the opportunity to put his cycling skills to the test. The leg went just as expected and, truth be told, just as he had desperately hoped. As the race progressed, he passed one rider after another, including six guys who appeared to be in his age group, and remained past them for the entire cycling leg. He played tag with three more riders, at various times passing them, only to be passed a mile or two later. The four of them played a game of cat and mouse during the second half of the course, each of them at different times putting on a burst of speed, daring the others to keep up.

After almost twenty miles and no serious attempts at a breakaway, it became obvious all racers were satisfied with their current places and would remain that way until they returned to the race site. Matt was reassured with his ability to keep up with the others while not feeling like he was exhausting himself to do so. On approaching the park, Matt heard music blaring from the PA system; it steadily became louder as they neared the gate. For the first time, he realized that, although it seemed unlikely, it was possible there were several more guys from their age group in front of them they did not know about. Mentally, he gave a fatalistic shrug of his shoulders, figuring that if there were racers ahead, there was nothing to do about it anyway. But there was something to do about the guys just ahead.

His plan for the first half of the run was simple: keep them in sight. Matt and two other racers left the transition area one after the other. Step after step, he maintained the distances established at the beginning of the run. Thankfully, they didn't seem to be speeding up, and at the moment, he felt capable of sustaining his current pace for the duration. As with the last few miles of the bike ride, it seemed all three competitors were content to preserve their current places, at least for now, which suited him perfectly. If he had his way, no one would press the issue until the last few hundred yards. He felt confident of sustaining his current pace but had doubts about what would happen if one of the others sped up now.

He tried to put his mind on cruise control, letting his body take over and allowing himself to be in the moment, and he stopped thinking about how the race had gone up until that point, about how the other racers seemed to be faring, and about what he would do to close the distance should one of them take off. He focused on what the bottoms of his feet felt like each time they contacted the hard-packed dirt path, feeling the rhythm of each step. Breathing deeply, he felt the material of his racing suit stretching across his chest as his lungs filled to capacity, and he reveled in how easy the race seemed right now, feeling as though he were gliding on a carpet of air, his feet not even touching the ground. He was soon flooded with a sensation of positive feelings about his chances of making the podium, and maybe even winning his age group.

For stride after stride, the three men continued their pace. It seemed Matt was correct in his estimation that none of them wanted to take a chance at peaking too early. For quite a while, the plan worked beautifully, and he was even able to gradually narrow the lead beginning from the mile-four marker. Unfortunately, the course took a sharp turn at the mile-five marker, and as the other runners turned the corner, they happened to glance back and see how close Matt had come. There was a brief look of panic on their faces before both took off as though they had been shot out of a cannon. Cursing his bad luck, Matt responded with his own burst of speed. He had dreaded trying to go too fast too early but knew that with about one mile left there was no choice but to maintain the distance and trust in his training.

Without consciously thinking about it, he kicked himself into a higher gear, noticing as he did so that the others did the same. But at least now he was almost close enough to reach out and touch them. The finish line popped up off in the distance, and Matt decided to go for broke and test what they all had left. "Wadda ya got?" he silently asked while increasing the pace again. Slowly but surely, the arch over the finish line became larger and larger in his field of vision. *Now*, he thought, *if they can just play along and not speed up until we're almost to the finish line, that'd be great.* Too bad for Matt, they did not play along; just as he was getting ready to make his move, the lead runner turned around and saw both Matt and the other runner. A few seconds later, he took off as if he were powered by a jet engine. Matt mentally tipped his hat to the leader and began running all out.

As it turned out, the leader's tactic paid off. He was too close to the finish line for anyone to catch him in time, which made the race a matter of who was going to come in second. Matt and the other runner ran shoulder-to-shoulder for the last fifty yards before Matt's competitor managed to put on a final surge and crossed the finish line a mere two seconds ahead of Matt. The leader was standing a short distance past the arch, watching to see who would pull through in the end. Both runners' momentum brought them to where the leader was, and after finally catching their breath, the three shared handshakes and brief half-hug. They couldn't help laughing as they revealed what each of them had been thinking throughout the cycling and running portions of the race.

The other two were amazed Matt hadn't had much previous experience and was able to finish in the top three so early in his triathlon career. "Yeah, well … when I decide to do something I go for it 100 percent. Plus I've been cycling for years, so I knew I would do well on that part," he countered.

The second-place finisher, Peter, then threw out, "With that being the case, it seems like you're a natural-born endurance racer. You should think about Hawaii—I mean, once you've got even more races under your belt."

The winner, Victor, heartily nodded his agreement.

Before Matt could affirm or deny their assessment of his skills, a race organizer made the announcement that the awards ceremony would be starting in a few minutes, which shifted the conversation away from Hawaii and back to the race. When it came time for their age group to be announced, Matt experienced a momentary bout of anxiety. What if his times had been off? What if he hadn't been in the top three? Fortunately, he didn't have long to ruminate on his fears; shortly after naming the age group, the announcer was providing the finish time for third place and calling out Matt's name. He breathed an audible sigh of relief as he walked over and stepped up onto the podium. Bending over, he shook another race organizer's hand as she draped the third-place medal around his neck and handed him an engraved plaque made of bronze and dark wood. He was barely cognizant of the second- and first-place winners being announced, or of the people standing in front of the podium taking pictures. His mind was three thousand miles away, standing on a podium in Kona, Hawaii.

"Whoo-hoo! You're on your way! First race as a pro!" Lisa exclaimed enthusiastically, thrusting her hands in the air, palms up.

Sarah grimaced and shook her head. "Would you get a grip! Good grief, I haven't done anything yet. For all we know, I might be a complete flop."

Connor couldn't help but laugh at the exchange as he looked out the backseat window at the other cars pulling into the shopping center parking lot and people walking into the vacant grocery store that had been converted into the race expo. Sarah was equally as nervous as Lisa was excited. *Sure*, she thought to herself, *you can be all hyped up. It's not your future that's on the line.* But she didn't dare say that out loud. She knew what she would get from Lisa—a litany of all the reasons why Sarah had to do this now. The worst part of it was that Lisa was actually right for once. That still hadn't made it an easy decision, especially when it came to her parents—most of all her mother.

Although Lisa continued to chatter away, Connor picked up on Sarah's mannerisms. As they got out of the car and walked toward the entrance, he held Lisa back momentarily, whispering in her ear. Sarah couldn't tell what he said, but as they approached the double glass doors, Lisa simply hugged her, gave her a big smile, and kept her mouth shut. They slowly approached the table that had a sign taped to the edge with "PRO" written in dark, blocky letters. Sarah had great difficulty forcing her feet to move the short remaining distance to the table, feeling as if her shoes were glued to the floor. All she could do at that moment was stare at the "PRO" sign, knowing that as soon as she said her name, she would be starting down a road that would lead to uncharted territory and even more conflict than what she had encountered already. Lisa came up behind her and took Sarah's hand in hers, giving it a firm but gentle squeeze, for once not jabbering like some squawking parrot. Even with Lisa's support, all Sarah could think about right then was the conversation with her parents from just about one year ago this month.

"*You're doing what!*" came the expected reaction from her mother. Well, actually the first reaction was her mother laughing at Sarah's declaration that she was not going to take the position her father (although in truth with much manipulation by her mother) had gotten for her in his friend's company. When Sarah told her parents *why* she wasn't taking the position and what she intended to do instead, that's when the real reaction came. The question and emotional tone were expected; what was unexpected was her mother jumping up and dropping her teacup on the floor, shattering the delicate porcelain. "How? … What? … Who? … I … You … Gerald, say something!"

Sarah could almost feel sorry for her father; no one who knew Sarah's mom wanted to be in her crosshairs. She knew he was trapped. He turned to Sarah and took the physical stance he always did when making a show of supporting her mother but inwardly wishing he could be somewhere else. "Now, Sarah, are you sure you've thought this through? You've done so well as an intern I'm sure you'll have no problem doing well there, and the opportunities for advancement are almost endless." Sarah had a hard time not laughing. He said it with such an apologetic tone of voice, almost as if he were wishing he were the one who had just made an announcement that would take him far away from Sarah's mother.

"That's it? That's all you have to say!" There was a brief pause as Sarah's mother drew a deep breath so she had sufficient air to deliver what was sure to be a long-winded diatribe. "Honestly, Gerald, just once in your life I wish you'd be strong enough to be firm with her. You've always been too easy on her, and now look where it's gotten us." Rounding on Sarah, she continued. "Now you listen to me, young lady. I *forbid* this; do you hear? I don't know who put this crazy idea into your head—probably that … that … girl … what's her name?"

"Her name is Lisa, Mother!" Sarah interjected. "And she has nothing to do with this!"

"Well, I don't care who filled your head with this nonsense; it's not going to happen! Honestly, a professional triathlete? Do it on the weekends if you like it so much, but it is time for you to grow up, get a real job, and settle down! I did not work this hard to see you throw it all away on some childish whim!"

Sarah's initial feeling was one of intense anger and indignation at still being treated like a child, even though she was now twenty-four years old and a young adult. However, years of her mother throwing her proverbial weight around left her absolutely trembling on the inside at the thought that she was standing up to her for the first time in her life. She geared up for her own verbal onslaught by placing her fists on her hips and leaning slightly toward her mother. "I ... I ... I ... That's all you care about! That's all you've ever cared about—*yourself!* You can't 'forbid' me to do anything! I am an adult, and I can choose to do what I want, when I want, where I want, and how I want. And if I choose to throw my life away, then that's my choice! *Mine! Do you hear me?*" Not trusting herself not to say anything further that might get her into even more hot water, Sarah stormed out of the room. The last image she had was of her mother standing in front of the love seat, broken teacup at her feet, with her mouth so wide open her jaw was on her chest.

Another squeeze from Lisa brought Sarah back to the present. She swallowed hard once more and took two long, purposeful steps toward the table; and when the volunteer behind the table looked up, she said in an emphatic tone of voice, "Sarah McKittrick."

The woman inspected a clipboard with several sheets of paper attached. "Let's see ... McKittrick ... McKittrick ... ah, here we are! McKittrick, Sarah. May I see some ID please?" Sarah held out her wallet, which held her driver's license in a clear plastic frame. The woman gazed at the picture, looked up at Sarah, squinted her eyes at the picture, and said, "OK, thank you." The woman called out "Seventy-three!" over her shoulder without bothering to check to see whether someone was paying attention to her and heard the number. Her confidence in the other volunteers was well placed, as within a matter of seconds a boy who appeared to be in his teens hustled to the table with a bag in his hand. As he gave it to the woman at the table, Sarah noticed a sticker on the bag with the number seventy-three on it. The woman cautioned Sarah as she handed her the bag. "Make sure everything is in the bag that you'll need for the race. There should be a timing chip with a Velcro strap for your ankle, a sticker with your number for your helmet, a number that goes on your bike, and a race bib with your number on it to wear on the run. If something is not in there, come back here right away and we'll get it for you. Good luck!"

Sarah took the woman's advice, and as she, Lisa, and Connor began walking around the expo, she pulled the items she was going to need out of the bag and passed them to Lisa. "OK, here's the race bib ... bike number ... helmet sticker ... timing chip. OK, looks like I've got everything."

Turning to Lisa, she said, "Next stop is the hotel, and from there the race site so I can figure out how to get from the hotel to the race. It's going to be dark tomorrow morning, and I'll need to see what the route looks like in the light." On the way, she flashed on that image often seen in movies and TV—the one where a good figure, usually an angel, is perched on one shoulder, while a bad figure, usually represented by a devil, is perched on the other. The devil continually made remarks such as, "Your mother is right. You're an idiot to think that you should be doing this. What are you thinking? This is no future for you." Periodically the angel would counter with "This is the perfect time of life for you to do this. You're young, and you have your whole life ahead of you if this doesn't work out. Think about all the excitement you'll have at the races and being able to travel all over the country." Most of the time, Sarah didn't know which voice to listen to; sometimes she wished they would both just shut up and leave her alone.

Time passed quickly after Sarah got back from the race site, what with swimming, going to dinner, and then sitting outside in the pool area, talking and relaxing. Sarah had a brief jolt of anxiety when she got a text from a friend wishing her well tomorrow and saw that it was time to go to bed. She didn't know how much sleep she would be able to get, still being very nervous about not just her performance but also what tomorrow signified for her life. "Time for me to get some shut-eye," she informed Lisa and Conner. "Stay up as late as you like," she finished, scooting her chair back from the table.

"OK," replied Lisa. "We shouldn't be too much longer, since we have to get up early too."

Sarah walked to their room as slowly as she could. The small talk around the pool hadn't lessened her anxiety at all, so she tried taking measured deep breaths while walking. After arriving back to the room, she continued her relaxation strategies by doing some light stretching and then taking a hot shower to melt away the knots in her muscles. She was feeling very physically comfortable by the time she climbed into bed. "Now if I can just get my mind off mother, I should be fine," she verbalized softly. Lying on her back and closing her eyes, she continued focusing on her breathing while attempting to empty her mind of all thoughts. Just when she felt she had achieved success, the scene with her parents in their living room burst into her awareness, ruining her brief nirvana.

The sound of music coming from her cell phone jarred Sarah awake, and she quickly turned over and fumbled with it until she hit the right button, and she then went into the bathroom as quietly as she could and spent several minutes loosening up her muscles under the hot, pulsating shower. Drying off, she could hear sounds through the wall of Lisa and Conner talking. By the time she had put on her triathlon suit and a warm-up suit over that, they were dressed and ready to head to the race. Sarah couldn't stop a chuckle on stepping out of the bathroom and encountering Lisa, who was practically bouncing on her toes and clapping her hands.

"Ooooh! Here we go! This is so exciting! Your very first race as a pro, and we're here to see it. Oooh, someday when you're famous, we'll be able to say we were with you when it all started."

Sarah shook her head. "Lisa, get a grip, would you. Jeez, you're more excited than I am. Oh, and when I get famous? Are you kiddin' me? Nobody ever gets famous as a triathlete!"

Lisa wasn't about to allow Sarah's realism to temper her enthusiasm. "Whatever," she responded. "I still think it's very exciting, and I'm going to be the first one to congratulate you when you cross the finish line, even if your family isn't going to be there."

Conner didn't need to look at Sarah to know what effect that statement was likely to have, and he quickly grabbed Lisa by the arm and led her to the door. "We'll meet you in the lobby" was his brief statement as he almost shoved Lisa out into the hallway. Sarah fought back tears as she stood up and grabbed her prerace food bag. Closing her eyes, she took several deep breaths while a cacophony of thoughts and emotions sped through her mind. It took more than a few moments for her to process all that she was experiencing, but when it was done, she had a certain peace about what was starting today. "It is what it is," she said, for the first time eager to compete in her first race as a pro.

Time seemed to rush by like a video that had been put on fast-forward. According to clock time, it took two hours to get to the race site, find her number on the bike rack, get her station set up, and warm up until the race started. But to Sarah it felt as if all that was crammed into a few minutes, so when the race announcer called out into her megaphone that the race was going to start in fifteen minutes, Sarah had an overwhelming sense of not being ready yet and wanting to ask for more time. Sighing and resigning herself to the inevitable, she yanked off her warm-up suit, stuffed it into her gear bag, and headed over to the lake.

As with all Sarah's previous races, the race announcer made a few last-minute announcements and then gave the male pros the three-minute mark, followed by a two-minute warning, before calling out, "Sixty seconds!" After a short pause, she yelled, "Thirty seconds! ... all right, let's hear it! Ten ... nine ... eight." She allowed the crowd to finish the countdown, and on one, an air horn sounded. The race announcer repeated the countdown process with the female pros. As before, the crowd picked up the countdown, raucously yelling each number, along with a few names being called out at the same time. Just before the air horn went off, Sarah took a final deep breath to steady herself, not only to prepare for the sudden increase in physical activity but also from the urge to run out of the race site and back to the hotel.

Owing to her extensive swimming background, Sarah was one of the first three women to exit the water. She watched the other competitors out of the corner of her eye while jamming her helmet on her head and sliding her feet into her shoes. All three athletes had the appearance that they were well versed in getting through the swim-to-bike transition, and they all ran in unison toward the "BIKE OUT" sign that was at the end of the transition area closest to the street. With the understanding there was still a lot of race to go, Sarah exercised some good sportsmanship and allowed the other girls to go ahead of her, even though she could have easily elbowed her way past them.

For the first eight to ten miles, all three riders kept their positions and a steady pace. Over time, one after another racer caught up to them, until a group of about eight riders formed a loosely packed knot of cyclists. By mile twenty, although there had been a few halfhearted attempts at a breakaway, no one had seriously tried to leave the others behind; Sarah took that as a sure indication they all knew fifty-six miles is quite a distance to cover. The riders churned through mile after unrelenting mile; the only break in the sounds of heavy breathing, chains running through gears, and tires on the asphalt was the occasional cowbell and cheers from spectators who were standing in their front yards. The group remained together for the duration of the cycling leg, including cruising into the transition area en masse.

As Sarah dismounted from her bike and ran to her station, she tried to count how many women were in the transition area, but that proved too difficult. Forcing herself to focus on her own race, she snatched her visor and sped off toward the "RUN OUT" sign at the opposite end of the transition area. The run course paralleled the transition area and race expo tents before heading out into the surrounding residential neighborhoods and onto an asphalt hiking trail. Spotting her competitors was easier said than done. The path wasn't all that wide, and runners were constantly jockeying for position, such that it was difficult to be sure whether she was counting everyone or counting the same person twice. Several women were so far ahead that, from her vantage point, they all looked alike.

She began calculating the number of girls she had to contend with on the way to the finish line and finally settled on five as a reasonable estimate. Taking for granted that the two top spots were pretty much already sewn up, in her mind that meant five girls were competing for one spot: third place. She began by focusing on the closest girl in front of her. "Five runners to pass," she whispered. "So the big question is, When do I make my move, and how many should I go for?"

Sarah's plan coalesced into a series of short-term goals, the first of which was to pass the closest runner right after the turnaround point. She increased her speed just enough to be right on her heels as they made a U-turn around the road marker. After passing her, there were two girls within proximity. Sarah made passing the first one at the mile-eight marker her next small goal. Once that was accomplished, she saw that passing the next runner was not going to be as easy. In the time it had taken her to reach the runner she had just passed, the next one in line had increased her own speed. "Actually," she reasoned, "if I'm going to be serious about this pro thing, I may as well find out now whether or not I have what it really takes to be competitive."

Upon reaching the mile-ten marker, she decided that if there was going to be any chance of catching the next runner, and even the next one after that, she was going to have to make her move now. Within several hundred yards, she felt as if her heart was beating so hard it might burst out of her chest at any moment. Her breathing was so labored she didn't think it would have been possible to carry on a conversation. Although she was quickly approaching the next runner, it was obvious there was no way for her to maintain her pace for another three miles, so as disheartening as it was, she slowed down; she was still making up some ground, but not at the same rate.

She eventually passed the woman between mile eleven and a half and mile twelve. Perhaps the woman hadn't been paying attention to the locations of her competition the way Sarah had been, because she looked genuinely surprised while being passed. Once well past her, Sarah began searching for the next runner. When she found her, there was some good news and some bad news. The good news was that the runner was only about a hundred yards ahead; the bad news was that she had already passed the mile-twelve marker, meaning there wasn't much race left. Even though she was close, Sarah wasn't sure she had enough left in the gas tank to fuel another burst of speed.

The sound of shouting and music pulled Sarah out of her mental deliberations. She rounded a corner and, sooner than expected, saw the inflatable arch only a few hundred yards away, with the word "FINISH" in bright, bold letters on top. Seeing the finish line so close, and the next runner so far, sent her into panic mode. Without thinking about the consequences, she sprinted the remainder of the distance. The other woman was unable to match her speed, and Sarah zoomed around her just before reaching the finish line. She barely managed to get far enough away to avoid impeding other finishers before collapsing on the ground.

When she was able to hear something other than her own gasping for breath, she was vaguely aware of Lisa's voice. "You did it! I'm so proud of you! And the way you beat out that other girl at the finish line. *Wow!* That was incredible!" After what felt like an eternity, she stood upright and walked over to lean against the railing, not having the energy to do anything except stand and breathe. Lisa began a barrage of questions. "So … how do you think you did? Were there many girls that were as good of a swimmer as you are? How did you do on the bike? How was the run? We saw you pass that one girl but lost track of how many finished ahead of you. What place do you think you came in?"

Sarah just made eye contact with Lisa. It took some time before Lisa paused, finally picking up on her social cue, and acknowledged, "I'm talking too much aren't I? OK, I'll shut up and let you talk. So … tell me, tell me, tell me, how did it go?" Sarah held up one index finger while taking another deep breath and then pointed to the tables to indicate she needed to sit. On the way, she grabbed an energy drink from a large plastic container before starting an account of the race. When Sarah had exhausted every detail of the race, including her strategy during all three events, Lisa took Sarah's hands in hers, stared into her eyes, and emphatically stated, "I can't tell you enough how proud I am of you. I know it hurts that your parents aren't here right now, telling you the same thing, and I would change that in an instant if I could. I just hope that someday they'll come to their senses and realize how foolish they've been and tell you they're proud of you, because you deserve it." Tears began to well up in Sarah's eyes, and it was all she could do at the moment to mouth the words "Thank you" and squeeze Lisa's hands. After the exchange, Lisa stood up and proclaimed, "Enough of this. Let's go see if we can find out some results!"

Curt felt as if he had reached his two hundredth birthday while stepping out of his car, very cognizant of being hunched over while closing the car door. Squaring his shoulders and tipping his head back, he made a concerted effort to look and walk normally. For all his efforts in the parking lot, Shelley, the office manager, smiled as Curt attempted to casually stroll in through the double glass doors. He was almost past her desk when he noticed her facial expression. "What?" came his query.

Shelley continued to smile but attempted to deflect his accusatory question. "Oh, nothing" she responded, making a feeble attempt to appear engrossed in something on her computer screen.

"Don't 'nothing' me. You're smiling at me. C'mon, admit it. There's something you find funny."

After several shots at transforming her face into something more serious, she eventually conceded defeat and began giggling. "The way you're walking … You've been working out again, haven't you?"

Curt quickly realized he hadn't quite pulled off the facade he had intended. "Oh, uh, well … it shows, huh?"

Shelley gave him a sympathetic look. "Yes, it shows, but at least you're staying in shape, which is more than I can say for my husband."

Curt laughed, ceasing his endeavors at walking normally, and shuffled to his office. After taking a few moments to stretch and shake out the soreness as much as was possible just then, he trudged to the small staff lounge to fill his coffee mug. Geoff's office was on the way to the staff lounge, so he had no choice but to hope that Geoff would be on the phone or looking at his computer. Curt heard a loud laugh just past the doorway, with Geoff out of his field of vision. *Crap*, he thought to himself. *Do I pretend I didn't hear it and face the music as I walk back, or do I face it now?* After a brief pause, he opted to get it over with, so he turned sideways and stuck his head into the doorway. "Yes?" he asked, pausing to see what Geoff's exact response was going to be.

Geoff laughed again. "You look like you're eighty!" he exclaimed.

Curt feigned insult. "I am not eighty," he retorted in as haughty a voice as he could muster, sidling into Geoff's office.

"Hah!" Geoff snorted. "I didn't say you *were* eighty; I said you *looked* eighty, which you do. C'mon, admit it. You're walking around like you're one step away from a nursing home."

Curt sat down, maintaining his defense. "I don't have to admit anything." He wanted to say something else, deliver some snappy comeback, but drew a blank.

Geoff was quick to jump into the lull. "Let me guess; you worked out again this morning, or maybe last night, and you're still feeling the effects."

Curt knew he was backed into a corner and conceded defeat. "Both, actually. It wouldn't have been that big of a deal if I hadn't taken off a week and a half in between workouts."

After Geoff inquired as to what type of workouts Curt had done, and received a concise description of each one, he posed one more question: "I get that you do this to train for your triathlon hobby, but *why* do you do it? Why punish yourself? I don't get it."

Curt rose from the padded chair with considerable effort. "Tell you what. When I find out the answer to that question, you'll be one of the first to know." They shared a laugh as Curt left his office and completed his mission of getting his coffee.

Geoff's questions popped into Curt's mind when the alarm clock went off at 5:00 a.m. the next morning. He groggily rolled over, fingers fumbling around the top of the clock in a vain attempt at locating the off button. Once the clock was off, he lay on his back for a while, wondering whether getting up so early was worth it, especially since it was still dark outside— and cold. He did not like the cold. It didn't get nearly as cold in Fairview as it did in the north, but for local standards, it was cold. He sighed while rubbing his face. "Maybe I'll skip it this morning. One morning can't hurt much," he reasoned, the entire time knowing one morning would soon turn into two, and then three. It took a decidedly conscious effort to throw the covers to the side and slide off the bed as quietly as possible.

His question of "Why am I doing this?" was compounded once he was outside and walking along the sidewalk. His gloves provided some warmth for his hands, but not completely, being thin wool. His usual route included walking to a multiuse trail the city had constructed a few years ago, and then running once on the trail. There was almost no one out on the trail this morning, which didn't surprise him in the least. Living up to its name, Fairview saw very few people going out in adverse weather. Traffic did increase as it got lighter outside, and he passed someone every few minutes during the second half of his run. Although he didn't have any answers to his questions, his mood was much brighter on the way back to the house. It was so much improved, in fact, that he began planning his workouts for the weekend, recalling that a local cycling group had rides every Saturday morning.

Riding to the location the cyclists were meeting at, Curt tried to wipe his mind of all the negativity that had built up over his lack of progress and focus instead on what he was trying to accomplish on this particular ride. Knowing that, at three hours, it would be the longest ride he had done so far, especially this early in the year, his first goal was simply to finish. There were five riders assembled when he rode up, and they were chitchatting about past races and upcoming training opportunities while waiting for more people to arrive. Curt just listened, occasionally asking a question but mostly remaining quiet. Within about ten minutes, four more rode in, and after checking the time and asking around to determine whether anyone knew about others who had said they would be coming, the group decided to get started. Curt allowed the other riders to take off before pushing off and bringing up the rear.

They followed a major street that led out of the city and into the foothills. There were no real mountains near Fairview—at least not what most people would consider mountains. The highest peaks reached only about 2,500 feet in elevation—barely enough to get snow in the winter. Those cyclists wanting to get some workouts that included steep climbing had to drive at least an hour, but since there weren't many of those types around town, few people complained about the lack of serious hill work available. Besides, a nice side benefit of the area was that it didn't get as cold in Fairview as back east or in the north. In fact, Curt had read in the news that morning that many parts of the north and northeast had gotten snowed in, and here they were riding their bikes.

It was probably about twenty minutes before the rider just in front of Curt, whose name was Donna, hung back a bit to strike up a conversation. As it turned out, Donna had done several triathlons herself. Curt explained about his injury and about seeing the race in Hawaii on TV and thinking at the time how crazy "those people" were for doing such a thing. "Now here I am, one of them," he finished. He then quickly added, "Well, partly one of them. I'm still not so sure about doing those long races."

Donna nodded in agreement. "Yeah, every once in a while I start thinking about trying it one of these years." She paused. "But then I lie down until the thought passes, and I'm OK again." They both had a good laugh—one loud enough to garner the attention of the next-closest rider at the back of the group.

"Uh oh, sounds like there's too much fun going on back here. Don't you know this is supposed to be work?"

Donna chuckled, "We're workin', we're workin'."

The man, Peter, sounded skeptical, "Uh huh, then what's so funny?"

Curt and Donna began talking at the same time; Donna allowed him to finish explaining about their reservations concerning doing an Ironman-distance race. "So why not?" Peter interjected. "Hundreds of average joes do it every year, many of them a lot older than we are. In fact, I remember reading an article a few months ago about a guy that did it at seventy-five years old. Seventy-five! If he can do it, so can we!"

Both Curt and Donna rode in silence for a few moments before Donna got a sly grin on her face. "So I guess that means we can expect to see you there this year, right?"

Peter barked a quick laugh. "Well, not so fast now. Remember: common folk like us have to put our names in a lottery and then hope that our names get drawn. The only other way is to win our age group in a qualifying race, and I don't know about you two, but I don't think I can devote enough time to training to compete with the big dogs."

Curt listened intently as Peter enlightened the pair on getting to the race, and he then asked, "So let's just say one of these years we do become interested. What are our chances of getting a lottery pick? How many spots are there?"

Peter hesitated before responding. "Let's see … last time I read about it, I believe there were about a hundred fifty spots available by lottery. But remember: even if you do get picked, you still have to finish a race over here on the mainland. The only advantage is you don't have to actually win your age group."

"A hundred fifty spots, huh?" Curt mused. "Have any idea how many people put their names into the lottery each year?"

Peter was mute, looking down at the ground as if he were searching for something on the road. After several long moments, he said, "Not really sure, now that you ask. My educated guess, though, is that it has to be in the thousands by now—probably even tens of thousands. But … who knows … From your questions, it sounds like you're thinking about trying it out yourself."

Curt's hands almost slid off the handlebars. "Me? Now? No possible way; I just barely got involved in triathlon. I haven't even done half those distances—not even in training!"

Peter used his skeptical voice once again. "Hmm, mmm, OK. But I didn't say now. It'll always be there when you're ready." And with that he accelerated away to rejoin the lead group. Curt opened his mouth to say something, but nothing came out. He had to admit that the idea of doing it, which had once seemed like the very definition of insanity, now had sort of an appeal to it. He had to acknowledge, though, that watching it on TV led to a certain amount of romanticizing the event, and he purposely reminded himself of all the athletes sitting on the side of the road, lying in first-aid tents, and running in the dark and falling on the road a mile from their goal.

"So … is he right?" Donna asked playfully.

Curt glanced at her and then turned his attention back to the road as he hit a small pothole. "Right about what?" he asked back.

She laughed before responding, "You know what. Are you thinking about doing it?"

He tried weakly to feign ignorance. "Oh, that." After he described what he had just been thinking, they both agreed doing an Ironman race was something that sounded better when one was simply talking about it rather than in the middle of doing it. He finished with "Now that we're talking about it, I suppose if I do keep going with racing, at some point I would try it. But I absolutely want, and need, to get in a few good years and experience before I even consider it."

As is so often the case, life became a blur. Since Curt and Katie had school-aged children, it seemed as though their life cycle revolved around the school calendar. Each year, Curt found himself sitting in a classroom listening to Justin's and Ashley's teachers drone on about what they would be doing during the upcoming school year. And if that wasn't bad enough, once they both reached intermediate and then high school, with their schedule including six classes and six teachers, he would have to go through that process six times, for each of them. Time passed so quickly during this phase of his life each September that he often had the same thought: *Weren't we just doing this last week?* The sole reprieve came when Ashley entered high school, which meant back-to-school night was the same for both children, and he and Katie were forced to divide the agony.

No longer needing childcare removed some of the parental responsibilities from their shoulders, but instead of granting a sense of relief, it added to their sense of life rushing by, as it heightened their awareness that they were now moving into the next stage of life. The only break in the normal grind of work, chores, weekend, work, chores, weekend, ad infinitum, was the family managing to cram a vacation in each summer. Once that was over—*wham!*—the school year began anew, whereupon Curt found himself sitting at a desk that was not built for adults, wondering, *Weren't we just doing this last week?*

For Curt, in addition to all those necessities of life, there was also the factor of his training and racing schedule to further impact his own personal sense of time. With each passing year, his workouts melded together until he couldn't remember how many miles he had biked or run since he'd started. Since he usually did the same races every year, those, too, began to merge. Whereas he could once recall his exact finishing times for each race and each year, now it was very difficult to recall how many times he'd done them all. An unpleasant side effect of reaching the milestone of a decade of racing was the beginning of the experience of a sense of ennui at the end of each season. Several times he considered giving up the sport, or at least not racing for one year, just to determine whether he could retrieve the passion he once had.

After gliding into the driveway one autumn Saturday morning after a solitary two-and-a-half-hour bike ride and pulling his shoes out of the pedals, he stood motionless with his upper body hunched over the handlebars. The entire time, from getting dressed to coasting into home, had been dull and lifeless—a complete and absolute chore—giving him a sense of being completely emotionally drained. He would have cried then and there if he had been the kind of guy to cry very much. But he wasn't, so he stared down at the front wheel for who knows how long, ruminating on how dejected he had grown.

Tottering into the garage, he hung his bike up on the wall rack and shuffled down the hallway to the bathroom. He struggled to pull his cycling shorts and jersey off, not only because he was sore but also due to his lack of emotional willpower. Standing in the shower so the water stream would massage his neck and shoulders, he began to sort through the plethora of nebulous thoughts and feelings. Every now and then, a whisper of an idea would pop up, but before he could grasp it firmly the thought would float away without leaving any trail. An image sprang up of him in a meadow, trying to grab a butterfly with his bare hands.

Finally a whisper came unbidden. Instead of chasing it, he pictured himself standing still, allowing the idea to come to him. When it finally did, he put both hands out to the tile to steady himself. *Hawaii? Oh, hell no, that's never going to happen! Those people are insane, and they are in much better shape than you will ever be in. That's crazy … that's ridiculous … that's …*

He paused his silent ravings. *Let's consider this honestly and realistically.* Was he ready now? Absolutely not, but the next installment wasn't for another year. Could he get ready in one year? It would be a lot of very hard work, but again, if he started now, he might have enough time.

He knew even before broaching the subject with Katie that he would have to come up with a sound plan that would not put the family in a financial bind. A trip to Hawaii could be pretty pricey. Although their status was solid, he had to acknowledge she had a right to be concerned about a major expenditure like this would be.

Just then the door from the garage opened and closed, and he heard footsteps walking down the hallway toward the kitchen. "That would be Katie. Now, the big question is, do I bring up Hawaii now or wait until I have a definite plan for how I'm going to pay for it?"

Angie cruised at a steady gait around the large city park, the only change in her exertion level occurring when the road inclined slightly upward or gently sloped down. She loved this time of year so much; it was the one time when the weather was perfect in both the morning and evening. It would still be mostly dark and chilly upon waking, but by the time she got dressed and began running, the sun was peeking over the mountains in the east and providing just enough warmth that a light, long-sleeved shirt or windbreaker was enough. She sighed out loud at the thought of wishing the weather would stay the same throughout the entire year.

The cell phone in her running belt suddenly began vibrating and then, within a few seconds, started ringing, interrupting her in-the-moment bliss. She barely had time to answer before she heard a shrill voice shouting through the speaker, "Mom? Mom!" It was Jonathan.

There was just enough of a pause to allow her to quickly answer, "Yes!" but she couldn't get anything else out before he shouted again.

"Mom, she's started." Angie pursed her lips to ask who had started and what was starting, but she was interrupted once more by Jonathan's obviously excited and urgent voice. "It's Tiffany, Mom! She's in labor! The contractions started about three hours ago and have gradually gotten closer together. We just called the doctor, and she told us to head over to the hospital. I'll call you when we get settled and get a room. Bye!"

It took her several moments to recover from the shock and realize she was just standing there, in the park, miles from home. "What am I doing? I've got to get going!" Throwing aside her normal training regimen, she ran as fast as she could, huffing and puffing the entire way home.

The only opportunity she had to catch her breath came while she was standing in the shower for a few brief moments—just long enough to soap up and rinse off. Her phone rang as she finished drying off and had wrapped the towel around her body. "Mom!"

This time Jonathan sounded slightly more composed, giving Angie a chance to respond. "Jonathan, how are things progressing?"

There was a short pause before he replied, "As good as it can be. We're at the hospital, getting ready to go into one of the maternity rooms. They said when you get here to just give the information desk our names, and that person will tell you the room number and directions. See ya when you get here!"

Angie pulled into the parking stall in the hospital parking lot, not entirely sure of how she had gotten from point A to point B. She recalled opening the door into the garage and sliding into the driver's seat of her car, but everything that followed was a complete fog. It was gratifying when, after checking in with the information desk and being directed to Jonathan's and Tiffany's room, she discovered she was the first one to arrive. Tiffany was smiling and sitting up as Angie said, "Knock, knock," pausing briefly before pulling the curtains aside and entering the birthing room. She couldn't help but smile—not at the kids, but at the thought that birthing room décor hadn't changed much in twenty-eight years.

She slid one of the few padded chairs in the room to the side of the bed, inquiring as to what had transpired since Jonathan's last very fleeting phone call. Every few minutes, Tiffany would wince and begin labored breathing through her mouth.

About an hour after Angie had arrived, Michael made his appearance. When he noticed Angie sitting next to the bed, he stood holding the curtain aside without coming further into the room. There was an awkward pause in the flow of conversation until Jonathan broke the ice. "Hey, Dad, come on in."

Michael cleared his throat before taking a few tentative steps toward the end of the bed. "Thanks" he replied, and then, to Tiffany, he said, "Hi, Tiffany … So how are you doing? All things considered, that is." He nervously glanced at Angie as Tiffany and Jonathan repeated the information they had provided Angie. Finally, with a facial expression that looked to Angie as if he were reaching out to grab a rattlesnake, he nodded in her direction and squeezed out "Angie."

"Michael, how are you?" she responded as civilly as she could, being proud of herself for her tone of voice. It held just the right amount of genuineness—not icy at all. For the kids' sake, she really did hope it would put him at ease, although from the corner of her eye she could see Jonathan and Tiffany exchanging looks with raised eyebrows. Michael smiled and nodded again but made no verbal comment. Tiffany then had another episode of contractions, for which they were all thankful. Angie took the initiative. "Michael, it looks like Tiffany's contractions are increasing in intensity, which suggests she is almost at the point to begin pushing. Whadda ya say we head on over to the cafeteria and grab some coffee?" As if right on cue, the doctor entered the room, and after hearing Tiffany describe her contractions, and Angie's remark, emphatically stated, "Well, it looks like the future grandma is spot on. I'd estimate we've got about half an hour before this all gets serious."

The pair knew they were approaching the cafeteria from the smells emanating from around the last corner. They separated as each went in search of something to curb their hunger, and they then sat in the cafeteria long after they had finished their breakfasts, talking about a variety of topics but always keeping the conversation very superficial. Angie wasn't sure how long they had been in the cafeteria when suddenly Sandra plopped down next to her. "Hey, mom! Hey, dad!" she chimed, giving Angie a side hug and relaying the information that by the time she had arrived, she wasn't able to go into the room, as the birthing process had already begun.

The trio debated how long they might have to wait and whether it would be more comfortable in the cafeteria or the labor and delivery waiting room. Angie, being ever so practical, pointed out they were sitting in hard plastic chairs and the waiting room would most certainly have padded chairs. Michael and Sandra quickly agreed, and after grabbing some drinks and snacks, they headed back to the birthing wing of the hospital.

Hour after hour marched past, and with each one, Angie wished Jonathan could spare some time to let them know what was happening. After several hours, Sandra spontaneously threw out a question about how Angie's last triathlon had gone. Angie nonchalantly described the race and how she had fared compared to others in her age group. She was mildly shocked that even Michael joined in with a question now and then, not only because he was asking about it but also because he seemed genuinely interested. Toward the end of her account, a young man from another family asked, "You do triathlons? That's the swimming, then biking, and running thing, right?"

Angie smiled, responding with a simple, "Yes." She had noticed he perked up as they were talking about it, but he had appeared to be politely waiting, not wanting to interfere with a private talk.

"That's crazy!" he exclaimed, leaning forward in his chair as he did so. "I was watching some of that on TV. They were in Hawaii, swimming in the ocean, and then the guy on TV said that part of the biking and running took them through lava fields! Lava fields! He said the temperature and humidity would be like sticking your head in an oven! He also said they were riding their bikes something like over a hundred miles, and then running a marathon in those conditions! That's insane!"

Angie leaned back until her head contacted the wall and laughed heartily. "Yes, I've heard of that one, but I've never done it, and from the sound of it, I would never want to even try it. I agree with you; that does sound insane. No, I just do local ones that are far easier and less strenuous."

Conversation dropped off, and there was a lengthy silence before Sandra blurted out, "Why not?"

Angie was taken aback with the suddenness of the question. She gazed at Sandra with a puzzled expression. "Why not what?" she queried.

Sandra shot her a "What, are you kidding me?" look, replying emphatically, "Why *wouldn't* you try it?"

This time it was Angie's turn to shoot Sandra the "What, are you kidding me?" look. She sighed and shook her head before answering. "Do you realize how far they go? And you just heard about the weather conditions! Do you have any idea how much training it would take? I would have to do nothing but eat, sleep, and train. No thank you!"

Sandra smiled impishly. "OK, OK, don't get your knickers in a twist. I understand you don't want to even try it; you're afraid you couldn't do it. There's no shame in admitting you can't do something."

Angie leveled her gaze at Sandra, trying to give her a "Don't mess with me" look. After debating how to respond, she countered with, "If you were attempting to goad me into doing something which I have absolutely *zero* interest in, you failed miserably."

The room had quieted down for only a few minutes when one of the nurses from Jonathan's and Tiffany's room popped her head around the doorway and, recognizing Angie, announced they now had a granddaughter. Angie didn't care about anyone else's reaction; she let out a cry of joy. The other family laughed and expressed their congratulations. The nurse smiled. "Everything went well; baby and mama are doing fine. Give us just a little more time to finish cleaning up baby and mom, and you should be able to visit a few minutes before they both will need some quiet time to get some rest."

With the knowledge that the baby was a girl, the talk about what types of things to buy and in what colors resumed. The pickup in communication made the time pass quickly, and soon they were in the delivery room, admiring their granddaughter and niece. Jonathan did his best to field each question fired at him in rapid order. Tiffany allowed him to do all the talking, although it appeared she wouldn't have been capable of talking much even if he hadn't been there. She cuddled with the baby, stroking her face and hands, trying unsuccessfully to stifle a yawn now and then. Finally Angie informed her everyone understood how exhausted she was and said she shouldn't try to hide it. Tiffany smiled broadly at the acknowledgment, whereupon Angie, once again the practical one, was the first to proclaim the new parents needed some bonding time with the new addition to the family and it was time to leave.

Angie filled Sylvia in on her granddaughter's birth during their weekly jogs, inadvertently mentioning Sandra's comments about the triathlon in Hawaii while in the waiting room. When she had recounted the interaction to Sylvia, she was floored when Sylvia said, "I kind of think she's got something there. Maybe you should try it."

All Angie could do was stammer the beginnings of questions: "Who … how … what …?" Finally, after catching her breath, she asked, "Where on earth do you get the idea I could do something like that? Do you even have a clue as to how far it is? What the conditions would be like? Seriously?"

Sylvia answered Angie's questions in rapid order. "First, I get that idea from the fact you had absolutely no confidence you would be able to do short runs, let alone triathlons, but you have. No, I have no clue how far the distances are. No, I have no idea what the conditions are like. Happy?" She didn't wait long for Angie to respond before adding, "I'm just making a suggestion based on having observed that quite often humans do things … *amazing things* … things that they never, ever dreamed possible, yet many times when they work hard, they surprise themselves, and others, by succeeding. *And* I know you. I've seen how much progress you've made in all areas of your life in the last ten years, and I really believe you have not hit your limit yet. *So* … at least give it some thought. Look into it and see what it would take."

The two friends ran in silence as Angie did her best to come up with a rebuttal to Sylvia's contentions—not to the part about making progress; she knew Sylvia was completely accurate in her assessment of Angie's poor self-confidence. No, she was determined to find a solid argument as to why it would not be plausible to take another step and do Hawaii. Minute after minute after minute passed, with no spoken word uttered between the pair. "Can't do it, can you?" Sylvia challenged.

Angie was too taken aback to formulate a response. Eventually she queried, "Do what?"

Sylvia broke out into an extremely self-satisfied smile. "Think of a reason why you couldn't do Hawaii. That is what you were doing for the past few minutes, right? Trying to come up with some reason why it wouldn't be possible to do it?" Angie refused to give her friend the satisfaction of knowing that was exactly what she had been thinking.

Before she could defend herself, Sylvia continued. "Look, Ang, we've known each other for a very long time. You know me as well as I know you. You know good and well that if I didn't honestly think you could do it, I wouldn't build you up with some false sense of confidence just to see you come crashing down. Find out exactly what the distances are, what kind of conditions are expected come race day, and what it would take to train for it. If you decide it's too much to undertake, either right now or perhaps ever, then you'll never hear another word from me."

Angie mulled over her reassurances. "OK, I hear ya. I'll take your advice and start by investigating the details of the race before making up my mind one way or the other. Happy?" she asked with a smirk.

Sylvia chose to ignore the verbal taunt. "Yes, I am, completely."

Days turned into weeks, and weeks turned into months. With Angie being so caught up in seeing Charity, her granddaughter, as often as possible and recording every small milestone, she entirely forgot about not only Hawaii but racing too. She did continue to work out, but only because it had become part of her lifestyle. She wasn't training for any particular race; in fact, one race came and went without her realizing she had missed it. It was only when Sylvia noticed after the fact and observed she hadn't talked about how the race went, as she typically did, that Angie sheepishly had to admit having forgotten about it.

Later that night, while on her computer and getting ready to turn it off, she recalled her conversation with Sylvia from earlier in the day. Instead of clicking the shutdown icon, she logged into her internet account and went to the race's website. Each aspect of the race—including previous race results, training and nutrition, and directions to the site—had its own portion of the website. Angie quickly learned one had to qualify; it wasn't as simple as filling out an entry form. By the time she had read over everything pertinent to the race, it was well after midnight. After she stumbled into her room and into bed, it wasn't long at all before she fell fast asleep, her dreams filled with visions of competing in Hawaii.

By the next morning, she had forgotten about her investigations into Hawaii, even though her fatigue should have been a reminder of having stayed up so late, and why. As before, her work schedule and spending time with Charity served to remove her focus from her hobby. Over the next several weeks, she began receiving several emails every day from races throughout the state, companies that sold bikes and other equipment triathletes commonly used, and companies that sold nutritional products. It took her awhile to make the connection that the influx of emails was more than likely due to her visiting the various Ironman Triathlon websites. One might think that realizing the new emails were the result of searching for information about the race in Hawaii would create a renewed interest in finding out more details about it, but any epiphany was completely lost.

"There it is! Exit 194B—Valleyview Expressway," Sandra notified Angie, pointing to the large sign on the side of the freeway. "OK, got it," Angie responded.

Sandra glanced down at the directions to the race site as Angie eased the car into the lane leading to the off ramp. "According to this, when we hit the light at the bottom of the off ramp, we make a right and head straight for almost four miles."

"Turn right, then straight four miles," Angie repeated, making sure Sandra knew she was paying attention to her navigation efforts.

It was easy to spot where the park was, as tall trees jutted up from the houses and smaller trees dotting the vista. Sandra spotted a sign a few hundred yards from the park, and by the time they reached the park entrance, they saw it was a sign with the name of the race and the race company's logo emblazoned across the top. Although far from a traffic jam, there was a steady stream of cars pulling into the park entrance from both directions. It was natural to talk about the race, and racing in general, while they waited in line to get the bag that held her race numbers and other assorted race-related items. But once she had her bag and they were almost back to the car, Angie tried to steer the conversation away from racing and toward other topics.

It took several changes of subject away from triathlons and to other aspects of their lives before Sandra seemed to comprehend what Angie was trying to do. Although she did not verbalize her observation, she eventually stopped asking questions or making statements about racing. During the drive to the hotel, while checking in, and throughout dinner, the pair discussed all the things they hadn't had time for back home. As they were getting into bed, Sandra even remarked she was glad she had come along and had the chance for the "alone time." Angie expressed similar feelings and held it together until Sandra turned the light off. The last thing she remembered before drifting off was wiping a tear of joy from her cheek.

Angie was woken from a disturbing dream by the sound of musical chimes emanating from her cell phone. Each stage of the race had gone horribly wrong. She had felt as if she were swimming through honey or syrup, while everyone around her whizzed by. After a number of riders had passed her on the bike, she finally looked down to discover her bike had training wheels. During the run, she felt as if her feet had been encased in concrete. She breathed a deep sigh of relief while rolling over to turn the alarm off. Sandra mumbled something but then fell back asleep, awaking only when Angie was dressed for the race and ready to leave.

They arrived at the park while it was still dark, the headlights from each car piercing the inky blackness. The scene reminded Angie of playing flashlight tag when she was a young girl. As they had the day before, they followed the procession of cars to the parking area. Although the sky across the horizon was beginning to show some color, it was still so dark there were several portable floodlights positioned around the bike racks. As it was, Angie and Sandra had to squint to locate the numbers on the edge of each rack. From that moment on, Angie's sense of time seemed to be out of whack. Everything started happening so quickly; her mind flashed to the scenes movies in which a person stands still and everyone around the person is moving so fast they are just blurs in the person's field of vision. It seemed they had just gotten to the water's edge for the first wave to go off when the announcer gave her age group the two-minute notice. Given her experience from past races, though, she was able to take it in stride, knowing this was a common dynamic to racing.

Breathing a metaphorical sigh of relief that her dream was unfounded, she glided through the water with ease. Her exhilaration increased while passing a few swimmers, and she almost pumped her fist in the air in excitement when she climbed up the slope out of the river and, upon turning around, estimated about a third of her age group was still in the water. Once out of the transition area and on the course, even though she was riding at a brisk pace, Angie couldn't help but look down at her back wheel. She laughed out loud when she realized she had been checking for training wheels. The humorous moment provided the necessary spark to reduce her anxiety and channel that emotional energy into her pedaling.

As with the swim, she was able to perform at a higher level than expected, making the bike portion enjoyable for once and seeming to take only a few minutes. Approaching the park entrance at the completion of the cycling leg, she felt her legs were still felt somewhat fresh, rather than sore and achy as in past races. Just a few hundred yards into the run, her stride felt stronger and more efficient, at least during the early stages of the run. Not wanting to press her luck, she maintained her speed even though she was passed on occasion. Mile after mile they ran, along a compacted dirt path parallel to a river. She continued to feel in good shape at the turnaround marker, but her cautious personality kept her from feeling too confident. As the runners passed the mile-six marker, the path curved to the right, bringing the finish line into view. She estimated there was now only about three hundred yards to go and boosted her speed, pulling even with two other women.

About a hundred yards from the finish line, she drew a deep breath and kicked off, putting as much power into each step as she could possibly muster, not needing to look back to know the other two women were now doing the same thing. There was just enough room along the chute funneling the runners toward the finish line for three people to run abreast with each other. She spied out of her peripheral vision that the women had caught up to her and were running even along the final fifty yards. The trio put on their last burst of speed and crossed the mats containing the timing sensors almost at the same time.

All three shared laughs and hugs as they stumbled to a spot just beyond the finish line. Angie was now starting to feel the effects of her exertions but did her best to get out of the way of the athletes finishing just behind her and the others. After a few moments spent getting her breathing under control, she aimlessly headed in the general direction of the tent containing food for the athletes, taking deep gulps of air as she walked. "Mom! Mom!" Sandra was running toward her, dodging athletes and spectators alike while gesturing wildly, obviously making no attempts to contain her excitement. "Mom, Mom, that was fantastic!" she exclaimed, pulling up just short of knocking her over. "Unbelievable!" she continued. "What a finish!" Angie barely had a chance to brace herself before Sandra grabbed her in a suffocating bear hug.

Not wanting to curb her elation, Angie allowed Sandra the opportunity to express her pleasure even though she desperately wanted to sit down. Eventually she squeaked out, "Sandra … Sandra … can't breathe."

Sandra released her grip and took a short step back, holding Angie by the shoulders. "Oh, sorry Mom. It's just that I couldn't believe how well you did." After another quick hug, Sandra went in search of results while Angie hobbled to the food tent and then sat down at a table near where they had met earlier. About twenty minutes later, Sandra came running. "Mom! Mom! Guess what! You finished fourteenth in your age group! Fourteenth! I told you, you did fantastic!" she gushed. "See, now are you going to have confidence in yourself? Look at what you can do when you put your mind to it!" Angie could respond only with a smile and a nod, being speechless at her own performance. Although she knew she had been well prepared, she never in her wildest dreams had thought of finishing so high up in the standings.

Sandra's eyes suddenly widened, and she grabbed Angie's shoulders. "Oooo! I just thought of something! You know how we were talking at the hospital about that race in Hawaii, and you said no way? I know Sylvia has been bugging you about it, right? Well … look how you did today. I think it's time for you to step up and take the challenge," she asserted, with crossed arms. Angie was so flabbergasted she was incapable of formulating a response. Sandra took the opportunity of her silence to add more fuel to the fire. "Look, you didn't think you were going to do this well today, am I right? Of course I'm right! Sure, doing that other race is going to take more work, but you showed you can do it when you want to, right? Listen, think about it. Sylvia and I will do everything we can to help you train." Sandra paused, peering expectantly at Angie for a response. Angie still didn't think she had what it took to do that big of a race, but she didn't want to let Sandra down either. With a deep sigh, she conceded. "OK, tell you what. I'll look into it, and if it seems feasible, I'll do it."

All In

As was his habit, Matt coasted in to work, gently applying the brakes as he guided the bike parallel to the curb, unclicking his shoe out of the pedal just before coming to a complete stop. He had ridden to work so many times it had become second nature. Carrying his bike through the back door and across the carpet of the physical therapy room so as the avoid the wrath of the office manager had also become second nature. Once he had put his bike and lunch away and had pulled his client's files from the file cabinets, he sat down next to Stephan and opened the first file. They had both gotten in early enough to take their time preparing for the day, engaging in small talk more than reading files.

The majority of the conversation was taken up with discussing life outside of work, and eventually the conversation drifted to Matt's ongoing exploits in his time-consuming hobby. "Oh, yeah, so what's doing lately in the world of triathlon?" Stephan asked.

Matt related brief descriptions of two upcoming races he was training for, adding, "I've done so well at what I've done so far I'm giving some thought to doing longer races."

Stephan raised an eyebrow. "Longer races? Like, how long are we talking?"

Matt, who had been reading a file, paused before sliding it over and making eye contact.

"A 2.4-mile swim, 112-mile bike, and a 26.2-mile run" he matter-of-factly stated, picking up another file. Stephan's chin almost hit his chest. "OK, the ones you are doing now I get, seeing as how you have taken to the sport and exceeded expectations, but are you really serious about doing the really long one!"

Matt paused once more before replying, "Actually, yes, I have considered it, although I haven't made any plans yet."

Stephan launched into the expected reprimand. "Are you kidding me? You know you barely have a life now! If you start training for the longest race, you are going to be forced to do nothing but train, leaving no time for anything, or *anyone*, else. Am I right?" Stephan hadn't come right out and said it, but Matt knew one of his major objections was his training interfering with Matt's first girlfriend since high school.

His conversation with Stephan remained on his mind all throughout his date with Hannah. He relayed their conversation and asked for her opinion. She paused before responding, "If you start training for longer races, you *would* have less time for other things and other people. Looking at it from a selfish perspective, if our relationship is going to become exclusive, that would mean less time for me. While I don't think I'm a diva, I do want some time with the person to whom I'm committed." This time it was Matt's turn to slowly lift his glass and take a sip. "I hear what you're saying," he acknowledged.

"The truth is, I've never really given much thought to getting married, or even getting serious with someone, or about having kids. I've just sort of drifted through life, taking it as it comes. The only thing I've ever planned out was becoming a physical therapist. I can see where you're coming from; it wouldn't be fair to anyone to say one is a boyfriend or girlfriend, or especially something more, and then neglect the other person. If we do get serious, and I attempt to do a longer race, then obviously I have to work on my time-management skills. I think I could do both; I've always been pretty good when I've had to discipline myself in some way."

With work staying as busy as ever, continued focus on training, and now a relationship to occupy his time, the months flew by. Matt kept competing in medium-distance races and more often than not was able to achieve either a podium finish or at least a top-ten finish. As most races drew the same guys year in and year out, he got to know them quite well, at least from a competition standpoint. As it happened, one of the races took place a few weeks after the race at Hawaii had been televised. Almost all the guys had watched it, and as they were talking about it, one of the guys that, like Matt, had been able to achieve several podium finishes made eye contact with Matt and asked, "So when are you going to stop playing games and go for Hawaii? You've already proven many times over you can do the short- and medium-distances. When are you going to really challenge yourself and go for an Ironman?" Matt felt as awkward as he had in quite some time as all conversation suddenly ceased and all eyes were focused in his direction.

Matt halfheartedly promised them he would look into it, more as a way of deflecting attention than speaking of his true intentions. The next day, he won third place, and several guys laughingly reminded him of his promise to get serious about Hawaii. Eventually he managed to yell over the din, "I'll think about it!" which earned him even more catcalls.

Matt had Hannah over for dinner a couple nights later, and since she hadn't been able to go with him, she asked how the race went. He filled her in on just a few of the specifics of each portion of the race, ending with his having been able to finish third in his age group. His recounting of the race jogged his memory of the good-natured confrontation in which he had taken part right after the award ceremony.

He noticed Hannah perk up as he described the verbal jousting. When he had dismissed the man's remarks with a wave of his hand, she interjected, "But it is something you've talked about before, even if it has been quite some time. Does this mean you're planning on doing it this time instead of simply talking about it?"

He cleared his throat before he replied. "Honestly, I have been thinking about it for the past two days, but I haven't reached a decision yet. On one hand, it is the ultimate, and I would love the challenge. On the other hand, I don't want it to dominate my life to the extent that it would jeopardize what we have."

Hannah smiled a cautious smile at his statement of thinking of their relationship and how his decisions affected her. After a few moments of quietly mulling it over, she smiled again, this time wider, with a cheerier facial expression, and exclaimed, "Then I think you should go for it!" He was dumbfounded and unable to do anything else than sit with his hands in his lap and stare at her until he came to his senses with a shake of his head. "You think I should go for it?" he asked. "You know what that will mean? Even if I focus on training smart, and not necessarily hard, I'm still going to have to increase the amount of training. At least a couple days a week, that is." Hannah giggled at his reaction but encouraged him, saying that she understood what it meant for both him and them.

The first task for competing in Hawaii involved more mental than physical work, as Matt had to sift through dozens of websites to determine when qualifying races were scheduled. He hoped to find one that was close to the race in Hawaii so there wasn't much downtime between races. In the end, he discovered one in late July; this was a little farther off than he desired, but he decided he could plan on what to do in between races later. At first there was a whirlwind of activity with registering for the race and, since it was in another state, booking a flight and hotel room. Once the logistics were completed, life settled down into the normal humdrum of work and training, until he received an email from the race organization informing athletes there was only two weeks to race day.

The message served as sort of a psychological slap in the face. He read it several times before admitting time had run by faster than expected. As a result, during the following week leading up to the race, each day seemed as if it were only a few minutes long. What made it even worse was a sense of unreadiness that remained with him over the next few days as he prepared to ship his bike to the race site and check his equipment list a dozen times. No amount of preparing or busyness could shake his feeling of unease. In the end, all he could do was chalk it up to extraordinary prerace jitters, given this was the biggest race of his life, at least to that point. It was still with him as he sat in the airport and boarded the plane— not that he expected it to go away.

Fortunately, the tasks of deboarding the plane, wending his way through the airport, and navigating an unfamiliar car through freeways and streets he had never been on served to ease the butterflies somewhat. By the time he strolled into the lobby and saw the potted plants, smoked glass doors, and dark wood registration counter there, they were almost gone. The next day, getting lost while driving to the race expo site provided further opportunities to divert his fears. The building seemed to be a temporarily converted furniture store. The name of the race was emblazoned across a huge banner hung over two glass doors. After briefly standing in line at the registration table and providing his name and driver's license, he received his race numbers and claim voucher for his bike. After being advised to check his numbers before leaving the expo, he was verbally directed to the left of the tables and cheerfully wished good luck. After inspecting his race numbers and voucher, he entered the expo itself.

Once through the expo, he made his way to the bike claim area. A volunteer asked Matt to open his container to check and make sure he had the right bike, and that everything he had packed into it back home was still inside. A quick scan told him his bike had arrived in the same condition as it had been back home. On returning to the hotel, the first thing he did was take care of business, which meant putting the bike together. Once that was accomplished and he was satisfied with walking out of his room the next morning with his bike in proper working order, he took advantage of the extra free time at the pool and jacuzzi. He had several dreams throughout the night but could remember only one. In that dream, he had attempted to complete the swim with a child's inflatable ring around his waist. When he went to get on his bike, he discovered it had training wheels, and after struggling the first few yards on the run, he looked down to see he was wearing huge clown shoes.

The sudden sound of music playing from his phone intruded on his dreams. Barely suppressing a groan while rolling over, he fumbled across the top of the phone until he located the off button by accident. His mind flashed on the ending of the one dream he was able to recall. Everything appeared as it normally did during a race as he approached the inflatable arch and finish line. It wasn't until after crossing the finish line that he became aware of one huge difference from usual races: there were no people—no couples or families having picnics, no one walking a dog, not even any children playing on the swings and slides. He finally spied one lone figure in the parking lot. He lumbered through the finish area, making his way to the man. As he got closer, he noticed the man was sweeping the parking lot with a broom! The man either heard or saw Matt walking toward him; he stopped sweeping, holding the broom upright in one hand while draping his other arm across the end. If he picked up on the fact that Matt was wearing a triathlon suit and a pair of clown shoes, his face didn't show it; nor did he say anything.

Matt stopped a few yards from the man, nodded, and said, "Afternoon." The man simply nodded in return and said, "Afternoon yourself," whereupon Matt asked, "Where is everybody?"

At first, he wasn't sure the man had heard the question and was opening his mouth to ask again when the man asked, "Where is who?"

Matt was incredulous and stopped just short of calling him an idiot. "What do you mean, who? Everybody—all the people! There isn't a single soul in this park except for you and me! Where did all the people go?"

A look slowly crept across the man's face that strongly suggested he was thinking Matt was the idiot. "What do you mean 'all the people'? There's never anyone here at this time of the week, jus' me and my broom."

Matt bit off the beginnings of a laugh, asking instead, "The people competing in the triathlon, the people putting on the race, the people watching the race—those people! Where are they?"

The man burst out laughing, causing Matt to feel rather insulted. Before he had the opportunity to express his feelings, the man continued. "The triathlon? That was done and gone over a week by now! Everybody done left long ago!" The man shuffled away, heartily laughing and sweeping as he went.

Matt put the dream out of his head while going through the normal routine of dressing for and driving to the race site, which—as seemed so often the case—included a park. By the time he had pulled everything out of his bag and set it into its proper place, the sun had risen to just below the foothills in the distance. Once his station had been set up, he walked over to the lake. As he was scanning the surface of the water, the announcer's voice began providing the racers with details about the racecourse. He began by informing the congregated participants that the swim portion would consist of two laps, with each lap being 1.2 miles in length. They would have to exit the water and run along the water's edge for about twenty yards before reentering the water and beginning their second lap.

The next hour plus was the typical blur of time, thoughts, and emotions. Once the horn sounded for the beginning of the first wave and the start of the race, Matt experienced that fatalistic sense that it didn't matter how he felt he had prepared for the race; there was no longer any time to worry: it was go time. By the time his wave entered the water for their, start his nervous energy had already kicked in. When the announcer began the ten-second countdown, as a group, all the men faced forward, instantly becoming hyperfocused on the task awaiting them. Throughout the first lap, they kept their pace; there was no passing—at least not in his immediate area. The completion of the first lap, which necessitated sloshing out of the water and running along a sandy beach to then reenter the water for the second lap, gave him the opportunity to scan the field front and back. The action was happening much too quickly to get an exact count, but it seemed most of the ten to twelve guys ahead of him at the beginning were still in the lead.

The positions remained largely unchanged throughout the second lap. For the final several hundred yards, Matt was content to ease back on his throttle a bit, allowing the others to gain a few more yards. By the time he exited the water and ran up the banks of the lake toward the transition area, they were about fifty yards ahead of him. He smiled, knowing that short distance would be nothing once they were all on their bikes. His spirits, lifted by a better-than-expected swimming leg, provided him with all the impetus needed. He passed a number of riders during the first twenty-five to thirty miles, which he figured were the average athletes from the first three waves. Between mile thirty and mile fifty-six he caught up to, and passed, several riders from his own age group. Having long ago lost count, he was hoping this put him in the top five, but he couldn't be sure.

From about mile seventy to mile eighty-five, Matt struggled with maintaining the motivation to keep up the pace. During that stretch, the course led them out into the countryside, which, he discovered, consisted of completely light brown undulating foothills with a few sparse groves of trees here and there. The only break came when they passed an aid station, but those were spaced roughly twenty-five miles apart. About an hour later, they neared the last ten to twelve miles of the course, riding through inhabited parts of the surrounding countryside once more. Within another thirty minutes, they had entered the city limits, and there were a few people standing out on the streets cheering and ringing cowbells.

The running course paralleled the transition area for about a hundred yards before veering slightly to the right and roughly following the outline of the lake. In the beginning, Matt kept an eye out for the two runners in his age group, choosing to stay behind, knowing it was going to be a long race. His only concern was not letting them get out of his sight. Mile after mile they ran, with neither his opponents extending their lead nor Matt losing ground behind them. At about mile seven to eight, the course became more challenging. What had been an almost completely flat, level course was transforming into a series of slight up and down grades.

About halfway through the run, from mile twelve to about mile seventeen, the course flattened out again. The respite in effort gave him the opportunity to take stock of his physical condition, which became very important when he spied an aid station at mile sixteen. He felt good enough to be certain of catching up to his competitors even if he slowed at the aid station and they didn't; the last thing he wanted was to get cramps from dehydration close to the finish line. He slightly decreased his speed, jogging through the aid station as he drank cup after cup of both water and a sports drink.

Once through the aid station, a quick calculation showed there were about forty yards separating the leader from the next runner, and about another fifty yards between himself and the second-place runner. Even though the run was now more than halfway complete, Matt stayed with his philosophy of wanting to keep sight of the men and make his move at the end. At mile seventeen, the road resumed its gradual inclines and declines, and from about mile twenty to mile twenty-one, it felt as if the road had leveled off and they were running on flat ground once more. At mile twenty-three, the other runners were not showing any signs of weakness or struggle. Matt started doubting whether he could catch them at this pace, but just about the time that uneasiness was starting to creep in, he caught sight of the lead runner slowing down, then starting to walk, and then starting to hobble while grabbing his right hamstring.

Matt recognized those signs in an instant. For whatever reason, the man was getting cramps—and getting them badly enough it became necessary for him to stop. It was all Matt could do to keep from shouting out in triumph and pumping his fists in the air as he ran past the man, who was still shuffling while holding the back of his leg. With only two miles to go at that point, he was certain, unless there was someone ahead he hadn't seen, to win a spot on the podium. Just to make sure, he increased his pace until the gap between him and the new leader was about ten yards. He maintained his position even when the pair reached the mile twenty-five marker and could see the vague outlines of the race site in the distance.

He was getting ready to increase his pace again, enough to draw even with the leader so they could engage in a congratulatory conversation, when another runner caught up to and then passed them both. Initially he wasn't overly concerned, but he thought his eyes were going to pop out of his head when he looked down at the man's calf and saw that the number put him in their age group. When the other racer turned around to see where he had come from, Matt was sure the look on his face mirrored his own. The other man was so stunned he forgot his pace, allowing Matt to catch up to him in a few strides. "Holy crap!" he exclaimed. "Where the hell did he come from?" All Matt could do was shrug and chuckle. "I have no idea."

Being certain they would pick up spots two and three, they coasted across the finish line. After tracking down the winner, the three men compared strategies and thoughts about the race, continuing their dialogue while eating a typical postrace meal. Knowing the award ceremony was still a few hours away, Matt spent the remaining time stretching and watching others finish the race. In contrast to the past few days, time seemed to crawl, but things started picking up as soon as the ceremony began. The race organizer making the presentations gave the customary congratulations to all the racers, made a few remarks about how the race went overall, and dived into handing out the awards. When it was their turn, he joined the other two on the podium, smiling and waving to the well-wishers. Then, almost as soon as it started, they were stepping down to make way for the next trio. As he and the two winners were parting company, the second-place finisher got the attention of Matt and the first-place finisher and called out, "See ya in Hawaii!"

"Australia! You're going all the way to Australia? For a race!" Lisa exclaimed so loudly and emphatically Sarah felt as if she were in the room. "Are you kidding me? You couldn't find one closer to home? At least on the same continent?"

Sarah couldn't resist the opportunity to needle her close friend. "Oh, so you know Australia is a continent? That's good, Lisa." She didn't have to be on the other end of the phone to know what Lisa's facial expression would be.

"I'm serious. What made you decide to go all the way to Australia to compete?"

Sarah took a sip of a protein shake. "Well, I had a conference call with all my sponsors, and they were so happy with my performance in the races I've done so far that they were willing to spring for the airfare and hotel. Oh, and are you ready for this? My parents are chipping in for the meals."

There was an audible gasp in the earpiece, followed by Lisa's incredulous "Noooooo way! How on earth did you ever get them to do that? I thought your mom was still dead set against you racing and was waiting for you to admit it was all one huge mistake?"

Sarah finished her shake in one final gulp. "I didn't exactly get them to do it. And really, I'm sure it was all my dad's idea. He'll probably never admit it, at least not in front of my mom, but I think he's excited about my current career choice. Occasionally I'll catch him out of the corner of my eye, and he's got that 'proud father' look."

Lisa sighed. "Well, maybe one day your mom will finally have a change of heart. In the meantime, we still on for the run tomorrow?" Sarah had to remind herself what day of the week it was. "Oh, yeah, at the gym. Right, see ya there."

Sarah and Lisa were joined by several members from both the running and triathlon clubs, and while cooling down Lisa informed everyone about the news she had received from Sarah the day before. One of the guys in the group had done an Ironman race a few years earlier and was one of the more serious triathletes in the club. "So are you going to use that as a springboard for Hawaii?" he queried.

All peripheral conversation stopped, and all eyes focused on Sarah, who felt her face getting red. "Don't know," she replied once she had recovered her composure, hoping that would be enough to divert some of the attention off her and toward someone else. But she had no such luck.

"Come on," he pushed. "You've been a pro for what, four years now?" He paused briefly for confirmation.

Sarah held up three fingers. "Three ... and a half." The entire group laughed at her feeble attempt to minimize his point.

"OK," he conceded before continuing. "Three—and a half—seasons, and you're suggesting you have never thought about getting there? Even though that's the Holy Grail, the Super Bowl, the World Series, for the pros, and you haven't made plans to get there? Why am I finding that hard to believe?" He smiled broadly to take some of the heat off, but his implicit accusation was obvious to all.

"Fine ... whatever ... OK, I have thought about it, but not seriously at this point in my career. While it may be true I have won a couple races, they were all halfs. This will be my first full Ironman-distance race, so if I do well on this one, depending on how well I do, then maybe, *maybe*, I can begin looking into the possibility of Hawaii."

The man who had asked her about her plans could sense her digging in her heels, and he held his hands up. "OK, OK, we get it. You want to be cautious. Just remember one thing: we may not be pros, but we are veterans, and we've seen other pros in action. We're not just saying this because we want you to feel good about yourself. We honestly believe you could make it." As one, the group profusely agreed with his assessment of Sarah's skills, reassuring her of their support for her endeavors.

The flight to Australia from the continental US made a stop in Hawaii to pick up extra passengers. As they departed, she felt wistful watching the island of Oahu fade from view out of the small plane window. Seeing the islands now during approach and departure, she mentally kicked herself for not trying. It also made her put Hawaii on her to-do list. *Someday*, she thought as the plane banked and the islands were completely lost from view.

After the longest flight of her life, landing and getting off the plane was rudimentary and unremarkable, until she emerged from the tunnel and entered the terminal. A short distance from the door, a young woman was standing with a small sign that had "Sarah McKittrick" written on it in bold letters. Sarah put her hand on her mouth and giggled as she sidestepped the other passengers, making her way to the woman.

"Hi! I'm Sarah McKittrick!" she said, waiting for the woman to take the lead from there.

"Hi, I'm Michelle. Nice to meet you, Sarah. I'm from Down Under Productions; they're sending people out to pick up the pros and get them settled into the hotel. I'll show you where to get your luggage, and if it's OK, there's someone else coming in about half an hour from now, so would it be all right if we wait for him and then we can all head to the hotel together?" Sarah was just tickled at the rock star treatment, so she responded with "Absolutely!"

Sarah used the time waiting for the next pro to arrive to pick Michelle's brain about race and weather conditions. Back at the gate, Michelle took her position in front of the door to greet the other athlete. Sarah grinned from ear to ear while observing a young man (whose name was Roger), appearing to be in his midtwenties, timidly walk over to her and put his hand on his chest. Even though she couldn't hear what he said from the short distance, she was sure he was introducing himself. There was no doubt in Sarah's mind that her face had looked exactly the same when she had seen her sign.

The two athletes had completed introductions and discussed background information by the time the trio reached the oval luggage conveyor belts. Sarah smiled but didn't say anything as Roger began grilling Michelle over race and weather conditions, just as she had earlier. Sarah gave her a wry grin when Michelle made eye contact with her and repeated the same facts. On the short ride to the hotel, Sarah and Roger informed each other of races they'd done in the past and their hopes for the upcoming race. Michelle facilitated checking in, which was fine with Sarah. She suddenly felt exhausted after the long travel day. When she got to her room, she flipped through the emails printed from the race organizers, discovering that the first event was set for the next day at 10:00 a.m. She opted for sleep over food and set her alarm for 9:45 a.m.

The next morning Sarah chuckled as she stepped in line right behind Roger at the hotel café. Apparently, he had chosen sleep over breakfast as well. Once they had their orders they discovered Michelle waiting for them in the hotel lobby.

"How was your first night down under?" she queried.

"Wonderful!"

"Outstanding!"

Sarah and Roger exclaimed their responses on top of each other:

"Glad to hear it," Michelle replied, introducing three other pros standing nearby and informing the quintet they just had enough time to get to the location of the first event, which was an orientation and informational meeting.

On the way to the event, Sarah and Roger chatted with the other three pros: Keith, who was from Canada; Stan, who was from England; and Sonia, who was from Germany. As Sarah and Roger had done earlier, they traded stories with the others. Once they learned Keith had done this race before, they eagerly tried to get as many tips for the course as possible before they got to the event location.

They had just gotten out of the van and entered the large warehouse-type building when a voice boomed over a PA system. "Welcome, triathletes! Welcome to the land of down under!" The last greeting was issued with special gusto, leading the assembled crowd to cheer in response. The speaker went on to encourage the athletes to take their seats, as he had a lot of information he wanted to convey but didn't want them to spend their valuable time in meetings. Sarah tried to estimate how many were in the room but quickly lost count. They didn't have to wait long to learn an exact number, as the speaker's first statement once everyone had found a place to sit informed the group there were 165 athletes, representing twenty-three different countries. The man paused briefly before launching into all the information they would need over the next few days. As he was talking, several people handed the person on the end of each row a folder, which the man explained included all the material he would be talking about that morning.

Sarah absentmindedly listened to the lecture while inspecting the other females in the cavernous room. They were all very lean and muscular, some even appearing rather masculine. Their mannerisms suggested confidence and sureness. One and all, they reminded her of lionesses or tigers; their movements had a certain feline grace about them. In a brief flash of insecurity, she wondered about looking the same to the others, which led to questioning about whether she belonged. Her mother's voice suddenly echoed in her mind: "Someday you'll realize I was right and you made a terrible mistake. You just wait and see!" Doubt began creeping in like ivy curling itself around and through a fence. As it took hold, she froze, feeling as if she were in a whirlpool, going around and around, and sinking a little further with each revolution.

It took a tremendous strength of will to remind herself that she'd had experience and had exceeded expectations. In fact, if she hadn't done as well as she had, the sponsors never would have funded this excursion. Plus, she had already competed against other pros, as well as elite age groupers, and had come out on top. Slowly the vines loosened themselves, and she took a deep breath. A veil of darkness lifted from her eyes, and she now regarded those seated around her as equals.

After the meeting, they were driven to the race site. Company staff and volunteers were just starting to set up big tents and the poles that would hold up the plastic barriers separating the transition area from the finish chute. After walking around a while and getting a feel for where they would leave the water and enter the transition area, Sarah and the four men discussed their options and decided to drive the course to get a visual on what they could expect on race day. After getting to the turnaround point halfway through the bike course, they were all thankful the course did not include any major climbs. The way back to the race site took a slightly different route, but the terrain was largely the same as it had been when they were going out. They completed their foray by driving along the road that would hold the running course, and they again were pleased it was almost entirely level. "Looks like this is going to make for some fast times come race day," Roger remarked, receiving enthusiastic head nods and various murmured assents.

Race day came too fast for Sarah's liking. By the time she had dressed and left her room, there was already a large group of athletes standing just outside the glass lobby doors, waiting for the shuttle that would transport them to the race site. As was typical among triathletes, the talk soon gravitated toward expectations, especially considering how they had done in previous races of this distance. The athletes became more talkative and animated the closer they got to the race site. "Good luck!" she called out to the guys as she located her station; then she got right to opening her bag and arranging each item into its place. After warming up, she rummaged around for her goggles and swim cap, and she then ambled along the carpeted path to the platform. There were a few people jumping or diving off; she donned her cap and goggles and joined them.

With the countdown to the race start quickly approaching, she returned to her station, giving it one last examination. Being satisfied everything was in order, she leisurely walked toward the water. There was decidedly less banter and conversation now than when they had all arrived on the buses, as the athletes were now focused on preparing themselves mentally for what the next eight to ten or eleven hours would bring. Many of them wore steely-faced expressions, staring straight ahead with an appearance of extreme determination.

There was a set of large speakers positioned on a grassy slope behind the platform. A steady stream of chatter from a race announcer issued from each speaker, providing the spectators with information about how many athletes there were, both pros and age groupers, how many countries were represented, and so on. By the time he had completed his breakdown of race participants, the male pros were all either on the platform or in the water, warming up. After a brief pause, the race announcer notified the male pros they had approximately ten minutes until the start of the race.

The next several minutes saw the males jockeying around the ramp, some choosing the area closest to the platform, while others chose to be at the opposite end. They had just reached somewhat stable locations when the race announcer called out, "Two minutes to go! Two minutes to the start of the male pros!" By now the crowd needed little additional encouragement to cheer on the athletes. It got even louder when the race announcer gave them the one-minute warning, and the cheering remained at a fever pitch until he instructed the spectators to join him in the final ten-second countdown. As one, all assembled picked up the count: "Ten ... nine ... eight ... seven ... six ... .five ... four ... three ... two ... one!"

The males dived in unison, giving the appearance of one huge, elongated splash. As they headed for the first buoy, those at the extreme ends angled toward the middle, giving the appearance to those on shore of a large diamond. After the males had left, the race announcer gave the female pros their five-minute notice. A few women jumped into the water to get a last-minute warm-up, but Sarah felt she was ready for the race to get started and remained on the platform, shaking out her arms and legs.

Although she might have lacked confidence in her ability to bike and run, given her background she had total certainty about her swimming prowess.

The race announcer was soon notifying those in the water that they had to get back to the platform, as they had only two minutes until the start of their wave. They barely had time to get out and take their positions before he called out the one-minute mark, and in a flash he was yelling for the crowd to count down: "Ten ... nine ... eight ... seven ... six ... five ... four ... three ... two ... one!" As before, the announcer's voice was masked by the roar of the spectators and the air horn. Sarah didn't really hear either, as she was focusing on diving as far out from the ramp as she could. She glided underwater briefly before surfacing to explode in a burst of activity.

The swimming leg turned out to be a fight between Sarah and three other women. Knowing this was her strongest event, she put extra effort into establishing and maintaining a lead. It proved difficult, but she was up for the challenge and was barely cognizant of the race announcer yelling her name as being the first female pro out of the water. Exiting the transition area, she caught a glimpse out of the corner of her eye of the woman who had been just behind her coming out of the water.

The knowledge that she wasn't as strong at cycling and running as she was at swimming led to a very different strategy for the remainder of the race. After some mental calculations, she decided on five as the magic number. She would use just enough energy on the bike and the first twenty or so miles of the run to stay in fifth or maybe sixth position, trusting there would be enough left to finish in the top three by mile 26.2. It didn't take long at all for the woman who had been second out of the water to overtake her, but Sarah stuck with her plan, allowing her to pass and then using just enough effort to stay several bike lengths behind. Within the next ten to fifteen minutes, several more women passed, but each time, Sarah kept her speed constant while keeping a tally of how many women were ahead.

At about the halfway point, the number had reached nine. Not only that, but some had passed her at a speed that made her feel as if she wasn't even moving. After the ninth woman passed her, all the old doubts bubbled up. She put her head down, not being able to judge if the moisture around her eyes was from sweat or the beginning of tears. It came as no surprise when her mother's voice careened around inside her head and she could perfectly hear "I told you this was a mistake!" For a few moments, Sarah vacillated between determination and defeat, at danger of coasting to a stop at the side of the road, her head hanging over her handlebars in a blithering mess. But at that moment, right before she stopped pedaling, another voice burst into her mind, and she heard Lisa telling her how great she was. On the heels of Lisa's voice came the voices of several others—members of the triathlon club and other pros.

There was a transformation in that moment; instead of slowing down and coasting to a stop, she gritted her teeth and growled out loud, bearing down on each revolution of the pedals. Taking advantage of her renewed spirit, she stood up once more to close the gap between her and her nearest competition. Not only did she overtake the next five women; she eventually pulled to within about thirty yards of the three to four women in the lead group. It wasn't until she was that close, and still bearing down, that she thought to herself, *What am I doing? I'm going to use all my energy on the bike.* She eased up slightly, keeping her current distance from the leaders, once more feeling confident about her chances of maintaining the pace and being at least somewhere near the front at the finish line.

The places remained stable during the last fifteen miles on the bike course. From Sarah's vantage point, she was able to observe the leaders continue to ride where they were relative to each other, with no one attempting to pass even as they arrived back in town and approached the transition area. Knowing it was going to be a long run, she tried to forget about where the other women were; there would be ample time to get a bead on the others. They had to make several turns to get out of the transition area and onto the running course, but once they had done so, the course was straight for as far the eye could see. Sarah used the same strategy as on the bike course, running just fast enough to remain a constant twenty to thirty yards behind the nearest woman.

Sarah used the women ahead of her as her own personal pacers. At about the mile-six marker, the course took a ninety-degree turn. Since there were buildings on the corner, she couldn't see ahead until she rounded the corner and was once again running on a straight path. She began making mental calculations. *Let's see. We just passed the mile-six marker, which means we are one quarter of the way through the run. Where's the competition?* She noted that all four women were almost exactly as far apart at the turn as they had been for the last several miles, which provided a sense of encouragement. *Now,* she thought, *If things can stay this way until the last mile or two, I should be in really good shape.*

Mile after mile they ran, long strides eating up asphalt. The only thing breaking up the steady measure of feet striking the pavement was their grabbing water proffered by the myriad volunteers on the course. As Sarah approached the mile-eight marker, some of the men pros came running the other way. Roughly thirty minutes later, she was able to make out groups of people standing up ahead, some of whom were standing in the middle of the road with the ever-present sandwich board signs with U-turn arrows on them. Nearing the turnaround point afforded her a glimpse of the three women ahead.

Her nerves were mostly calm, as none of them attempted to put distance between themselves and their competition. The gaps remained the same on the way back even as they reached the turn, but this time they were turning right instead of left. Although the race was progressing very rapidly, there was still about six miles left, which was a long way to try to gain a lead and hold on through the finish line. Approaching the mile twenty-three banner, Sarah began feeling the strain but had the one small advantage of being one of those simply keeping up, not the one who was trying to establish the pace.

Right after the mile twenty-four banner, first one and then another woman began faltering, their strides appearing much more erratic. Although still content to be the pursuer, Sarah now began formulating her own plan of attack. It was a given she was going to put the hammer down at some point; the only question was when. Debating the timing of her push, she began to pick up on a low rumble, which grew as they ran, and she soon realized it was the noise of the spectators cheering on the racers at the finish line. "If I can hear them, then it must mean we are close," she hypothesized. "And if we are that close, then it's time to make my move. We can't be more than a mile away by now. It'll take quite some doing hitting it now, but I think I've just enough left to make it."

She breathed a mental sigh of relief upon spotting the crowd a few minutes after making her push. Her own breathing was becoming more and more difficult, but she didn't dare slow down. The banners serving as the finishing chute were the most beautiful sight she had ever seen in her life. After turning a corner, it was a straight shot to the finish line. Sprinting the final hundred yards, she held her arms high in victory and crossed underneath the large inflatable arch, discovering only two women standing there waiting for her. She had done it! They allowed time for Sarah to catch her breath before they embraced in a group hug, all three winners congratulating each other while wearing huge smiles.

The announcer began the awards ceremony by calling out the top pros. When it came to the women, starting with third place, Sarah's name was called first, followed by second place and then first place. As they were standing on the podium, Sarah's name was announced again as the first female out of the water, adding she had earned the swim premium of $500. As they climbed down and began going their separate ways, the first-place finisher raised her voice to get Sarah's attention. When Sarah looked her way, she exclaimed, "See ya in Hawaii!" She quickly picked up on Sarah's confused facial expression. "Hawaii … see you in Hawaii." When it was apparent Sarah still didn't grasp her intended meaning, she stated emphatically, "Hawaii … the race in October in Hawaii. You came in third; you earned a spot."

The reality of what Sarah had accomplished finally made an impact on her consciousness. "Oh, my gosh. That's right; I did. I entirely forgot about that. I was so intent on simply doing well here that I completely forgot about that. Thanks for reminding me, and yes, I will definitely see you in Hawaii." The two victors shared a laugh and parted ways, knowing the real battle lay ahead.

"C'mon, Ang, what's the holdup? You've been doing triathlons for ten years now; if it's not finally the time this year, then when will it be? What's the problem, huh, huh, huh?"

Angie issued a deep sigh, holding in what she really wanted to say. Instead she resorted to a mild chastisement. "First of all, it's only been nine years, not ten; and second … has anyone ever told you that you can be annoying at times?"

Sylvia practically cackled in delight. "Yeah, quite often, but that's my personality, and what's a gal gonna do, right?" She laughed again, leaving

RUSSELL KOOP

Angie to grimace in agreement. The few brief moments of silence were interrupted by Sylvia refusing to allow Angie the chance to avoid giving her a concrete answer, but at least this time she used a more tactful approach. "I'm not trying to make you feel bad or anything like that, but I've heard you talk about it for the last year, so I know there's been some interest in doing it. Is it the distance you're concerned about? 'Cause from what I've seen over the past *nine* years, you've been able to increase your distances and decrease your times well enough."

Knowing what Sylvia's response would be kept Angie from verbally agreeing to at least investigate what it would take to get to Hawaii. Her hope that it would ride for another day was short-lived. "Well …?" Sylvia asked, raising the tone of her voice at the end of the word, deliberately waiting for a reply to her query.

Try as she might, Angie could not figure out a way to continuing avoiding the topic. "OK, I'll look into it! Happy?" came the exasperated retort. Sure enough, Sylvia threw her head back, clapped her hands, and hooted again in an even more thoroughly annoying manner

As it was, the run ended way too early for her liking, though there was little choice but to stick with the short distance. Any hopes that her concession during the run would keep Sylvia off her back for a while were shattered as soon as they reached the front door. "OK, what do we do first?" she prompted. Angie briefly considered an attempt to put it off, but before she could get any words out of her mouth, she decided the best way to get Sylvia to drop the subject was to get it over with. "Well, I'm guessing it would be similar to other races; I have to register." Without a word, Sylvia grabbed her arm and led her to Angie's home office.

An hour later, they discovered it wasn't as easy as simply registering; it was necessary to win one's age group in a qualifying race. "Hhhmmmpphhh, that's not going to happen" Angie stated dejectedly. Sylvia opened her mouth but then shut it when Angie gave her a look that shut her down. Another few minutes of searching brought the knowledge that an interested person could enter a lottery and gain entry if they completed a race stateside. Before stopping to fully consider the ramifications of her actions, Angie filled out the forms to enter the lottery.

"Great!" Sylvia exclaimed. "What do we start with first? Oooh, I know, we'll start a workout schedule. Then we can research proper nutrition habits that will foster maximum physical performance. Then—"

Angie threw her hands up. "Whoa, whoa, whoa, hang on a sec! Who is this *we* you keep talking about? Did you forget who's actually doing the race? Speaking of which, I've just finished making a momentous decision here. At least give me some time to wrap my head around what it is I've done before you go blasting off with all the nuts and bolts of training and ... and ... and everything else! Besides which, odds are against me even getting selected!"

This time it was Sylvia's turn to throw her hands in the air. "OK, OK, message received—Take it easy for a few days. I do, however, want you to remember: this is not a solitary endeavor you are undertaking. We are a team, and I'm gonna be in your corner every step of the way. Understand?"

Angie stood up from the computer, taking Sylvia's arm and guiding her to the kitchen. "Yes, I understand. Right now, though, it's time to relax over a nice glass of vino."

After that evening, Angie almost completely forgot about the entire matter. The only times she recalled the issue were when Sylvia, Sandra, or Jonathan would bring it up. This occurred to the extent that when the day came for the race organizers to notify the applicants about whether they'd been chosen, she totally forgot to check her email until she was getting ready for bed. In fact, she was in the act of pulling back the sheets to climb into bed when something, and she was never quite sure what, jogged her memory that this was the day. She stood looking down at her bed, a thousand thoughts racing through her mind. She became paralyzed with indecision; a part of her was eager and excited to discover whether she was headed for Hawaii, while another part was in dread over the amount of training, commitment, and dedication it would take. As she stared at the bed, though not really seeing it, an awareness crept in that part of the fear was all about a nagging belief she wouldn't be capable of pulling it off—about getting close only to fail.

After taking a deep breath, she strode purposefully down the hallway and into her office, her hands shaking while pushing the button to awaken her computer from its sleep mode. She took another deep breath and was just about to exhale when she spied an email from the race organization.

With very shaky hands, she positioned the arrow and clicked. She then threw her hand over her mouth while staring at the screen, transfixed by the message. She had been chosen!!! She spent the next couple of minutes reading and rereading the message to make sure someone hadn't played a practical joke on her or that they weren't informing her she *hadn't* been chosen.

As far as she could tell, the message had indeed come from the race organizers and not from some third party, and the message was quite clear: she had been randomly chosen from a field of applicants and was now faced with the requirement of completing a qualifying race to make her acceptance into Hawaii official. Her heart continued to pound in her chest as she struggled to soak in the full implications of this momentous undertaking. Waking up the next morning, she had to fight an urge to race to her computer to read the message for the umpteenth time. The same thoughts from the previous night rushed into her mind. "Relax!" she said out loud emphatically. "Let's just take it one step at a time. You're in; leave it at that for now."

Although she was feeling somewhat childish, she passive-aggressively waited several days before telling anyone, choosing Sylvia to be the last person she informed. "No way!" was the predictable reaction. "Seriously? You wouldn't mess with me on this, right? It's too important of a deal to try to prank me with, correct? So, you really got in? I am *so* excited right now I can't begin to tell you!"

Angie chuckled at her friend's excitement. One would think she was the one who had been chosen in the lottery. "I'm glad you're excited, but remember, I'm only going to Hawaii if I finish a race. I keep telling you I have to finish a long-distance race that I've never done before."

Sylvia's response was expected. "Oh, c'mon, Ang. You always do this. You're always saying, 'Oh, I don't know if I can do this, I've never done this before,' and then you go right out and do it; isn't that right? Go ahead, try to tell me I'm wrong." Angie wanted desperately to do just that, simply for the sake of winning the argument, but she knew Sylvia was telling the truth.

She spent the next two days just getting used to the idea she was well on the path toward making a pipe dream a reality, wanting to take a metaphorical breath before launching into her training plan, knowing she'd have to follow it religiously for the next seven months. When the alarm went off at 5:00 a.m. that first morning of the new training regimen, she rolled over and, with bleary eyes, fumbled around the top of the clock radio until she found the correct button, more by accident than anything else. She pushed off the night table and lay on her back, staring at the ceiling in the darkness. "Why did I ever want to do this?" she moaned.

There was barely time to begin her new training program before Sylvia, true to her nature, called to inquire as to whether she was ready to look at qualifying races and make travel plans. "Well, at least she gave me a couple of days" Angie replied with a deep sigh. Once the travel arrangements had been taken care of, Sylvia launched into rambling about what they would have to wear, how much to pack, and on and on, whereupon Angie abruptly interjected they had done enough planning for one day and wasn't interested in discussing any further details of their trip, adding that she needed to get to bed early since tomorrow was one of her 5:00 a.m. workout days.

As the days turned into weeks and weeks into months, Angie became thankful for the part of her personality that included the rigidity of creating a plan and sticking to it at all costs. All too soon, the day came to leave for the qualifying race. Despite misgivings about being prepared, she reminded herself she had been training for several months for this exact moment and could do no more. The flight and drive to the city hosting the race was uneventful, and she experienced no more instances of apprehension throughout the trip.

The next morning was a mandatory meeting, which didn't last all that long—only about forty minutes. Then came the usual standing in long lines while checking in, picking up her bike, and setting up her transition area. Laying out her shoes and hat, she noticed several people tying balloons to mark their areas and made a mental note that before dinner she would have to find a store that sold balloons. She had never done that before, but then she had never competed in a race with this many people either. Any little thing to make the race go smoothly would be a decided plus.

On race morning, Angie's cell phone alarm woke her from a deep sleep, which was surprising given her expectation from the previous night of being so nervous about today that she would be awake before the alarm could go off. She squinted at the slit in the curtains, detecting a small bit of light coming from the large illuminated sign of the hotel. Other than that, it was still completely pitch-black outside. "Well, it is 4:00 a.m.," she mumbled. There was complete silence while they drove to the race site and found a parking space. The sky had almost imperceptibly grown a little lighter, but for all intents and purposes it was still night outside. The race organizers had to bring in several banks of lights on tall poles so the racers could see what they were doing. It was still somewhat dark by the time Angie had her station set up and had begun stretching and warming up, but the sun had risen far enough to provide a little light.

As had been the case at so many previous races, there was someone from the race organization keeping up a constant stream of chatter over a loudspeaker system. In addition to his general comments about what the weather was expected to be, the water temperature, and so on, about every ten to fifteen minutes he advised the athletes on how much time they had left until the first wave went off. The women in Angie's age group were one of the last waves to get started, since the younger groups typically went first, with each successive wave being the next-older age group.

Being so involved in her preparations resulted in Angie losing track of how fast time was slipping by. She was at the edge of the transition area when she heard something that caught her attention. Fortunately, the announcer said it again, "Fifteen minutes until race start. Those of you in the first few waves, if you aren't already at the water, you should be leaving the transition area and getting to the starting line. Everyone else should be out of the transition area in five minutes. *Fifteen minutes!*" There was a noticeable flurry of activity in the transition area in response to the latest announcement.

Angie spent the rest of the time before her wave went off shaking out muscles and rubbing in sunscreen. She thought she would have all the time needed, but once the first wave left, in keeping with past races, her perception of time seemed to change. Each minute seemed to last only a few seconds, and she had just gotten her wetsuit adjusted and swim cap on when the age group in front of hers went off. En masse, the cluster of women in her age group slowly migrated toward the imaginary start line that extended from a flag at the shoreline. As Angie was adjusting her goggles, the announcer began the ten-second countdown. As he and the crowd of spectators reached "one," there was an outbreak of motion, with the water churning, resembling a feeding frenzy of sharks.

Within a few hundred yards, the pack had divided enough that all the swimmers had their own space in which they could stretch out with every stroke. This enabled Angie to switch focus to the circumstances of the race, and before long she reached the turnaround buoy, which was a little more than half a mile downriver. During the rest of the way back toward the start area, several people passed her. With each few people, Angie felt a pronounced tendency to mentally beat herself up. Approaching the starting line and the beginning of the second lap, she was able to hear the race announcer calling out the names of those participants who were just then exiting the water and running up the mats toward the transition area. *That'll be me in … I don't know how long, but I'll get there sooner or later. All I have to do is not stop*, she thought encouragingly.

"But first you have to finish the second lap. C'mon Ang, gotta go, gotta go!" she said, spurring herself on to pick up the pace. Although she had felt her speed drop off only slightly on the way out, by the time she had rounded the turnaround buoy to head back toward the start area, fatigue began to kick in. *It is what it is*, she thought, resigning herself to the necessity of limping in instead of finishing strong. Her arms hung limply at her sides like cooked noodles. The vitality that had been mostly sapped by the swimming was restored when she heard the race announcer bellowing her name, which really stood out, since at least two-thirds of the field had already finished the swim and were on the cycling course.

Using newfound exhilaration, Angie performed her best sprint through the transition area to her station. Wheeling her bike toward the gap in the fence, she suddenly became aware of Sylvia standing by the exit, whooping and hopping up and down. "Whoo-hoo!" she screamed. "One third down, only two thirds to go! You got this! Go, go, go!" Angie paused just long enough to give Sylvia a vigorous high five, and then she pushed off as she hopped on her bike, cranking hard while clicking her shoes into the pedals.

The bike course wound its way through the small town, and it didn't take long to leave behind rows of quaint houses and move into the surrounding countryside. Following chalk lines and arrows on the roads, the riders made a number of turns before hitting a stretch that was relatively straight. After another half hour, the course made a right turn, directing them through what seemed to be the main street of another small town. Speeding past a coffee shop, post office, gas station, and other businesses typical of small towns, Angie couldn't help but be invigorated by throngs of people standing on the sidewalks, cheering loudly, some ringing cowbells. And then, as soon as it all began, it was over.

Almost without warning, the shops and businesses came to an abrupt halt, and a short couple of minutes later Angie was riding among vineyards. After two more turns, the course left the valley behind and entered the first climb, meandering through foothills, paralleling the valley below. After she had been curving through the hills for about forty minutes, the landscape opened to reveal the valley below. A few miles of riding brought her to the city in which the race would end. Eventually she rounded a corner and spied a gathering in the street up ahead. Upon growing closer, she was able to make out cones and banners, and once there it was easy to spot two large signs: one with an arrow pointing to the right into the parking lot of the community event center, and the other with an arrow pointing left below the words "SECOND LAP."

The second lap seemed to go by in a flash; once past the center of the city, the course headed in the general direction of where the swim had taken place. In no time at all, she was riding through the vineyards and before long was riding through the small town once more. There were noticeably fewer people standing on the sidewalks than earlier, but still quite a large number. They yelled out her number if they were quick enough to spot it as she zipped by; if not, they just called out broad praise. And of course there were the cowbells—the ever-present cowbells. As before, the hoopla didn't last long.

Reaching the base of the foothills brought a grimace to Angie's face, as she knew what lay ahead. Oddly enough, even though she had ridden about ninety-five miles by that time, the hills seemed easier the second time around. When she finally reached the valley floor, keeping in mind there was still a marathon to run, she restricted her output and reduced her exertion again when rounding the final corner and seeing the finish of the cycling course in the distance. She coasted the last forty to fifty yards and braked to a complete stop. Scanning the transition area containing rows and rows of bicycles, she eventually spotted her balloon, and she said a silent prayer of thanks for the strategy, being certain it would have taken her quite some time to find her station without the visual aid.

It was somewhat of a surprise to Angie to see and hear Sylvia near the start of the running course, whooping and yelling. Feeling very confident about being able to meet the overall race cutoff time, Angie hesitated long enough to give Sylvia a double high five and a hug, and she responded to her outbursts with several of her own. "OK, wait, I'm not done yet!" she reminded them both. "We'll celebrate when I cross the finish line!"

"No problemo! You got this!" she heard Sylvia scream from behind her as she took off. Once through the race site itself and out on the running course, reality set in and she had to consciously temper her emotions with facts. Even without all that swimming and biking, a marathon was a very far distance to run.

Angie fell into a rhythm during the first and second of four laps. She was able to keep at a steady pace, passing the mileage markers and aid stations at very regular intervals, resulting in a sense that the race was progressing very nicely. All that came to an end as she began the third lap. It was as if she were running through knee-deep water. She would grunt and exert energy, only to find herself barely able to make any headway. Panic began to set in, and she started worrying about what was going to happen on the fourth lap if she was feeling this way on the third lap—and not simply *on* the third lap; it was just at the *beginning* of the lap.

She fretted from the first mileage marker all the way to the turnaround point, and she then slowed even further, wondering whether she might be able to make better time by walking fast instead of moving at her current slow jog. Her progress was further impeded by the necessity of wiping away tears of frustration, fear, and defeat. She felt relief when the volunteers at the aid station thought she was wiping away sweat, which was masking the fact that most of the moisture on her face was from crying. She was almost to the point that the crying would soon be transformed into a complete breakdown. Even then—even when every fiber in her body told her she should concede the day and walk the rest of the third lap, or that she should skip the fourth lap, find some grass somewhere, lie down, and end this unnatural endeavor—something inside kept her going.

As Angie was nearing the end of the third lap and approaching the turnaround point to begin the fourth lap, her gut told her to put a stop to this insanity and head for the race pavilion. *It would be so easy*, an inner voice crooned. *Relax, get something to eat and drink, put your feet up. So what if you don't finish. You can always tell people you gave it your best shot.* But despite that thinking, her body rounded the board and headed out for the fourth lap. It was almost as if her body were running on autopilot, doing whatever it was going to do regardless of what her brain was thinking.

A newfound resolve replaced the despair, slowly at first but then gathering momentum until it completely expelled any and all negative thoughts. The first awakenings of her transformation began with the thought that she was indeed on the fourth and final lap of the run course. Next came a reminder that it wasn't just about this race; in fact, it wasn't even *primarily* about this race. This was about her chance to make it to Hawaii—something most triathletes never got. She felt emotionally as if a thunderstorm had suddenly ended, quickly supplanted by the bright sun behind it.

Although still not making much speed, at least for the rest of the fourth lap, she no longer felt as if her legs had weights tied to them. Passing the last mileage marker, she could hear the faint noise emanating from the finish line. The increasing volume of the music and occasional announcements of racers crossing the finish line while drawing ever nearer to the race site resulted in a boost in energy. Tears welled up in her eyes as she made her way through the neon barriers creating the lane toward the finish line. Even at this late hour, there were hundreds of people leaning over the barriers, cheering the athletes, most of whom raised their arms high while crossing the finish line. Angie was too exhausted to copy their example, but she managed to sprint under the arch into Sylvia's waiting arms. She began crying again, this time not out of frustration or defeat, but from knowing she had been tested and had triumphed. "Next stop, Hawaii!" she bellowed while raising her arms high in the air, not caring about the possible reactions.

Curt coasted into the driveway, absentmindedly easing the car into his side of the garage, somewhat oblivious to his surroundings. The only object that caught his attention was his bike, which was leaning against the opposite wall. It had served him well but was looking more and more beaten up, and he became increasingly antsy about the arrival of his new bike. True, it was only the last day or two of the expected time period for the delivery, but he just couldn't resist hoping it would get there sooner. After changing out of his work clothes, he went into the kitchen, where Katie was preparing dinner. He slid his arms around her waist from behind and gave her a firm hug, kissing her on the neck as he did. "You'd better be careful; my husband should be home any minute," she joked, her laugh transforming into a shriek as he bit her neck.

"Anything I can do to help?" he said, craning his neck around her shoulder to get a glimpse of what she was making.

"Not right now," she said after a short pause. "You can do the dishes after dinner," she added.

"Dishes?" he snorted. "That's what we have children for." She shoved him out of the kitchen without any verbal comment. Eventually Katie called for Ashley to come set the table, and during dinner the family engaged in their customary chitchat about the day's events. Ashley and Justin had told them about their plans that weekend, but Katie and Curt expressed uncertainly about theirs when asked by the kids. After several half-hearted statements, Curt said, "About the only firm plan I have is to go out riding Saturday morning. Sure would be nice if the new bike arrived by then."

Ashley suddenly looked up from her plate. "Oh, it's being sent here? So that might explain the big box on our porch." Curt stopped his fork midway to his still open mouth. It took him a few moments to fully comprehend her statement. "Big box? What box? There's a box on our porch? Why didn't someone tell me?" he exclaimed. He rushed toward the front door and ripped it wide open to discover that there was, in fact, a big box behind a pillar. "My bike!" he squawked, before even checking the shipping label, although he didn't really need to check. He jammed his fingers into the gap between the flaps on top and pried the two pieces of cardboard apart.

The bike had been disassembled into several pieces, so he ripped the cardboard down the side and kept pulling the box apart until the bike was completely exposed. Once the components were free from cardboard and plastic, he leaned the frame and wheels against the wall to get a better look. "Ooooh, sweetheart" he purred.

Katie, who had been standing behind him, harrumphed and said, with quite a bit of disdain in her voice, "You never call me sweetheart."

Curt paused in his admiring gaze, for the first time becoming aware anyone was standing behind him. It took a few moments to process her comment and formulate a reply. "I call you other things," he remarked, with as much of an ingratiating smile as he could muster.

"Hah!" Katie barked, turning on her heels and heading back into the kitchen.

Curt switched his focus back and forth between the bike and the direction of the kitchen. "Most of them are good," he called out. When no further response was forthcoming from Katie, he quickly returned his full attention to the bike. He was so engrossed about the bike he forgot to finish his dinner, instead scooping up all the parts and transporting them to the garage. He devoted an hour to tinkering with assembly and adjustments. He would ride for a few minutes at a time before returning to the garage to move one part an inch and then another part half an inch. Just as the evening sky was turning to dusk, he stood back while surveying his efforts. Suddenly recalling his earlier interchange with Katie, he began formulating plans on how to appease her before incurring any more of her wrath.

Now in possession of a new ride, Curt's next step in renewing the passion for his hobby was entering the lottery in hopes of securing a spot at Hawaii. His exhilaration was tempered as he explained to Katie how many spots were available and the expected number of entries. Although his emotions were muted by the long odds, that knowledge seemed to enhance Katie's mood. "This discussion is basically a moot point, because the chances of you getting chosen are slim to none, so I don't have to worry about it." As much as he hated to admit it, she was right. The only thing to do was sign up and wait until the names were picked.

Time slipped by like months being rapidly torn from a calendar. Being so wrapped up in the necessities of everyday life, Curt completely forgot that the day for lottery entrants to be notified of the results was fast approaching. In fact, when he received the email from the race organization, his first thought was *What is this about?* It wasn't until clicking on the link and waiting for the message to pop up on his screen that he remembered the significance of the month and date. He felt very juvenile for having done so, but in the moment, he couldn't control his actions. Before the message came up, he squeezed his eyes shut as tight as possible and, pressing his lips together, held his breath. Just when he thought his lungs were about to explode, he forcefully exhaled and took another deep breath before opening one eye. It took a few moments of scanning before he caught sight of the relevant part of the message: he had been picked!

"Sonuvabitch!" he shrieked, clamping his hand over his mouth. "Sonuvabitchsonuvabitchsonuvabitch!" he continued to whisper, the stream of words coming out as a muffled scream. He closed his eyes again, and a brief thought flashed through his mind that he had read it wrong and reading it again would reveal the error. But after taking a third deep breath and reading it again, there it was: he had been chosen! The implications of the message came crashing into his mind like a flash flood, and he began almost hyperventilating. In an effort to dispel the sudden surge in energy, he jumped up from his chair and began pacing in front of the computer.

It took several minutes for Curt achieve the goal, and upon plopping back down on the padded chair, he felt as though he had been on a short sprint and fought back tears of joy while repeatedly reading the message over and over. Once the initial rush of being chosen ran its course, he settled back in his padded office chair and returned to thinking about what the next few months would hold. Knowing for certain he had been picked increased his commitment to make sure he was putting as much into each workout as possible. It would be inexcusable to be given this rare opportunity only to see it slip through his hands by not taking his training seriously.

Katie was elated for her own reasons. "Ooooooo, I don't really have anything to wear to a tropical climate! Looks like I'll have to go shopping for some new clothes. And of course I'll have to get the accessories to go with them! I'm so excited!" Curt began to say something about Katie having plenty and not needing to spend money on new clothes, especially outfits she might only wear once or twice in her entire life, but he then remembered the amount of money they would be spending on the race itself. "Of course I really am thrilled for you," she quickly added. "I know you've worked very hard to get the chance to do this. Congratulations!"

The next order of business involved finding a race that included all the distances Curt would be doing in Hawaii. Some quick searches revealed several, but the closest one was in the next state over, and even then it would be quite a long drive. "Oh well," he mumbled. "Better a long drive than sitting around airports." He spent the next hour and a half registering for the race and booking a hotel. Once that was accomplished, Curt resumed his focus on training. Although he initially felt as though he had plenty of time, the months passed by in such a rush that he felt as if he were surfing on a tidal wave, unable to shake the persistent anxiety about not being ready.

The day they were due to head over to the race, he hardly slept, and he woke up before the alarm went off. The sense of impending doom persisted throughout the morning until he acknowledged he had done everything within his ability and could do no more.

With the advantage of current technology, in the form of GPS on his cell phone, the drive to the race site proved uneventful. Throughout checking into the room and then relaxing in the atrium in the center of the hotel, Curt spotted a few people he felt sure were there for the race. The telltale signs were everywhere: lean figures, well-defined calves and thighs, muscular arms. The same dynamic remained that night at dinner, as they rubbed shoulders with dozens of what appeared to be athletes. Curt did his best not to compare himself with others, but as the evening progressed, it became increasingly difficult. Katie picked up on his nonverbal behavior and steered him to the hotel atrium and a cocktail.

They had the luxury of sleeping in late, since Katie had had the foresight to suggest they arrive two days before the race. After a late leisurely breakfast, Curt attended the mandatory race meeting and then checked in and put the numbers on all his equipment. They spent the rest of the afternoon strolling through some quaint shops near the hotel. The restaurant they chose that night was filled with more athletic-appearing people, resulting in Katie engaging Curt in conversation about anything and everything but racing. Her efforts, and the necessity of having to go to bed early, left Curt little time for wallowing in his anxiousness.

In fact, it felt to Curt as if he had just laid his head on the pillow when he heard bells chiming from his phone alarm. "Can't be," he protested groggily, hoping he had set the wrong wake-up time. Once his eyes were able to focus, he saw that yes, it truly was 4:30 a.m.: game time! Now that it was here, he didn't know whether he should be excited or crawl back under the covers in trepidation. "Well, I didn't do all that work for nothing!" After getting his muscles moving with a warm shower, he dressed, slung his bag over one shoulder, and wheeled his bike out of the room, down the hallway, and toward the lobby. An advantage to staying in the race hotel was the opportunity to grab the shuttle to the race site itself.

Even though this was the biggest race so far in his career, with considerably much bigger stakes, Curt couldn't help but smile at thinking that the process was still the same: locate his transition station, get everything set up, go through some warm-up exercises, and then walk to the water and wait for his age group to go off. Once there, he stepped to one side, allowing others access to the path leading to the banners at water's edge, wanting a moment's respite before the chaos began. Big race or small, the methodical pattern to each triathlon soon took over. The race announcer would give each age group their warning, a veritable rainbow of swim-capped triathletes would wade into the water to await their countdown, and the process would be repeated until the last age group took off.

"The only difference," he reflected, somewhat regretfully, "is that I won't be kicking back, drinking a beer, and relaxing four hours from now. I'll just be getting started. What have I gotten myself into?" There was no way in hell he would back out now, but even at this moment in time, he was still at a loss as to why he was doing this.

Just then the horn for the start of the race blew, tearing him from his introspection. With the last vestiges of contemplation slowing slipping away, he promised himself he wouldn't simply treat this race as nothing more than a stepping stone, something to be endured for the sake of a greater goal rather than to be relished in and of itself. He vowed to take in every part of the race: all the sights and sounds, his fellow competitors, the volunteers, the crowds yelling their encouragement, and, yes, even the temperatures and discomfort that were sure to accompany engaging in such an endeavor.

Getting into the spirit of the event not only made it more entertaining but also made the passage of time even quicker. Standing near the water, waiting expectantly for the next group to assemble just beyond the banners, he suddenly noticed the entire group was wearing the same color swim cap as his. "Hey! It's my turn!" he unintentionally exclaimed aloud. In contrast to previous races, the time between the one-minute mark and the start of the ten-second countdown seemed to take forever. But just when he started thinking, *What's taking so long?* there came the familiar refrain: "Ten … nine … eight …"

As usual, he allowed the faster swimmers the opportunity to get into the water first, and he then waded in himself until waist deep. His last conscious thought before splashing in was "Here we go!"

He swam as fast as he could without taxing himself too much, wanting to keep up with his age group but also not wanting to use all his energy in the first event. His subconscious kicked in and reminded him that 2.4 miles is a very long way to swim.

The only thing breaking up the monotony of the constant stroke, stroke, stroke was the need to turn around the buoys at each end of the swim course.

He tried to keep his positive attitude going, but it seemed as if the buoys were moving soooo slowly each time he peeked across the water. As he finally made it around the buoy signifying the halfway mark and then passing the buoy for the three-quarters mark, the growing crowd noise served as another distraction to the endless repetition. This time, however, scanning the surface of the water to gauge his progress, he spied a few swimmers in the distance sloshing out of the water and running up the embankment. Twenty minutes later, when he made a quick inspection across the water to ensure he was swimming on course, Curt was quite surprised to discover the finish area just ahead. *Damn!* he cried out inside his head. *One more burst of speed and I'm done with this part!*

Curt was always thankful when exiting the water and leaving the swimming behind, but this time, given the extreme distance, he was especially grateful. "Enough of that noise," he mumbled to himself, ripping the goggles off his face and trudging up the slope toward his transition station, consoling himself with the knowledge that for him, the hardest part was over. "Now for some real fun," he said with a grin, content to walk part of the way up, using it as an opportunity to catch his breath. He threw on his cycling gear in an efficient, but unhurried, manner. "A few seconds on a race this long aren't going to matter," he reassured himself.

The first mile of the cycling course wound through the recreation area centered on the lake. Many of the spectators had already made the trek from the lake up to the park, hollering, blowing horns, and ringing cowbells whenever a competitor raced by. Curt pictured the cycling course map in his head, recalling that the route was essentially a large oval around the lake and consisted of two fifty-six-mile laps. Along with the street map, he mentally called up the diagram of the elevations they would encounter. Somewhere on the other side of the lake was a relatively steep climb, but the rest of the course included only gradual inclines.

The length of the course provided a sort of psychological beat-down. If it had been shorter, they could have simply hammered all the way, been done quick, and moved on to the run. The only factor mitigating the suffering was eventually making it to the end of the first lap. He chose to coast to a stop and down a banana and bagel while straddling his bike, finishing that off by leisurely gulping from a bottle of sports drink. The second time around, familiarity assisted his sense of tedium. He was able to use things he had seen before as checkpoints. Being on the lookout for race markers and landmarks, such as particular houses or billboards, rather than simply focusing on grinding it out, divided the race into shorter segments that were easier handle.

Once back in the transition area and switching out of his cycling gear and into his running shoes and hat, he made his way to the "RUN OUT" sign at the opposite end of the transition area. As he was just about to run through the opening in the plastic fence, he heard, "Whoo-hoo! Way to go Curt! Go! Go! Go!" At first, given his current physical and mental condition, he thought there must have been someone else in the race named Curt and kept going without looking around. Katie called his name again, using his first *and* last name just to be sure. Hearing both his names stopped Curt dead in his tracks. Not knowing which way the sound had come from, he did a complete 360-degree turn. Spying Katie, his first reaction was "Katie! What are you doing here?"

She laughed and shook her head. "Watching you, silly. How have things gone so far? How do you feel?" He moved aside quickly to avoid being in the way of another runner leaving the transition area, taking a few moments to give her some highlights of both the swim and bike. He was just starting to make another comment about the bike when Katie broke in. "Huh, Curt, can I point something out?" she paused when he froze in midsentence. "You're not actually *done* with the race yet. I'm flattered you want to sit here and talk, but you still need to run, don't you?"

Finally reality set in. "Oh, huh, yeah, you're right. I ... huh ... I'll be right back." He came in close, as if attempting to kiss her, but she backed away, her face a picture of disgust. "Eeeeeewwww! You're all sweaty and stinky! Go finish the race." He laughed but spun and scampered in the direction the other runners were going.

Curt kept to a slow run for the first few miles, needing his legs to get acclimated to a new activity after being on the bike for seven hours. This time, instead of thinking about having to endure an entire marathon, he reversed his reasoning. After leaving the transition area, rather than ruminating about having to run twenty-six miles, he split the run into twenty-six fragments. Fortunately, the race organizers had made this task more uncomplicated by placing banners at every mile. When Curt reached the mile-one banner, it became a matter of running until reaching the mile-two marker, and so on. Arriving at the mile-six marker, he celebrated, knowing the race was about one quarter over. He performed the same mental trick at mile thirteen ("Outstanding! Halfway there. It's all downhill from here!"), and at mile twenty (Three quarters! Almost there!").

Curt was almost giddy when running past the mile twenty-five banner. "I've done it!" he pushed out loud while exhaling. There was a faint sound of music, as well as some other sounds that weren't yet discernable. Running past the mile-twenty-six banner, he could see the arch at the finish line, the music was louder, and he could now decipher the other sounds as cheering and an announcer calling out names as participants ran under the arch. During the last hundred yards, it became difficult for Curt to catch a breath, owing to how hard he was laughing and pumping his arms in the air. He was so jazzed that he kept up the pace even after crossing the finish line, until several volunteers jumped in front of him with their hands held up, yelling "You're done! You're done! Stop! Stop!" Another volunteer handed him a cold bottle of water, and Curt sipped it while scanning the crowd for Katie.

Not seeing her right away, he tottered around the finishing chute, on a bearing toward the food tent. "Honey! Honey!" he heard someone calling out. A few seconds later, he finally got a glimpse of her waving her arms, and he politely pushed his way through the throng. Still keeping her distance, she nonetheless beamed and squealed, "You did it! I'm so proud of you!"

Picking up her hand, he kissed it instead of her mouth or cheek. "And I couldn't have done it without your support. I want you to know how much it means to me that you were behind me this whole way. Now ... on to Hawaii!"

Katie smiled mischievously. "I know. Looks like I have some shopping to do."

Logistics

Lisa lounged on the couch chitchatting aimlessly while Sarah finished getting dressed, making sure her voice was loud enough to carry into the bedroom. According to Lisa's stated purpose, they were going shopping to find Sarah some "appropriate island attire." The true purpose, which remained unspoken, was to find Lisa some skimpy outfits to attract a hot guy while Sarah was taking care of race business and out on the course come race day. Sarah was only half listening; the other part of her consciousness was already a few weeks ahead, preparing for the race. Coming out of the bedroom, she shook her head as she grabbed her purse off the coffee table. "You have a one-track mind," she admonished her friend.

Lisa took two steps before coming to a sudden halt. "Well, so do you," she countered. "The only difference is the track we're on."

Before Sarah could respond, her phone vibrated and played the melody she had chosen for her mother. She froze in midstep, torn between answering the call and getting it over with, and putting it off. She did not want another conflict with her mother to ruin her outing. What with training for Hawaii and making final preparations, she hadn't had a day off in what seemed like months. She glanced at Lisa, instantly recognizing in her facial expression her understanding of Sarah's inner turmoil. A few moments of silence passed before Lisa said, "Your call," with a sad smile.

Sarah tilted her head back, gazing at the ceiling, regretting they hadn't left the apartment earlier with her forgetting the phone. Her eyes were slightly watery as she returned Lisa's rueful smile. "Might as well get it over with." Retrieving the phone from her purse, she cleared her throat. "Hi,

Mom," she exclaimed in her best bright, sunny voice, in contradiction to her emotions.

"Hi, sweetheart," came the response. "Listen; I know you're probably busy, but I couldn't remember when you were leaving for Hawaii. Is it this week or next?"

Sarah visualized a calendar. "It's just a little over two weeks, like two weeks and two days—something like that." Her mother began asking her questions about how many days before the race she was going over there, whether she was feeling ready, what the weather was likely to be on race day, and many other things that suggested she had a newfound interest in Sarah's chosen occupation.

As the conversation continued, Lisa began looking confused. Even though she could hear only one side of the dialogue, it was obvious from Sarah's answers that her mother was asking her questions only an involved parent would have, and her mother had proven repeatedly she was anything but that. Over time, Sarah's face transformed into a look of suspicion, then worry, and then back confusion again. Several times she mouthed "What?" as Sarah answered her mother's queries. Just as she began thinking it couldn't get any weirder, her mother quickly blurted out, "Well, I just wanted you to know that even though I haven't always approved of your profession, I am proud of you for what you have accomplished so far. I'll call again before you leave for Hawaii, but I just wanted to tell you that now. Bye bye."

Sarah couldn't muster a reply before her mother hung up. She stared straight ahead with eyes glazed over and mouth wide open, her fingers barely grasping the phone. Lisa's expression intensified, and she sat bolt upright. "What? What is it? What happened? *What did she say?*"

Finally Sarah whispered, "She said she was proud of me."

Both girls sat dumbfounded, not really believing the message. Lisa broke the quietness. "Bullshit!" she burst out. Quickly realizing what had been said and how, she clamped a hand over her mouth. After regaining her composure, she attempted to make sense of what had just transpired. "Are you sure you heard right? Don't take this wrong, but could it be that you're hearing something you want to hear? She actually said, 'I'm proud of you?' Just like that?"

Sarah could no longer hold back the tears, which came streaming down her cheeks. "Yes, I'm sure. Yes, I'm positive I didn't just hear what I wanted to hear. I'm not making it up! She said she was proud of me." Once more the pair sat in disbelief. After several minutes spent in reflection of the significance of the statement, Lisa slid across the couch to embrace her friend. "She said she was proud of me. After all this time and all the grief and negativity ... she said she was proud of me" Sarah murmured. Lisa racked her brain to think of something to say. When nothing appropriate came up, she contented herself with the physical act of support.

Eventually they agreed that they were in a state of denial and that it would take some time to accept it for what it was—a heartfelt declaration of support. Upon arriving at their conclusion, Lisa pronounced, "Hey, we've got clothes to try on! Let's get going!"

Sarah shook her head again at Lisa's insistence on their physical appearance but chose not to make a comment. What she did do was stand up, hold out her arm in a gesture for Lisa to join her, and proclaim, "Yes we do. Let's do this!"

Curt shook his head while scanning the contents of the large suitcase lying on the bed. "Good grief," he muttered. "Only one week, and in a tropical location where it's gonna be hot the entire time—how much clothing does one woman need?" In his estimation, Katie had left him about one quarter of the space.

"What's that?" she asked, entering the bedroom.

Curt debated the wisdom of getting into an argument with a woman about how much room she needed before deciding it was preferable to keep the peace. "Nothing," he conceded, and he then waited until she walked into the bathroom to push her items toward one side of the suitcase, which now left him with approximately one third of the space.

For the umpteenth time, Katie asked, "What time are we supposed to leave tomorrow morning?" Curt took the opportunity of facing away from her to smile and shake his head. "Rise and shine at 4:30 a.m. Justin should be here at four forty-five to take us to the airport." He ignored Katie's groan, feeling the same; neither of them were morning people. But coming from a medium-size airport and traveling to a large airport to pick up a connecting flight to Hawaii left them with very few viable options.

The first flight itself was completely uneventful, from takeoff to landing. After getting off the crowded plane and exiting through the narrow gangway, entering LAX felt like a release from prison. "Let's find our gate first," Curt suggested upon arrival at their terminal. "This seems to be a pretty big place. Then we can get something to eat and still have plenty of time before our flight."

Katie readjusted her bag. "Sounds good to me. We haven't had anything yet except for a bag of peanuts and a Coke."

Even after taking their time eating, the departure time for the second flight was still about two hours away, but the seats around the gate were rapidly filling with fellow passengers. He chuckled to himself at the common theme of those certain to be heading to a similar destination as theirs. The colors varied, but there was no mistaking the floral prints dominating the clothing.

It took the doorbell chiming for Angie to realize she had been watching the coffee pot brewing. She vigorously shook her head on the way to the front door, attempting to jolt herself into a more alert state. Even with the effort, all she could manage was to turn the dead bolt and doorknob. The door swung open, followed by Sylvia's chirpy, sunny voice. "Whoo whoo! Who's ready for Hawaii!" At that time of morning, compounded by a mostly sleepless night, her voice grated on Angie's nerves like fingernails on a blackboard. Why did she have to be like that even when it was this early? Why couldn't she be like normal people and be groggy at 4:00 a.m.?

They talked about things to do on the island while waiting for Sandra to drive them to the airport. Within a few short minutes, Sandra arrived, walking into the house without so much as a "knock knock." As she rounded the corner into the kitchen, Angie saw why; Sandra appeared to be in a similar state as she herself had been earlier. She dropped onto a chair, folded her arms on the table, and allowed her head to bang against her arms. "Who gets up at 4:00 a.m.?" she asked, more to herself than anyone else. Although the drive didn't take long, the trio had awoken and were in brisk conversation by the time they arrived at the drop-off curb in front of the airport.

While retrieving their suitcases from the trunk, Sandra embraced Angie in a tight hug. "I am *so* proud of you and what you've accomplished so far, and I know you're going to go over there and have a good time. Oh, and finish the race, of course. No doubts about that!"

Angie gave her one last hug. "Thanks, Sandra. And I have always appreciated all the support and encouragement you've given me. I'll call when we're there!" Turning to Sylvia, she added, "Thanks again for all your support, and for coming with me. Getting over there would probably be lonely without some company."

Sylvia reached over to squeeze her hand. "Hey, that's what besties are for, right?"

Once the procedures of getting into the plane and at cruising altitude were completed, the friends continued their pursuit of events and other leisure interests for after the race. Upon finalizing their list, they discovered the flight was already almost over. Since neither woman had traveled much, upon exiting the plane they found LAX overwhelming. With each step along the way to the next terminal, they marveled at how large of a structure it was and yet how efficiently travelers seemed to be getting from one place to the next. "Speaking of travelers," Sylvia remarked, "Check this guy's clothes. I'm guessing Mr. Traveler is going to the same place we are, and he's not trying to hide it."

Angie looked in the direction she had gestured, immediately spotting a rather portly man in a floral print shirt—with matching shorts, no less. "Ow! It hurts my eyes to look at him," she joked. "I don't think I'm ready for this yet. Let's go get something to eat."

Sylvia gave a firm nod of her head. "Lead on," she said.

Hannah poking him in the side brought Matt out of his stupor. Trying to focus his eyes, all he could make out was fuzzy shapes. He became aware of music playing and wondered why someone was playing music while they were trying to sleep. Didn't whoever it was know they had to get up early the next morning? He felt another poke in the side. *All right, that's it*, he thought. *They'd better leave me alone; I gotta get up early.* Turning his head, he was barely able to make out the shape of Hannah's head, but no details, since it was only dawn and the sun wasn't yet peeking over the horizon.

"C'mon, wake up, handsome," she needled. "We've got a plane to catch, and they're not gonna hold it up for us." She gave him a quick peck on the cheek before heading to the bathroom.

He turned his head this way and that while rapidly blinking his eyes. "Wait; did she call me handsome?" he pondered.

Sleep had come late, and he had woken up repeatedly throughout the night, resulting in his falling asleep on the way to the airport while Hannah drove. He continued yawning throughout the process of checking in and getting through the security area, and he then fell asleep again while waiting for the plane and remained groggy until halfway through the flight. "Welcome back to the land of the living," Hannah playfully teased. Matt yawned once more, shaking his head to clear out the last vestiges of tiredness. "Man, that was not fun," he remarked. "Had to be from not getting enough sleep. I feel OK now. Still not a hundred percent, but I'll live." They chatted while getting something to drink and a snack from the flight attendant, and they then settled in for the remainder of the flight.

Matt had flown into large airports for conferences and his qualifying race, and Hannah had traveled some for business, so they weren't overly impressed with LAX. After deboarding and entering the terminal, they stood for a while, watching what seemed like thousands of people rushing right and left and surveying the airport. "Meh, seen one big airport, seen 'em all," he said with a smirk.

"Not very attractive, is it?" Hannah agreed. "Of course, it is pretty old, so …" They located a map of the entire airport nearby and found the terminal of their next flight.

The seating area around the gate had filled in considerably by the time they arrived. It took a few minutes to locate two seats together, and even then, those were tightly sandwiched between other passengers. "Looks like it's going to be a very full flight," Matt noted.

Hannah scanned the mass. "Hmm-mmm." She nodded in agreement. It didn't take long to notice something extremely similar about how many of their fellow travelers were dressed.

"Yep, not only is it going to be a full flight, but we are obviously going to a tropical location, and most of them couldn't wait to get there; they just had to dress the part early," he snorted.

"Hmmm?" Hannah mumbled, not having heard a word he had said.

He continued to himself since she had returned to her magazine. "Not gonna see me lookin' like a complete dweeb! Uh-uh! Gonna be bad enough I gotta be stuck on a plane with all of 'em for five hours. By the time we land, I'll have flowers burned into my retinas."

The flight was long and boring, at least from the standpoint of the four triathletes. Owing to the length of time sitting in one spot without movement, they stretched creaky limbs while walking through the tunnel leading into the airport. On entering the terminal, they were all struck by the fact that it was completely open, in stark contrast to all the other airports they'd been through, which were entirely enclosed with steel, concrete, and glass. "Now this is truly a tropical paradise," Sylvia verbalized. Several others shuffling toward the baggage claim area murmured their assent. Given they were on an island that catered to tourism, they had no problems finding transportation. As they pulled into the parking lot of the hotel, they saw myriad signs and posters that left no doubt this was race central.

Lisa had been to just enough races with Sarah to know what a typical race packet pickup event looked like, so when they entered the hotel conference room and saw all the huge signs and banners, along with the hundreds of photos of past races, her mouth dropped wide open. "OMG!" she exclaimed loudly, having forgotten they were in an enclosed area. The sound carried, causing many of those standing around to jerk their heads in their direction. "Sorry, Sarah, guess I got carried away." She then raised her head back up and continued in a loud whisper. "But would you look at all this ... It looks like some big event—like a political fundraiser or a New Year's Eve bash or ... something. Having never been here before, I wasn't ready for the size of it. It still has all the stuff other races have. Look; there are the check-in tables, there are booths for all kinds of things, banners all around ... it's just that this is all something ... *more!*" As she finished speaking, she spread her arms out wide before letting them flop against her sides.

Sarah laughed, sliding her arm through Lisa's. "Yes, it is more, isn't it? C'mon; let's go get checked in."

As they strolled toward the tables, Sarah reminisced about all the times she had arrived at the race sites, and she had to admit that, even from the very first race, she had never been overly impressed with banners, expos, or any of the other peripheral occurrences at the races. The only thing she got a charge from was informing the volunteers of her name and that she was a pro. The way she felt at her most recent race matched the intensity of the feeling from when she had made that declaration for the first time; she didn't think that part of checking in for a race would ever get old. Sure enough, when she approached the table to get her race packet and bags, she thought her face would crack open, given how wide she was smiling.

The two headed back to the room to drop off the race bags before walking the circuit of shops, restaurants, and other sights in the area around the hotel. "I think I'm going to go for a slow run and then stretch out so I can keep limber for the race," Sarah informed Lisa as they arrived back at the hotel.

"Sounds good," came the reply. "Think I'll hit the beach. Gotta take advantage of the sun to work on my tan."

Sarah shook her head. "Your tan, huh? You have a one-track mind," she said with a giggle. Lisa opened her mouth for the beginning of what was sure to be a snide response, but she snapped it shut without a word. After several moments, she muttered, "Whatever," resulting in a bigger laugh.

Curt froze upon entering the large conference room. Although he had read as much as possible about what the race would be like, from arriving on the island to competing in the race, he wasn't prepared for the reality of it all. There was a constant buzz everywhere he went, and all manner of visual representations of what was going to transpire in a few days. True, his qualifying race had been the same distance, but there wasn't the same vibe at that city. The only place he could sense anything was at the race site; the locals mostly acted like they either didn't know or didn't care about a race going on. This was something entirely different. He didn't think anyone, even those on the island for a vacation, could have missed what was happening. The athlete check-in area definitely added to that impression.

Athlete pickup at all his past races had consisted of a few tables pushed together under a large tent if they were outside. Maybe there were a few signs or banners with the name of the race or the names of race sponsors, but that was about it. What was before him now was almost overwhelming; it was all just so much! In fact, there were so many banners and blown-up pictures and other materials that seemingly grabbed his head and demanded his attention that he had to scan the room just to locate the check-in tables, finding it difficult to tear his focus away from the visual landscape. The initial process was as simple as it had been with other races, but even here, too, there was a procedure that made this race something more than other races. He felt a little foolish after asking the volunteer for the third time to repeat what she had just said.

She giggled, and then reiterated, "No I'm not making this up. Yes, I'm being completely serious; you don't have to set up your own bike. In fact, you *can't* set up your own bike. You put your number on your bike and bring it to the transition on Friday, and a volunteer will take it to your spot. If you want to go with the volunteer to see where your spot is, you can. But we do everything for you. Oh, and you won't have your bike and running gear at your station either; those will be in the bags. You'll notice one is marked for your bike stuff and one is marked for your running gear. Once you've put your things in each bag, you'll hand those off to a volunteer too. See, we've thought of everything!" Curt was stunned to silence, managing a mumbled "Thank you" as he backed away from the table.

A sudden image burst onto his consciousness; it was from the movie *The Jerk*, starring Steve Martin, in which the character discovers his name in the phone book and runs around yelling, "I'm somebody! I'm somebody!" That's what he felt like doing at that moment. In the other races he was simply one of many; here he was being treated as if he were someone special. The emotions of the moment got the better of him, and he walked at a very fast pace to the room. Katie was sitting in a padded chair on their patio when he arrived. "Katie! Katie!" he frantically called. "Look at this!" he exclaimed, dumping the contents of the race bag on the bed. "You're not gonna believe this!" he continued. He separated the pile into race numbers, his bike bag, and his running bag. Picking up the two clear plastic bags, he waved them in front of her face. "One bag is for my bike gear, and the other one is for my running stuff. Check this out! I put my race stuff in these bags, and volunteers take care of it for me! And guess what?" he asked. Without waiting for a reply, he jumped in. "On Friday I take my bike to the transition area and give it to a volunteer, and they put it on the rack for me! I don't have to do anything at this race!"

Katie did her best to show some enthusiasm. "That's great, dear; that should make it easier for you."

If he picked up on her feigned interest, he didn't comment on it. "I'm telling you, they really know how to make a guy feel like a celebrity!" She gave him a quick peck on the cheek before returning to the patio and her magazine, while Curt began organizing his race paraphernalia.

Throughout the course of their friendship, there were only a handful of times Angie could recall Sylvia being speechless—or, more accurately, relatively speechless. Now that she was thinking about it, she had never heard Sylvia truly stop talking. There were only momentary lulls in a constant stream of comments. This was one of the few times Sylvia paused for more than a few seconds. "Whoa," she uttered as they entered the conference room for Angie's check-in. She waited for the verbal barrage that was sure to follow given what they were seeing. When there was nothing but silence from her side, she turned to make certain Sylvia hadn't had some type of accident and was treated to the sight of Sylvia with mouth wide open, heading rotating back and forth, taking in the sights.

When she was finally able to speak, for some reason she whispered, which was not like her at all. "Ang, would you look at this! Have you ever seen anything like … like … this?"

Angie laughed while surveying the room herself. "Yes, it is quite something, isn't it?" she agreed. "No wonder everyone tries to get here at least once in their lives." She paused before continuing. "And we haven't even hit race day yet. Plus, imagine what the athlete banquet is going to be like if this is just the check-in."

Sylvia was still having trouble getting her mouth going until she saw the tables for the athletes. "Ooh, look; there's where you check in! C'mon, c'mon, c'mon," she insisted, pulling Angie by the arm. One would have thought Sylvia was the athlete and Angie was the tagalong.

Angie perked up when the volunteer began explaining to her how many bags were in her packet and what each one was for, and when she received the instructions to take her bike to the transition area on Friday instead of wheeling it over with her on race morning. As they walked away,

Sylvia was almost squealing in excitement. "Look at you! Oh, baby, they're treating you like royalty. Hey, you are, ya know! You are triathlete royalty! Does this mean I'll have to bow in your presence?"

Angie gave her a quick playful hit on the shoulder. "Syl, knock it off; you're gonna embarrass me." Sylvia let up on the teasing but kept on with the comments about the race.

"Unbelievable! They really know how to do this right. Too bad other races don't do things like this one. Speaking of which, you know it's gonna be hard to go back to doing everything for yourself after this experience. Kinda like flying first class and then having to go back to flying coach. Ugh!"

Angie wanted to add in her own thoughts but was having a hard time putting what was happening to her internally into words. Another thing making it difficult was that she was beaming from ear to ear and wasn't sure whether her mouth could even work right now. Finally she contented herself with a hearty "Yep!" at Sylvia's constant stream of exclamations about how the athletes were treated.

Hannah chose to lounge by the hotel pool rather than accompany Matt to check in and pick up his race materials, which was OK with him. In fact, he expected it. Over the years, he had learned that her support of his hobby went only so far. The last couple years, she had stopped going with him to his races, except for his qualifying race. He asked if she wanted to go only out of politeness and not wanting her to say something afterward. She wasn't planning on going—he knew it, and she knew he knew it—but it was a little game they played, just as so many other couples do. "Women," he said with a grimace while strolling toward the conference room. He could have found it even with his eyes closed. The hotel was mostly quiet, except for a combination of music and very loud talking emanating from the direction in which he was headed. The closer he got to a set of very large wide open doors, the louder the clamor became.

As he stepped through the doorway and into the cavernous conference room itself, the racket was almost overwhelming, both visually and auditorily. There were posters and humungous pictures everywhere, plus banners on poles. There was a set of speakers on poles set against one wall, playing music he guessed was supposed to be uplifting, and a small mob of people were talking to each other in loud voices so they could be heard over the rhythmic tunes. He was forced to stand in place for a while so his senses could adapt to the dramatic change in stimulation. A little voice deep inside told him this was all part of the race experience; he felt that instead of following his initial urge to get his stuff and get out as quickly as possible, he should stand back and take it all in.

And take it in he did, ambling around the perimeter of the room, studying each picture, and reading the captions underneath. As with many other first-timers, he had to have the volunteer explain the contents of the bag twice. In all his past races, there had been one race number for his bike, one for the front of his body, and occasionally one for his helmet, all together in one bag. He repeated the instructions out loud to make sure he was understanding them correctly. What really blew his mind was having volunteers do almost everything for him. He had expected that kind of treatment for the pros, but to receive the same courtesy as a simple age-grouper—that was something else entirely. Stepping away from the tables, he verbalized the instructions several more times, figuring that if he misunderstood something, there would be an opportunity to go back and ask while still in the room.

Curt half stumbled through the lobby on the way to the café to get a pair of coffees for him and Katie, being just at the point of entering the café when a commotion outside caught his attention. He changed course to stand on the fringe of the lobby, attempting to make some sense of the cheering crowd standing on the sidewalk. "Can't be the race; it's only Thursday," he reasoned, fighting his confusion. A few moments more didn't do much to alleviate his bewilderment, so he gravitated to the check-in counter. "Hey, do you know what's goin' on?"

The clerk didn't have a response until Curt motioned with his head toward the street. "Oh, that," he said with immediate comprehension. "That's the Underpants Run," he said with an air suggesting Curt should already know what the Underpants Run was.

"Underpants Run? You mean that's really a thing? I heard about it but thought it was all a big joke. You know, something to tease the tourists with." He stared off, considering the logistics of the issue. "Well, I guess the cops couldn't very well arrest several hundred people, could they? That's the funny thing about it. If one person were out there walking around in their underwear, they'd get busted for indecent exposure, but a few hundred …? Too much," he chuckled.

Katie was equally amused when he related what had occurred just outside the hotel. "Oh bummer, you missed it. Wait! Is it still going on? You might be able to still get in on the action. It'd make a great picture for everyone back home," she goaded.

"Very funny," he dryly replied. After a brief pause, he corrected himself. "Hang on a minute. If this is something for the racers in general, then there must be lots of young girls in their underwear. Hmm, maybe I will join them," he finished with a leer.

This time it was Katie who put the kibosh on his participation.

At the prerace banquet later that night, Curt and Katie lingered around the makeshift event area, inching their way through the buffet line, and chose a table at random. Curt had guessed there would be a plethora of floral clothing and discovered his hypothesis about attire was spot on. Most people were wearing extremely bright prints of various kinds of flowers and palm trees. By contrast, those who weren't almost looked out of place, as if they hadn't gotten the memo. Regardless of garb, almost everyone was quick to strike up conversations with those around them, feeling an instant sense of kinship. Animated conversations were eventually interrupted by the emcee introducing some hula dancers and guys twirling batons of fire.

After the entertainment, several people stepped up to the dais and shared either words of encouragement or stories of past experiences while competing in the race. After listening to the speakers, one athlete affirmed, "If I ever had doubts about doing this race, they're mostly gone now. I can hardly wait for Saturday."

Curt agreed wholeheartedly. "I'm with ya; if it weren't dark, I'd say let's get started now!" The next morning, before they had gotten out of bed, Katie reminded him he would be getting up very early the next day and should think about sleeping in. He agreed with her logic, but his brain wouldn't cooperate. He kept hearing the messages from the banquet, and the more he thought about them, the more his body got amped up. He finally threw off the covers with a disgusted snort, conceding defeat. After assembling his race bags, he walked his bike over to the race site and delivered the requisite items to awaiting volunteers, and he then accompanied the volunteer with the bike to his station.

After Curt accomplished the last prerace details, he and Katie spent the remainder of the day walking around and lounging by the pool. Even though he had stated the previous night he was ready for the race to start right then, as the minutes and hours ticked away, a growing sense of unpreparedness began to settle in. In contrast to earlier sentiments, he began wishing time wouldn't pass so quickly, but to no avail. He almost jumped when Katie announced the time and suggested they get an early dinner so he could get to sleep at a reasonable time. Upon returning to their room, and still being unable to settle down for the night, he went out to the patio. His mind was racing so fast he couldn't make coherent sense out of anything, simply staring straight ahead.

Katie coming out and sitting on his lap served to break his disjointedness and switch awareness to his surroundings. When she saw his facial expression, she quipped, "Penny for your thoughts?" There was a long pause before he responded.

"Good question; there are so many things going through my mind right now, from all the way back to when I first starting racing to now." Another long pause ensued. "You know, when I was a kid, I played Little League baseball a couple of years ... we sucked. Then, in junior high and high school, I kept playing baseball and football. We sucked."

Katie broke in to this stream of thought. "Oh, looks like there's a pattern here." Curt glared at her. "Sorry," she squeaked. "Continue."

He remained silent for a while before doing so. "I don't think I've ever been a part of a winning team ... ever. I've never won or been close to winning *anything*. But tomorrow I'm going to stand toe-to-toe with a couple thousand of the best athletes on the planet, and I don't have to beat them. All I have to do is finish, and I'll be a winner." He finished speaking with a satisfied look on his face.

Katie harrumpfed. "You'll be a loser." Curt's facial expression morphed into one of hurt and confusion. "Listen," she continued with an emphatic tone of voice. "Just the fact that you've done the races you have makes you a winner. The fact you do something that only about 1 percent of the population does makes you a winner. Working your butt off to get here makes you a winner. Even if for some reason you don't finish tomorrow, *you are still a winner!* But you're too thickheaded to get that!" She punctuated her words by stabbing his head with her finger.

He rubbed the spot she'd jabbed, attempting to find a suitable answer to her arguments. But when none were forthcoming, all he had was "Oh."

"Now, I don't want to hear any more talk about what finishing or not means. All you're going to focus on is going out there tomorrow and doing your best. Got it?" she demanded, with a challenging glare.

"Yes ma'am," he replied meekly, still massaging his head.

"Good! Now, is there anything I can do to help with that?"

Curt dropped his hand. "I don't know. I need to get some sleep?"

Katie stood up. "OK, that I can help with."

The next thing he was aware of was his vision being blocked by something covering his face. He pulled it off to discover it was Katie's bikini top. It took a few seconds for him to figure out what the fact her top was off meant. Once he deduced the intent behind her actions, it took only a few seconds more for him to get into the room, shut the sliding glass door, and pull the curtains shut.

Sarah was able to stay in the moment while they ate, and for the hula dancers and fire twirlers. But when the emcee began speaking about what everyone had been through to get there, she zoned out. Hearing his descriptions of common stories gave her flashbacks to her own experiences, and she was so caught up in her memories she wasn't seeing or hearing anything around her. She jumped all the way back to competing in that first race with Lisa, continuing with it as a hobby while she completed her college degree, and her first few races as a pro. Recollections of comments made by her mother when she shared the news about her decision intruded into her consciousness; she felt her body steel itself in response. Taking deep breaths and actively working on relaxing her muscles broke her train of thought, and her awareness came back to the banquet.

The next morning was largely a repeat of the previous morning, with the main exception being Sarah taking her bike and race gear to the transition area. Ordinarily she would have set up her area and left, but as with everything else, this race was anything but ordinary. After shadowing the volunteer to her station, she lingered to arrange a few items and scan the rows upon rows of bike racks. After returning to her room, the first half of the afternoon consisted of a very light workout and lots of stretching. The two friends then spent the remainder of the time lounging by the pool.

The weather outside as they ambled back to the hotel from dinner was the best it had been on their brief stay thus far, leading Sarah to grumble about having to go to bed instead of enjoying it. Lisa attempted to cajole her into staying up, at least for another hour or so. "It's very tempting," she said after giving it some consideration. "But I came here for one reason and one reason only. By tomorrow at this time … then I'll relax and cut loose."

Lisa stopped them in their tracks to give Sarah a tight bear hug. "I am *so* proud of you. It's still hard to believe you've gotten so far in what seems like so little time. There is not a doubt in my mind you are going to blow that course up tomorrow. Who knows—with a little luck, you may be reading your name in the papers on Sunday."

Sarah chuckled after being released from the tight embrace. "Thanks. Hope you don't mind if I stay more realistic."

Lisa laughed while nodding her head in assent, but during the walk and getting dressed for bed, she kept up a constant stream of encouraging statements.

"I feel like a complete dweeb," Matt lamented.

Hannah stuck her arm through his. "Oh, relax. If you look around, you'll notice almost every other couple is wearing matching outfits. Promise I'll only get one picture, just as a memento, and I won't show it to anyone without your express permission."

Once they had their beverages of choice, they randomly chose two seats facing the stage. Three other couples were already sitting, making idle chitchat. Matt guessed they were couples, since there were two pairs of identical tropical shirts and dresses. While they listened for the first few minutes, two men and one woman were sharing stories about how they got to Hawaii, so it was only natural for Matt to impart his.

The four had barely gotten into discussing the concept of "what's next" when the emcee began welcoming everyone to the event and giving directions about the dinner and the evening's festivities. Matt found himself thankful for the interruption, having never really given much thought to what came after this race. He pondered what athletes do after getting to a Super Bowl or World Series. *Do they shoot for another one the following year? For them it makes sense; playing football or baseball is their chosen profession.* He supposed for the pros that would be competing Saturday, the process was the same. But for him and all the other age-groupers, this was a hobby. Sure, it was a hobby that consumed a great deal of their time, but it was still a hobby—not an occupation. Once one reached the pinnacle of that hobby, then what? He mulled over the question throughout the banquet.

The words of the emcee barely registered on his awareness at the start of the program; he was still grappling with the issue of his future in triathlon. There was little problem with maintaining focus while several people got up to talk about past races and to encourage the participants regarding their own efforts at this year's race. A couple of videos also served to get his internal engine revved up. A quick glance around the table told him the other athletes were getting antsy as well.

When he got up Friday morning, the emotional charge from the banquet was barely noticeable. In its place was the customary prerace anxiety. *Par for the course*, he thought. After breakfast, he completed the day's only scheduled activity—taking his bike to the transition area. It was still difficult to wrap his head around the idea that almost every prerace function was being done for them. While walking with a volunteer to his station, he overheard a couple other guys expressing the same thoughts and feelings, and he joined in the conversation, adding the sentiment that it would be hard at the next race when they had to go back to doing everything for themselves.

Knowing there was nothing on the day's agenda, he took his time soaking in the surroundings—not just the sights but the sounds as well. If this was to be his only time here, he wanted to create as robust a memory as he could. He strolled through the transition area toward the spot where they would enter from the swim. Once he reached the water's edge, he scanned the immediate area, straining his ears to catch even the slightest of sounds and inhaling to absorb each and every scent. Taking mental snapshots of every turn and nuance, he made his way back to his station and then returned to the hotel in search of Hannah.

Over dinner that night, they developed a rough sketch of their next adventure, filling it in with a few details gleaned from searches on their phones. At one point, Hannah couldn't resist a little good-natured needling. "So is this going to interfere with your race calendar?" she asked with a wide grin.

"Very funny," Matt was quick to retort. "Next year's calendar is going to be very sparse compared to this year's, which you know very well was done to get me to this race. I think I've earned some down time."

After some idle chitchat, she leaned over to give him a quick peck on the lips. "I'm so proud of you. I don't have any doubts you're going to … go get 'em … knock 'em out … uh … do your thing …" she stammered, attempting to provide him with the type of encouragement she thought athletes received before a big event.

He stopped her. "It's OK. I know what you're trying to say, and thank you."

———

"Tonight? Whadda ya mean, tonight? It can't be tonight," Sylvia whined. "We just got here. We haven't done much of anything. Why does time go so fast when you're having fun?" she protested.

Angie laughed. "That's just the way it is, and yes, I'm sure it's Thursday, and I'm sure the banquet is tonight. Besides, what other plans did you have?"

Sylvia stuttered and stammered for a while before conceding she didn't really have any *specific* plans; she was just thinking they would have more time to enjoy the island.

"If you recall, we *are* staying here for a few days after the race, so we'll still have time to do more things," she countered. "Look; if it makes you feel any better, we have the entire morning and afternoon for something. What would you like to do?" she asked, while Sylvia sat with a scowl on her face.

Her first choice was surfing lessons, which was hastily quashed. "I came here to race, remember? How am I going to do that if I have a broken arm or leg?" After more grumbling about Angie being a "buzzkill," she found a snorkeling expedition that was close by and left them with enough time to get ready for the banquet. "That'll work," Angie chimed in eagerly. "Let's go!" Once back to their room from the outing, she had to admit it was the perfect way to enjoy themselves and get her mind off the race. While showering and getting dressed for the banquet, she couldn't resist humming some songs they had heard on the bus to and from the excursion.

As they mingled with the other athletes at the banquet, Angie was thankful they chose a table that consisted almost entirely of lottery winners, which provided all those seated with a lively discussion about their reactions to being notified of their selection. The experience served to further her positive outlook on her reason for being there, as she now had proof positive that others had gained entry the same way she had. It felt as if they had just sat down with their plates when the emcee returned to the stage to begin the evening's entertainment.

Angie derived great pleasure from watching the hula dancers, but her favorite part was the fire dancers. It was astounding they were able to go through the routines without catching their grass skirts on fire. It was one of those experiences that makes someone say, "Hey, I think I might try that," only to completely forget about it when they get home. They were having such a good time and had succeeded in spending the entire day forgetting about the race that she was momentarily taken aback when the emcee announced they were going to hear from some speakers and watch some inspirational videos.

She leaned forward as the first speaker, and then the next, relayed stories of personal struggles and triumphs, emphasizing that at one time they had been sitting exactly where the athletes now sat, had had the same thoughts and same misgivings, and had prevailed simply by refusing to give up. In spite of herself, Angie jumped up while clapping until her hands hurt, without waiting to see whether anyone else was going to give the speaker a standing ovation. The videos contained much the same message as the speakers': don't give up, keep pushing yourself even when you don't think you're at your best that day, keep fighting, and sooner or later you'll be crossing the finish line. By the end of the program Angie had temporarily overcome all negative thoughts and feelings and couldn't wait for Saturday morning.

The Moment of Truth

Sarah was relatively surprised at how easily she woke up and began her prerace ritual. A warm tropical breeze wafted over her as she strode out the lobby and into the early morning atmosphere. She paused, inhaling deeply while scanning the entire area just outside the hotel lobby. In keeping with her usual routine, she began walking around the race area, increasing her pace every few minutes until she was at a speed that might be considered a fast jog. By this time, the sun was fully over the horizon, and she didn't know for certain whether there was an actual increase in temperature or whether it was simply an effect of seeing the sun, but it suddenly felt very warm.

Knowing this was definitely not a race she would want to start dehydrated, her first task back at the transition area was to locate the nearest source of fluids and drink as much as she dared without drinking so much it would slosh around in her stomach. Once having accomplished that mission, she grabbed her swim cap and goggles and made her way to the swimming start platform.

Sarah had to admit there were times when she wondered why the pro men always went off first. *Many of the pro women are able to keep up with the men on the swim, so why not let us go first once in a while*, she reasoned. Today, however, she was content with the men beginning the race, much of that due to her being able to see the cannon as it boomed out across the bay. Unfortunately, she couldn't enjoy it for long, since the pro women went off only minutes after the men. In fact, mere seconds after the men took off, the women began rapidly striding into the water. Owing to the splashing of the racers and clamor of the throngs of spectators, she was barely able to hear the race announcer leading the assembly in the countdown, and she was still treading water when the women on either side reached out to take their first stroke.

Her plan was to hold back just a little while assessing how fast a pace the other women would be setting. She may have been one of the faster swimmers in the field, but Sarah knew she was far from the strongest cyclist or runner and wanted to preserve as much energy on the swim as possible. True to form, she didn't have much difficulty maintaining the same speed as those around her and tried as much as possible to focus on her stroke while keeping an eye on those in front. As the small lead group passed the first buoy, she made a rough count of how many were in her line of sight. "Let's see ... one ... two ... three ... four ... Is that five, or did I count the same person twice?" Regardless of the exact total, she observed that she was easily in the top ten.

They passed the first cone and made a ninety-degree turn to head parallel to the shoreline, with Sarah staying just far enough behind the leaders not to get kicked in the face. From rounding the corner of the first cone to making another ninety-degree turn around the second cone, the women stayed where they were, leading her to believe they were content to stay in those places and not challenge anyone—at least not yet. As they swam away from the cone and headed for the shoreline, she debated whether there was much to gain by her being the first one out of the water. She knew she had the speed but doubted that having a lead of, at most, thirty- to forty-five-seconds would do her much good. She decided to play it safe and kept her position.

The lead group maintained their spots relative to each other the entire time they were heading back toward land. Sarah glanced at her watch; she had been correct in believing she could have had a faster swim, but she felt certain that at least four or five, and maybe as many as nine or ten, of the women in the lead group would have passed her on the bike. All those around her managed to pull off their swim caps, jam helmets on their heads, and yank the bikes off the rack in less than a minute. The leaders held to their positions as they snaked through the transition area, hopping onto their bikes while crossing over the line signifying the beginning of the cycling course.

Beep-beep, beep-beep, beep-beep. Matt groggily bolted upright, looking around for the car heading his way. It took him several moments to realize it was the alarm on his phone. Groaning, he stabbed at the phone several times before finally hitting the button to turn it off and falling back onto the bed while attempting to focus his eyesight in the predawn darkness. Once dressed and heading over to the race site, it was obvious to him from the amount of activity that something momentous was about to take place. He completed his usual warm-up routine and then, not wanting to use too much energy, spent the remaining time walking and shaking his arms and legs.

About forty-five minutes before race time, he returned to the transition area to retrieve his goggles and swim cap to get in a few strokes. A few minutes into it, he paused and looked back to shore. Although he was not sure how much longer it was until race time, he had no difficulties making out what seemed to be several hundred athletes at water's edge, which was sufficient to make him swim at near race pace on his return. Once on land, he kept up with shaking out his muscles while listening to the race announcers, who maintained a constant stream of commentary about the race. The chatter served to make the time pass quickly, until at long last he heard what he'd been working for all this time: the instruction for the athletes to gather at the starting line.

Once the pros went off, Matt strode into the water with the other men in his age group, noting the imaginary start line in the water now crowded with more than a hundred men stretched out across the boundary. In the few minutes before the horn sounded, he shifted his position from being off to the side of the pack to a more central location. If he was correct about his belief, the horde would soon resemble an arrow tip. He was going to do his best to be a part of the tip, and that meant being in the middle from the very start. Yeah, it meant fighting for space in the beginning, but he knew there should be ample space to swim sooner or later.

Sure enough, they had just passed the second buoy when the swimmer ahead and to Matt's left surged forward enough to create of sliver of open water. Matt's eyes popped wide upon spying the crack; he motored past the person on his right and then swerved to avoid running into the swimmer on his left. As they turned around the first cone, his goal was to maintain the space between himself and the other swimmers. Rounding the second cone and heading back in, his next goal was to try to close the gap between himself and the men up ahead. Unfortunately, he was never able to achieve the second goal. Resigned to being excluded from the race leaders, he kept reminding himself he was a natural-born cyclist anyway.

As the swimming leg neared its conclusion, his fight against the rising apprehension became more difficult. He was much farther from the finish than desired when he made out several men rising out of the water and running toward the transition area. Reaching the swim finish himself and climbing out of the surf, he estimated through experience that he was somewhere between four and five minutes behind. He shook his head in disappointment while making his way to his transition station. "OK, not my best, but not my worst either. No sense in beating myself up. Let's get on that bike and blast off!"

As it turned out, Katie's efforts at helping Curt get some sleep were only temporary. He fell asleep right away but couldn't manage a sound sleep for the entire night. "Must be worry about the race," he guessed. A warm shower did wonders at reviving him from his fitful slumber. Owing to the proximity of the race site to the hotel, he didn't have to walk very far to the race site. The sound of the other triathletes making small talk and getting themselves psyched up was everywhere. At least one thing was similar to past races—there were a number of participants walking, jogging, or stretching. Curt followed their example and began warming up.

The sun was beginning to peek out from behind the horizon by the time he had done enough to work up a slight sweat. Returning to the transition area, he decided to use the light to reorient himself to the layout and take a few minutes to find his station. It wasn't until he noticed many of the athletes heading toward the water that he realized he had forgotten to keep track of time. Glancing down at his watch, he saw that the moment for the race start was soon approaching, so he hurried to the staging area. By that time, it looked as though almost everyone was ready to get started.

Boom!

He had been so focused on trying to see around those standing in front of him he was completely startled and stumbled back when the cannon went off. Once the entire field of professional men were in the water, he marveled at the controlled chaos. The scene reminded him of videos he'd watched of piranhas feeding. He followed suit as the age-groupers in front began inching toward the water. There was enough of an incline that he was able to spot the professional women treading water at the imaginary start line situated between two large buoys. Shortly after they left, the hundreds of age-group men entered the water. After several days of inactivity, springing into action allowed him to get out of his mind and concentrate on the task at hand.

Once in the water, the massive assembly of men congregated in a thick cluster along the start line. "I don't need to beat anybody," he reminded himself, pulling down his goggles and adjusting them around his eyes. "I just need to finish within an hour of the top swim time. After that, no worries." He knew that wasn't 100 percent accurate, given the length of the course and the climate, but even way back when he had submitted his name for the lottery, his concern was getting here and being disqualified for having too slow of a swim time.

Once underway, he recalled the map of the swim course, noting it was basically an out-and-back course. This meant having to swim a little over a mile in one direction, turning to swim parallel to the shore for a bit, and then turning again and swimming an entire mile all the way back. He also remembered seeing several buoys between the start/finish line and the turnaround point. Instead of trying to think about the swim in terms of going out and back, he located and fixated on each buoy. Upon reaching the first one, he scanned the water's horizon until he spotted the next one and aimed for it.

Stroke after stroke, minute after minute, he continued. Even with breaking the swim into smaller segments, he felt as though he spent the entire morning in the water, but at long last he was able to catch a clear view of the finish area. The proximity gave him a burst of adrenaline, and he dug in for the finish. Entering the chute that led to the transition area, he decided no news was good news, meaning that if no one stopped him to inform him of his missing the cutoff time, he wasn't about to stop and ask. "Well, that was lovely," he whispered. Knowing that he had successfully completed his weakest event, he allowed himself a few moments to recover before donning his bike gear. "Now this is where the fun begins!" he exclaimed, guiding his bike along the route leading to the transition area exit.

A sound tugged at Angie's consciousness, gradually bringing her out of a deep slumber. When she had awoken enough to comprehend the source and meaning of the commotion, a large part of her brain was telling her there was no possible way it was time to get up yet, as they had gone to sleep just a few minutes before. "I must have set the wrong time," she said, attempting to assuage a growing sense of being mistaken. "Ah crap!" she mumbled, upon discovering that yes, it was in fact time to get up.

Angie thought she had succeeded in getting dressed without an undue amount of noise, but as she opened the door, Sylvia said, in a voice that suggested she was wide awake, "Good luck. Don't think you'll be able to see me at the start, but hopefully you will when you get out of the water." Angie contemplated an apology but settled on "Thanks, see ya out there." Wanting to take in all the sights and sounds of the race, she chose to keep as close to the race site as possible while warming up.

The sun was just over the horizon by the time her warm-ups were completed. Continuing to stretch and shake out her muscles, she listened to the unending stream of commentary. What made this race unique, and fascinating, was hearing the perspectives of the various professionals. Not really getting into the sport as much as some others, she felt somewhat left in the dark when certain names were reported and most people around her began cheering. The sole connection with them, anyway, was being able to say tomorrow they had all done the same race. That is, if she finished.

"No! No, I *am* going to finish. The only thing that's going to stop me is getting hit by a car or a broken bone, and even then, unless the bone is in my leg, I'm still gonna keep going. Other than that, I don't care what happens; I'm not stopping until I cross that finish line!" After retrieving her cap and goggles, she meandered around the transition area, noticing that most athletes were beginning to gravitate toward the water. By now many, if not most, of the athletes had assembled somewhere around the beach. Watching them en masse, she was reminded of racehorses being led into the small, narrow starting gates at the beginning of a race. In a very similar manner to the horses snorting and pawing the ground, the athletes were shaking out their arms and legs, generally appearing to be very antsy to get the race started. "Oh my gosh!" she whispered. "This is it!"

She was very thankful to be in the last wave to go off, never being completely confident in her swimming skills. As minutes turned to seconds before the race start, she was reminded of the fact that this race had a cutoff time. Even without knowing what the exact time would be, she knew that, at least for the swim, she was competing against some world-class athletes. If she could just manage to make it out of the water on time, she then had the luxury of having to compete only against herself and no one else.

"*No!* I'm not ready!" came the silent protest as the horn sounded. Logically, she had known this moment was going to arrive for several months, and she had even begun steeling herself in the early morning hours while warming up. Unfortunately, all that mental preparation went flying out the window when the race finally started. In the beginning, she didn't bother looking around to determine her place in relation to the other racers; that was a sure-fire recipe for getting thrown off her rhythm. She simply made her best attempts at getting into some kind of groove. "Remember, remember, remember: you don't have to beat anyone. All you have to do is beat the cutoff time. Focus, Ang; you can do it!" There were a few women around her, so she had some company, and she noted that several were slightly behind her position, which gave her some encouragement. "If I do miss the cutoff, at least I won't be the only one," she reflected through gritted teeth.

Though she felt she was swimming at an optimal level, Angie had a slight moment of disappointment upon arriving at, and moving around, the first cone. Ordinarily she would have been excited at what it represented: her being almost halfway finished. This time, however, she felt irritation at being forced to slow down to make the turn. Once around the cone, Angie purposefully put forth a surge of energy into her stroke to reach her previous pace. Instead of feeling as if it were taking forever to make it from one marker to the next, she was now pleasantly surprised when a brief gaze over the water's horizon showed the second cone only a short distance away. "Awesome!" she blew out in exhilaration. "I'm sure to beat the cutoff time!"

Her renewed vigor led to one final push to ensure there would be more race after the swim. She passed the first buoy on the way back in, and then the second, and she sighted the arch on the beach shortly after that. If she had been on land, Angie would have jumped up and down; she was almost there! As she rose out of the water, past doubts suddenly sprang up, and she fully expected someone to notify her she had missed the cutoff time and her race was over. When the only response from those standing nearby was enthusiastic cheering, she excitedly yelled, "Yes!" and sprinted at best possible speed to her station.

Sarah grew somewhat frustrated at the lack of opportunity to get a good read on the other competitors. The course didn't contain any true hills, just "rollers" that went up and down gradually but were high enough at their peaks to hide the other riders from view. Although able to spot two or three in the valleys directly ahead while cresting the rises, she was sure there were several others in the valleys past the next rise. Knowing that emotions tend to mess with a person's race strategy, she channeled the nervous energy into her pedaling. At the very least, the turnaround point was still up ahead, and she would be able to get an exact count of how many women were in front there.

Biding her time, she ground out a steady pace, keeping sight of the closest woman rider. Mile after mile the competitors rode, through the muggy heat that felt like the inside of an oven. Taking periodic slugs from their water bottles and squeezing some over their heads barely lessened the impact of such an environment. Other than other tropical climates, there were only a few places back on the continent that could adequately prepare the athletes for this type of punishment. The only consolation was that everyone was having to race under the same conditions, though currently that offered very little comfort.

After about two and a half hours, Sarah saw a couple of male riders coming back in on the other side of the road. The sight piqued her interest. If the male competitors had reached the turnaround mark, the top female racers couldn't be all that far behind. In addition to keeping one eye on the rider just in front, she continuously scanned the opposite side in the hope of getting an exact tally of how many women were ahead of her. It didn't take long for a woman to come into view on her way back in. "OK, there's the first one. Keep an eye out for the others," she said aloud. Within less than a minute, she caught sight of the next rider, and then the next, and the next. By the time she had slowed down and rounded the marker to head back in herself, she had counted eight women racers. *Excellent!* she applauded internally.

Being passed by another woman a few miles past the turnaround made her realize she had inadvertently slowed down during the internal pat on the back. She picked up her pace again, but it wasn't enough to pass the other woman. From that point to the completion of the cycling leg, three more women passed her. Each time, she had to wrestle with the urge to follow suit; and each time, she had to repeat her mantra. In fact, she had to say it out loud as the second woman went cruising by, as her internal voice ceased to carry the same impact as it had earlier. The result was that Sarah coasted into the transition area a very frustrated athlete. *Relax! Relax! Relax!* she screamed inside while running much faster to her station than was typical for her at previous races.

Discouraged by his place in the pack after the swim, Matt fought hard not to try hammering the competition too early. He knew that would be a sure recipe to blowing out on the run, so despite his emotions he kept to a steady pace. During the first twenty miles, he was encouraged by passing several men who seemed to be in his age group, but as the race progressed, athletes of all ages thinned out. Without the opportunity to gauge his performance by how many riders he was passing, he had to content himself with keeping his computer glued to a speed he knew he could maintain for the duration of the cycling leg.

Mile after mile, he chugged along, alternating between experiencing irritation at his inability to properly assess his race position and taking a more fatalistic attitude. He knew, but didn't really want to fully acknowledge, that he was operating near full speed. No matter how many guys were in front, the only way he could know for certain would be to go entirely full bore for the next hour or two; but doing so meant he was sure to bonk on the run. There was absolutely no doubt in his mind that it was only a question of how many miles he could get in before he hit the wall; it was going to happen. Conceding to the inevitable, he bit off a string of profanities.

"Too bad this wasn't just a cycling race," he mused in one last bid to make something out of what could never be. "Then I could hammer and not have to worry about what comes next." But this wasn't just a cycling race, and he did have to plan for the run. Rather than resulting in a drop-off in performance, his resignation allowed him to switch his focus to the run. Nearing the end of the cycling leg, he slightly reduced his cadence and then slowed even further upon approaching the transition area. After racking his bike, he allowed himself the luxury of stretching for a few seconds. "A little bit of time now to make sure I don't cramp on the run might save a lot of time later." He knew he wasn't the best runner on the course, and he still wasn't sure how many of his competitors were already out on the run course. "Time to find out," he reasoned, trotting through the exit gate.

About two hours into the cycling leg, Curt was surprised at how much energy he was having to put into each small climb. "Maybe it's the climate," he told himself. "If I can get acclimated to the surroundings, I should be OK eventually." The thought bolstered his confidence, and he pushed on. Although not picking up any additional speed, over time he did feel as if the climbs took less effort. Another hour plus later, he also discovered newfound energy when a quick peek at his bike computer revealed he had only about ten miles to go to the turnaround point.

It took longer for him to reach the turnaround than he desired, but once heading back in, he felt ready to tackle the remaining half of the bike ride. Unfortunately, that feeling didn't last long. Thirty to forty minutes past the turnaround, he began experiencing a pronounced sense of weariness that was sure to be due to the high heat and humidity. A sense of alarm began building when fluids and nutrition did nothing to dispel the fatigue, yet he continued to push on. Mile after mile, he shoved his feet down on the pedals; the only concession to his exertions was coasting down the slight declines, which provided the opportunity to rest his weary legs. Toward the end, his sole motivation was just wanting to be done with this part, even with the knowledge that he had to run a marathon once he had completed the bike ride. Catching sight of the transition area, he coasted to a stop just short of the dismount line. At that point, the best he could manage was to hobble through the transition area to his station. "Ah screw it!" he said with a forceful exhalation. "I'm just here to finish, not beat anybody, so let's go! Let's get this thing over with!"

Angie followed all the other athletes exiting the transition area with bikes in tow. It seemed there were more turns than she recalled from when she had located her station before the race started, but she chalked it up to race-time jitters. Once out on the course, she regained her senses and challenged herself with the goal of maybe catching someone that had left before she had. She did her best to maintain her speed but could feel the pace and climate taking a toll. A couple hours later, her legs didn't seem to have the same force as they did during the first thirty miles, forcing her to revise her plan. "All right, let's just make it to the turnaround spot and we can reassess the situation then. Don't try to pass anybody; just do your best."

It became necessary for Angie to remind herself of that several times over the next fifteen to twenty miles. This continued to be true even when she reached the turnaround point. In consideration of her performance on the first half, she felt an urge to rethink her strategy yet again on the way back in. The condition of her legs and recollection of the long run constrained her, causing her to dial down her effort. She spent the next few miles focusing on how her body felt. The new strategy became an attempt to maintain a speed she hoped was sustainable for the remainder of the cycling leg. It was slower than what she had expected going into the race, but experience had taught her these things were fluid and one had to adjust to the realities of the present situation.

On reaching the one-hundred-mile banner, honesty dictated that Angie admit she no longer cared about her pace; she just wanted to be done. Even though she knew there would still be a long run to go, reaching the transition area would mean two-thirds of the race was over. That sudden realization brought about a touch of sadness. "I've prepared for this and planned to do this for so long; for some reason I thought I would enjoy it more than I have," she reflected. "Now all I care about is getting this over so I can go back to the hotel room and relax. This isn't what I wanted out of the experience."

It didn't take her long to decide a pity party was not going to help her achieve her longstanding goal. "Screw emotions!" she whispered fiercely. "The race doesn't care what you feel; the race is there to be finished!" Her newfound determination led to her increasing her pace, creating a sort of tunnel vision in which the only thought in her consciousness was on maintaining her present speed. Before long she could hear cheering, and soon after, she spotted the transition area. She reinforced the competitor attitude while jogging her bike to her station. "I am not done yet, and I am not going to give up and play dead. I'm gonna keep going no matter what it takes. I don't care if I finish in the dark; *I'm gonna cross that finish line!*"

It took almost two miles out on the running course for Sarah to realize she had started out at a pace she couldn't have sustained for the entire 26.2 miles. "You fool!" she berated herself. "The most important race of the season and you make a rookie mistake like letting your emotions get the better of you!" She reduced her speed, but given the humidity, maintaining even that pace wasn't a given. Other races may have had the same general temperatures, but the humidity was the real killer. Arriving at the first long straightaway, she spotted a woman about fifty yards in the near distance and another one roughly the same length ahead of that. She adjusted her pace to match that of the closest woman and kept that gap for the next few miles, wanting to determine her strategy.

Mile after grueling mile, the racers inched their way along the course. There were times she felt like a snail, as the gradual progress seemed that time-consuming. The woman just in front was too far ahead to provide much relief. If she had been only a few yards away, there could have been a sense of athletic struggle—a match of wits, as it were. "Mano a mano," Sarah mused. But there was none of that now. There was just the sensation on the bottoms of her feet from the constant pounding, and the sound of her breathing. The sole divergence from the pattern was her perceived physical condition.

Despite all her nutritional intake, she began feeling the effects of the environment. It wasn't a significant drop-off, but she could feel her vitality slowly ebbing away. At the rate it was occurring, she didn't feel much concern about her ability to finish the race; that was a given. Her apprehension centered on whether she would be able to put forth a big effort toward the end if needed. Prior to this race, she'd always had a little something in the gas tank for one final big kick to pass someone near the finish line. The way she was feeling now, she wasn't too sure that would be a possibility today.

Her sense of time noticeably improved when the lead males began running back in from the run turnaround. At least now there was something to interrupt the monotony. While there wasn't an abundance of athletes heading in, there were just enough for her to use the distraction of watching them approach and disappear to ignore the fact she was still having to grind it out and her progress wasn't any faster than it had been. Her demeanor improved even more when she spied the first woman heading in. Although she wasn't entirely sure how much of a time gap there was, simply spotting the woman boosted her spirits. "That means I can't be all that far from the turnaround, and *that* means the run will be half over. *Sweet!*"

Less than twenty minutes later, Sarah exhaled an initial sigh of relief while passing the turnaround. She remained cautiously optimistic for a couple of minutes but waited a while longer to get a firmer idea of how much she could push herself. Over the next few miles, she gradually increased her speed, reaching and passing the woman that had been the closest during the first half of the run. Past experiences made her certain the woman would respond—especially given how close they were to the end of the race. Self-doubt began to creep into her thoughts when the woman didn't increase her pace. "Am I doing something wrong? Going too fast? There's not much race left. I know bonking is possible, especially during the last few miles, but it kinda seems unlikely now. Why isn't she doing something? Waiting for the last mile?"

Even plagued by misgivings, she stuck to her strategy. Catching anyone else would be unlikely, but that didn't matter. She focused her resources on preserving her place, determined to do anything and everything at this point to make sure those she had passed did not return the favor. Despite the exhaustion permeating her entire body, she sensed that if the woman did try to make a move, the emotions alone would give her enough vigor for one final kick.

The road of that final mile was jam-packed with people cheering, ringing cowbells, and in general creating a raucous scene. Rounding the last corner, she almost burst into tears at what she had accomplished. Even without knowing her exact place in relation to the other women pros, she had finished so much higher than her grandest aspirations. Crossing the finish line, it was all she could do to remain upright, but at that moment the joy outweighed any physical discomfort. In addition to the overwhelming emotions, there was so much noise and uproar she had a hard time coping with it all.

"Sarah! Sarah! Sarah!" She searched the general direction from where the sound seemed to be coming. It took her several moments to locate Lisa, who was pounding furiously on the banner enclosing the finish area. Sarah hobbled toward her, stretching out tired limbs. "You did it! You are so awesome! I'm so proud of you!" Lisa hugged her so tightly Sarah had difficulty getting a breath.

"Lisa … Lisa! Ease up!"

Lisa let go of the bear hug but retained her grip on Sarah's shoulders. "You are unbelievable! All this time you were so worried about how you were gonna do: 'I'm a first-timer, don't expect too much, there're over a hundred female pros, yadda, yadda, yadda.' I'll have you know I was counting, and you came in at number twelve! *Twelve!* I don't know what else to say. Incredible!" Sarah stammered a few syllables but was unable to produce any real words. After all this time and countless races, she finally felt like a professional triathlete.

Matt squinted in the midafternoon sunlight. After hours—how many had it been?—of swimming and biking, he had little choice but to commit to completing his best run and wait to see how his body would respond to the conditions. It took only a few miles of running for him to begin experiencing the effects of the sun and humidity. He had started cycling at such an early age that his bike felt like a second home. It had become so second nature for him that even the tropical weather conditions hadn't fazed him much. The run, however, was a different story.

His perceived exertion level so early into the run told him today's race was not going to be easy; nor was it likely to be much fun. In fact, it became apparent by about mile five to six that if he wasn't careful about being well hydrated and taking in enough electrolytes, there was a very real possibility of cramping. On the mainland, there were many races in which he bypassed most of the stations; in this climate, that would be a huge mistake for anyone. Even with all the fluids, he experienced a gradual sense of struggle.

Passing the mile-ten marker, he focused his energies on simply reaching the turnaround. It took longer than planned, but at least he was able to maintain his speed while getting there—barely. He rounded the marker at the halfway point and had almost reached mile fourteen when the strain was too much to disregard. He fought to maintain his pace, and by the time he passed the mile-fifteen banner, every breath was labored, and every step took herculean effort. He had just caught sight of the mile-sixteen marker when his body decided to end the conflict. In hindsight, he felt it was almost as if his body said, "All right, if you aren't going to pay attention to me, I'll make you listen!"

At that moment, he was blindsided by a sudden depletion of strength. "Ah, crap!" He exhaled forcefully, knowing from descriptions that he was experiencing the dreaded "bonk." His only solace was that he was still able to run, although truth be told it was more like a jog than a run. At mile markers eighteen, nineteen, and twenty, he stopped at each aid station instead of running through them and drank twice as many cups of fluids as he usually did. As his race neared its conclusion, he began developing a change in philosophy regarding his level of output; passing the mile twenty-two banner, it gelled into a "go-all-out-or-nothing" attitude, and he picked up the pace.

His body was so tired and sore at the twenty-five-mile banner that there was no doubt in his mind he had given it his best shot. He slowed from the last banner to the chutes leading to the finishing arch. It wasn't until he rounded the last corner and had a clear view of the space beyond the arch that he took the risk of making a final push. Although it wasn't much, he made his best sprint for the finish line. Once past the arch and well enough away to not impede the finish of the other athletes, he allowed his body to give out and collapsed to the ground. A volunteer came over to inquire whether he was OK, and Matt gave him a thumbs-up with a smile. "Just restin'," he reassured the man. The guy nodded and walked away.

"Hey, what's this?" he heard a female voice call over the clamor of spectators. He leaned over on one shoulder to glimpse Hannah, who was smiling with her arms resting on the railing. "What is this?" she said, provoking him. "I thought triathletes didn't lie down until they got home! Doesn't look like we're home to me!"

Matt rolled over, taking a few breaths while on his hands and knees before pushing himself erect with a loud groan. He then shuffled to the waist-high fence, placing his hands outside of her arms. "Normally they don't," he agreed with a sigh. "But this ain't normal," he corrected her.

"I'm sure it wasn't," she concurred. "I got all hot and sweaty just standing out here waiting for you. Can't imagine what you must be feeling. How about you get something to drink, gather up your things, and I'll meet you at the lobby. We can take showers and get a nice dinner. You've earned it."

Matt considered her proposal. "Sounds good to me," he replied. "Good," she affirmed. "You stink!"

"I think after this I'll definitely settle for Half-Ironmans," Curt resolved. "At most," he affirmed after running past the mile-two marker. "Whose idea was this anyway? Oh, yeah, mine. Somebody kick me next time!" He had mistakenly figured that having done a race of this distance on the mainland to qualify would have made this race a little easier for him—if not physically, at least in regard to the mental aspect of knowing approximately how long he would be out on the course for the entire race. Unfortunately, that didn't help much; if anything, it served as a brutal wake-up call that he still had about three and a half hours of running until he could finally call it quits.

"Well, this very well could be the only time I'm ever at this race, so let's take in the sights and sounds and enjoy it as much as we can despite this weather absolutely *sucking!*" He waved at the spectators lining the road, briefly chatted with the volunteers at each aid station, and provided encouragement to any athlete that passed him with a hearty "Good job!" and "Lookin' good!" He had just exchanged pleasantries with another man about his age when they simultaneously observed the turnaround point in the distance.

"Outstanding!" Curt shouted as he jogged around the marker in the middle of the road. The realization that he was halfway through the run and almost done with the entire race rejuvenated his spirits. The sound of cheering and cowbells carried over the landscape and kept him going until he passed the mile-fourteen banner. Over the course of the next two to three miles, however, the conditions began their assault on his body, with the inspiration he had gleaned from the crowd at the turnaround rapidly dissipating.

"This does not bode well," he moaned. Each step was torture; the air was burning his lungs. He was able to keep running, but just barely. Somewhere between miles sixteen and seventeen, he wondered how fast he would go at a walking pace. "Walking? For the whole rest of the way? Wouldn't that be giving up at this point? Let's be honest; we're tired—*really* tired. And we hurt, we're sore, we ache. But isn't there a *little* something in the gas tank? I'm certain no one would blame you if you did. Sure, nobody back home would know, but you would know. So the question is, Curt ol' boy: could you live with yourself if you gave up now?" The answer was incredibly obvious even before the question was completed.

Passing the mile-twenty banner, he began counting down the few miles to go until he reached the finish line. Plus the time of day added a goal to increase his flagging motivation. He knew the athletes would have the opportunity to finish even after the sun had gone down, but he wanted to finish while the sun was still up. Even if it was on the horizon, he wanted to finish before it had disappeared. He knew that might be a minor, silly, prideful sort of thing, but he was willing to use whatever psychological tricks were necessary to keep himself moving.

The next few miles became a contest of mind over body. His body was screaming for an end to the madness, his mind attempting to bargain with it. "Look, we've come this far. We only have a little way to go. Besides, we have to get back to the transition area anyway, right?" The suffering became so intense he no longer paid attention to the numbers on the mileage banners. He simply shuffled through each station, taking whatever was handed to him without questioning what it was, until he arrived at the mile-twenty-five marker.

He was even with the table when a volunteer, obviously noticing his distress, called out some encouragement. "You're at mile twenty-five! Look!" she exclaimed, pointing at the banner.

"What?" he asked, having a terribly difficult time processing any information.

"Mile twenty-five! You're at mile twenty-five! You're almost there!"

Curt wheeled and peered at the sign. When his brain finally began operating enough to register what that implied, he threw his hands into the air. "Hallelujah," he cried. "That's it!"

The volunteer laughed at his response. "Not so fast," she cautioned. "You're *almost* there. Close, but you still have to reach the finish line!"

Curt pointed at her in recognition of her meaning. "Right, OK, here I go! This is me goin'!" He inhaled deeply as he made off to complete the race.

It would be a complete fabrication to assert that the final mile plus was easy for Curt, but with the knowledge he was at last so close to his goal, it did seem less of a struggle—less in terms of his mind having to fight his body to not give up, but not less in terms of how drained he felt. Approaching the finishing chute, he glanced over at the horizon, noting the sun was still above land. "Got you," he said, smiling in satisfaction. He entered the chute signifying the final couple hundred yards, tears welling in each eye.

Crossing the threshold under the arch, he vaguely heard his number and name being announced over the loudspeaker system, and he managed to accept a water bottle from a young girl before completely breaking down emotionally. He bent over and sobbed uncontrollably for quite some time, until he heard a voice calling his name. There were so many people, and his eyes were having so much difficulty adjusting through the tears, he had a hard time locating the source of the sound. Eventually he spotted Katie standing just outside the barrier. As he turned toward her and she saw the state he was in, she joined him with her own flow of tears. "I did it! I did it! I did it! I did it! I did it!" was all he could squeak out again and again. They tightly embraced, crying and laughing all at the same time.

"This way ... this way ... this way, run out ... run out!" the volunteers at the edge of the barriers bellowed as a steady stream of athletes left the transition area to head out on the running course. Angie trailed several other women through the gate and on to the open road. She was so grateful for the support of the crowd; at that moment, she felt as if she could sit down at her station and take a nap. The crowds thinned out as the athletes got farther from the race site, but at least for the first couple of miles they were still plentiful and provided rousing support. This afforded her with the much-needed boost to get her legs moving after having spent the last several hours on the bike.

The crowd reinforcement began to slowly wane as she made what felt like minimal progress. Today it seemed it took forever to reach the first mile marker, and it then took an equal eternity to reach the mile-two banner. While passing the mile-three banner, she had to concede the point that a marathon run did feel slow during the beginning stages. She kept her foot on the pedal for the next few miles, desperately hoping something, anything, would finally kick in. At the mile-six banner, her fears began mounting, as not only was she not able to run faster but was now going a little slower.

"That was mile six, right? OK, I'm just about a quarter of the way there. Not setting any land speed records, but there is light at the end of the tunnel—a really, really tiny light, but it's there."

She battled with the thought that this might be as good as it was going to get but still held on to a tiny bit of hope that something might change and she would be able to increase her pace. With each passing mile, that hope shrank until she stumbled into the mile-eleven aid station and came to an abrupt stop. The last flicker of hope for improving her performance was completely extinguished. "You gave it your best shot, Ang," she said, grimacing. "Let's just focus on making it to the finish line, regardless of how long it takes."

She did receive a shot in the arm upon reaching the turnaround point. The cheering of the crowd combined with the knowledge of being halfway through the run served to energize her for a couple of miles. She didn't run any faster; it simply felt easier, as if each step took less effort. Unfortunately, the boost didn't last long. By mile sixteen, she had reverted to the earlier sense of struggling to put one foot in front of the other, but she kept plugging away, an unknown streak of stubbornness refusing to allow her to stop. Another discouragement came around the mile-twenty marker, upon her noticing it was no longer as light outside as it had been.

Scanning to the west, she observed that the sun was getting closer to sinking below the horizon. It was still a complete ball, and while she wasn't sure how long it would take to disappear, she knew it was now inevitable she would be finishing in the dark. She managed to make it to the mile-twenty-two banner before the sun completed its day's journey, quietly vanishing from sight. Her humor continued unabated as she enjoyed the spectacle of sunset in the tropics. "Kinda makes running a little more romantic, and it's not so hot." She giggled, despite her exhaustion.

Twenty minutes later, she was close enough to hear the sounds emanating from the race site, and although the number of spectators had dwindled from earlier in the day, they were still plentiful. When she stopped at an aid station for the final time, a volunteer handed her a glow stick. "Can't be too careful at night," he offered with a big smile.

"Whoo-hoo! I got one!" Angie crowed. At the start of the day, she had viewed having to run with a glow stick as an emblem of shame; now, after having been through everything, she saw it as a symbol of triumph.

Rounding the last corner and spotting the arch over the finish line, she stopped jogging and began walking, but this time her slowed pace was not from exhaustion. With finishing the race an absolute given, she wanted to make the moment last as long as possible, so she began reaching out and high-fiving anyone and everyone who had a hand in the air. At that exact moment, she ignored the aches, disregarded the messages from her body that it was ready to shut down, and forgot about all the fears and misgivings she'd had about ever thinking of doing this race. A few yards from the finish line, she began weeping, not wanting her current emotional state to end—ever!

She continued walking under the arch and well into the finishing area before finally succumbing to the exhaustion and dropping to the ground. Her consciousness swirled in eddies, and she was having a very difficult time distinguishing thoughts from feelings, all of which led to a great deal of confusion. "Why do I hurt so much but feel so fantastic?" she pondered, wishing she could channel her emotions into some type of physical energy.

"Angie! Angie! You did it! You did it!" she heard someone yelling from somewhere behind her.

In her fogginess, all she could manage was "That voice ... I think I recognize that voice."

She glanced up while still on her hands and knees to see Sylvia jumping up and down at the railing. "Angie! You did it! Way to go, girl!"

She pushed herself into a standing position, adjusting her feet to ensure she wouldn't fall over. After being reassured of that, she hobbled to Sylvia, resting her arms on the rail. The fact that Angie had just completed an Ironman-distance triathlon in extreme weather was temporarily lost on Sylvia; all she could take in was Angie's physical state.

"Nothing personal, but ... you look like shit. Shall I walk you over to the med tent?"

Angie had just began formulating a snarky comeback when she noticed Sylvia's wide grin and her shoulders shaking with laughter. She relaxed, but she still delivered a retort to make Sylvia think she was offended. "I look like shit? Do you have any idea what I've been through today while you were sitting in some air-conditioned room sipping drinks and thumbing through magazines? Do you?"

Sylvia's face transformed from mirth to horror. "Ang, I'm sorry. I didn't ..." That was when she picked up on Angie's smile and laughter. "OK, I guess I deserved that. All kidding aside, I am so proud of you," she said while gripping Angie's shoulders.

"Thanks," Angie replied. "It was a lot tougher than I expected it to be, but I did it. Hey! I'm an Ironwoman!" She raised both fists high in the air.

"Yes, you are," Sylvia agreed. "Let's go celebrate!"

Printed in the United States
By Bookmasters